Dedication:

This book is for all those who see the darkness coming and have made the decision to be a source of hope.

"Light shines brightest in the darkness"

About the Cover:

Yamerpro is your one stop shop for great cover design and graphics artistry. I couldn't be more pleased with their work.

www.yamerpro.com

Preface:

Apocalyptic themes are popular today due to a general belief that our country, perhaps the world, is headed for implosion. Moral decay, corruption on a grand scale, and irresponsible economic policy, promote this speculation into more of an inevitable consequence.

Nightly news demonstrates how fragile our "thin veneer of social control" has become. It's chilling to imagine how people would act if law enforcement suddenly dissolved?

This book is a continuation of <u>Days of Ragnarök: end of the gods</u>. It follows Jason and Anna Connors as they wade through the aftermath of social failure following collapse of their government. It is not connected to the seven years of Biblical Tribulation and reflects what can easily occur before that time.

When the fabric of civilization tears, we are left to depend on God's providence. This is where grace prevails and faith grows stronger. I trust you will enjoy this story of victory and healing in the midst of chaos.

I'd love to hear your comments:

Tyler Woods
contact@the11hr.com

Realm of Ragnarök –
two worlds meet

By Tyler Woods

Bus Ride:

Terlingua has been our winter home for the past five months but staying here through summer would be an epic disaster. It's been eight months since the US economy collapsed and nearly seven months since an EMP killed the electric grid. It appears to be a lasting problem and coupled with the loss of social order, has cost the lives of hundreds of thousands. If we can be thankful for anything, at least the die-off seems to have slowed for now.

I'm Jason Connors, formerly an oil field engineer. My wife is Anna. She's a nurse but I guess the 'registered' part is history since there doesn't appear to be any government to keep record. We have a two week old daughter named Mandy who I'm sure is still a baby.

We started off as a group of fifty at a deer camp in a pocket canyon of Big Bend, Texas. Unable to heat our shacks through winter, we found better shelter at Terlingua, a little tourist village here in south Texas. Current food resources won't carry us through a summer in this desert so we sent a team to find us a place that is sustainable. They went as far as central Kansas.

Thanks to the kindness and resources of the small town of Hazel Creek, Kansas, we are traveling as one group in a sports-team school bus; 'appropriated' after the government collapsed. Rural Kansas high school teams travel long distances so schools often keep a dedicated bus with air-conditioning and larger fuel tanks. It's just under nine hundred miles from Terlingua to Hazel Creek. We don't need air-conditioning in early April but the longer range plus extra barrels of diesel should get us there with a little fuel to spare. There won't be any gas stations open along the way. The bus seats eighty so some benches have been removed to make room for supplies. Accompanying the bus are two pickup trucks. One pulling a trailer of goats, and another loaded with food and water.

A few of our initial group have homes to return to but we still number forty-two with Mandy. At two weeks old, she's the reason our departure is delayed. Maintaining radio contact with Hazel Creek has helped our two communities connect from a distance. Hazel Creek may be only eight hundred and fifty miles from Terlingua but their experience could not have been more different. Where we avoided adversity by being secluded in a remote canyon in Big Bend, they were dragged through the worst of human depravity. They carry emotional scars that run deep and will take time to only partially heal.

Keith Reed is from Hazel Creek and came down with our recon team to help bring us back. Long bus rides provide time to get to know people and as Keith tells of the days following the collapse, we get a glimpse of the awful toll our new neighbors have paid.

"Hazel Creek is pretty remote as far as things go," he says. "When the feds announced the default, we just kept on as usual. Besides the corner store, there's not much to spend money on in town. Two towns up the road is a hardware store, grocery, and a restaurant but most folks are used to shopping once a month or longer if someone else can bring you something you need. Everything happened in August and Back-to-School shopping was just starting. We thought the government would have things figured out by the time school started. About a week later, news reached us about riots in bigger cities but we're a farming community so it didn't affect us... we thought. Things just kept getting worse. There wasn't enough National Guard to put down riots in so many cities and no one was surprised when the governor declared martial law. What was a surprise was after a couple days of warnings and arrests, police began shooting at curfew breakers. Nobody thought it was right but we weren't there to know how bad it was." Keith shows no emotion. His dialogue is passionless as though he is reading a newspaper.

"There was no break in violence and then the power went out. We thought it was a regular outage; we get those from time to time, but it didn't come back on. The phones, T.V., radio, and internet were down too. Someone guessed they cut power to stop the riots but nothing made sense. In any event, we quit getting news. Some days later, we saw our first refugees.

That's what we called them. They were from the city;
Wichita, I think. At first, there was only one woman
with two small children. She said the city wasn't safe
for her and her girls so they were traveling to her
parents in Colorado. We should have asked a lot more
questions but we never thought about what she was up
to. Families helped her with food, water, and fuel; they
stayed at our house that night, and left the next day."

The bus comes to a stop as Randy Fowler speaks up.

"We're going to have to take some ranch roads to get
around a city up ahead. There are too many
obstructions to attempt driving through town so we'll
go around. The road is bumpy and dusty so if it gets
too bad, we'll run the air-conditioner but try to secure
what you can and watch for loose things that will
bounce around."

For the next few hours, our bus makes slow progress
but eventually we arrive at a service road along a
highway; it's jammed with empty cars. At a rest stop,
the leadership team discusses warning parents of small
children about the grotesque sights along the way but
there are so many that aside from covering every
window of the bus, it will be impossible to hide them
all. This is a terrible new truth and the sooner we
adjust, the faster we can move forward. Weaving
amidst abandoned cars along the service road, our
vantage point from a school bus makes it nearly
impossible to avoid seeing torn-apart skeletons of the
dead. Gasps become fewer over time as each morbid
sight only affirms what we must accept has happened.

Seeking diversion from the plight of unprepared

masses, Kathy Palmer asks Keith to continue telling of the days after collapse in Hazel Creek. It's not that she wants to hear about it as much as any distraction from scenes outside must be better.

"Where was I?" asks Keith.

"You were telling of the woman with two children that stayed with your family," she says.

"Yeah... her... She left the next day but two days later a Kansas State Police car drove into town. Something wasn't right about the two that got out. Their uniforms didn't fit and they didn't act like police. They were asking about the woman who stayed with us and said she killed someone. Then they wanted to know who she stayed with and went to our house to question my Mom. Dad and I were helping Elmer Tousley get the last of his hay in, so Mom and Emma were by themselves. Normally that wasn't a problem because next door was the Bennett place. They were in town that morning. It wasn't their fault." Keith's voice shows a bit of change but only slightly.

"Mom must have felt something wrong because she never let them in. It turned out the woman with the kids was bait. They were a gang of some kind and looking for food, alcohol, and drugs. Mom had a shotgun and they weren't going to get in. Karin Bennett was hiding in the barn and saw the whole thing but there was nothing she could do. She'd been watching Emma so Mom could get some things done and Emma had run to the house to go to the bathroom. The two men split up and as the one tried to distract Mom, the other tried climbing in a back window. Mom caught him half way in the window and peppered him with birdshot. It didn't kill him but he wasn't right in the head anyway. Next thing you know he set the house on fire and shot at any attempt Mom or Emma made to escape. By the time neighbors got there, the house was completely engulfed and both Mom and Emma were gone. They never had a chance."

"That's awful!" Kathy isn't sure what's worse; the story or the grizzly view outside. Equally awful is Keith's empty emotion. His demeanor is cold and lifeless. "Did you catch the men who did it?" she asks.

"Not right away," he says. "They took off just before anyone showed up. Poor Karin has never been right since. She used to be really happy and friendly. Now, she's cold as ice; like she's got no soul inside." Keith pauses for a moment.

"Next thing we knew, a whole pack of men with trucks and those two in the police car rolled into town with demands for fuel, alcohol, drugs, guns, and food. If we didn't give them what they wanted, they were going to burn the town like they did our place. Right behind them was that woman with the kids... laughing the whole time like she'd won a prize or something." For the first time, a hint of emotion shows in Keith's voice. It is a mix of anger and hate and it comes from deep down.

"They gave us 'til five that evening to deliver the demands or they would start with burning the store. There was no meeting and no discussion. Everyone knew what had to be done. As quick as we could, we got in position. One of them broke into the store and brought out three cases of beer and a couple bottles of wine. Kansas is one of the tightest states for beer and wine sales and when they found the beer, it didn't take them long to start a party. I can still hear that crazy cop saying there was a weenie roast coming and the whole town's invited. At five o'clock, they got on the police loudspeaker and said since we didn't meet their demands; they were going to start burning but changed their minds about the store and were going to burn the church first. That's when we opened up on 'em. They dropped like ducks in a barrel. Six managed to get cover in the store but three died trying to sneak out the back door and the other three made a white flag and surrendered; the woman with the kids, the crazy cop, and one other. The two kids were hunkered down next to one of the trucks. The woman turned on the others and said it was the crazy cop who killed the lady and an argument broke out between all three. That's when the crazy cop pulled a pistol and shot the woman's two kids. I didn't count the shots that followed. There were plenty but all three dropped together. I do know it was Karin who got the crazy cop. He was missing half his head when we buried him." Keith's lack of emotion is almost spooky.

"We buried twenty-three that day. Nobody wanted them in the cemetery and nobody cared to give them a Christian burial so we got a backhoe/front loader and put the whole lot in a pit we dug in Hazel Park. Dad and me set an outhouse as their marker. I spit every time I drive by the place."

Keith goes on to explain. "Stacking up the bodies gave us time to look that police car over and the uniforms on the two men. The name plates on their uniforms matched some I.D. we found in the car but the faces didn't match. They weren't police and may have killed the officers and stolen their car. There was some old blood on one of the uniforms. We used their trucks and cars to block back roads to town and a security watch was organized. Anyone trying to enter town is checked out really good; one lie will guarantee a fresh hole in the dirt. There's been several new graves since but none as many as that first time."

Landmarks:

Passing an old roadblock and bunker brings a cold chill for both Randy and Chris but they don't say anything about their experience here. It is good to be passed it.

Cleared bridges and overpasses serve for bathroom breaks. "Ladies on the left, men on the right." Is a repeated announcement from Harry or Fred.

Meals are cold. Nobody wants to slow the trip by stopping to prepare food. We begin at dawn and stop when it is too dark to see. We would drive through the night except headlights draw too much attention. We're conspicuous enough as a caravan with a big yellow school bus.

We move some food and water out of one truck to make another supply run to a town that supplied good resources on the way up. We continue on and they catch up with another fifty-pound bag of salt, another of sugar, assorted hand tools, several fifty-pound boxes of nails, and several more pair of work shoes and boots.

Evening comes and Pat Wagoner tries to reach Hazel Creed by radio.

"HC1, HC1, HC1, this is KF5OSI, do you copy?"

"HC1, HC1, HC1, this is KF5OSI, do you copy?"

"This is HC1, we can hear you. Where are you?"

"We're about two hundred miles out. We should be arriving about mid-day. How are things there?"

"Everything's fine here. The women have been tidying up vacant houses for your arrival. There are some available places in the next town just east of here if needed. We'll contact them if necessary. How is Keith doing?"

Pat hands the mic to Keith.

"This is Keith. I'm tired like the rest but doing fine. Is that you Elmer?"

"Yes, this is Elmer. Your Pa has been stayin' with me since you left. We'll all be glad seein' you when you get here."

"This is Pat again. It will be good to meet you tomorrow. Until then, we'll close for now. KF5OSI clear."

"Us too. See you tomorrow."

Sleeping arrangements are not planned well. Dawn finds us with stiff necks and backs from sleeping on school-bus bench-seats. The only one who's not cranky seems to be little Mandy, and that's a blessing for everyone.

Day two; the landscape changes. Browns give way to green and rivers and creeks show signs of having water. We should arrive at Hazel Creek before dark. It will be good to get off this bus.

Anna and I are enamored with Mandy. Our first child; she will definitely get a lot of attention; not only from her parents but from her grandparents, and from the rest of this big extended family.

Anna has seen for the first time, hard evidence of the gruesome reality that comes when populations come unhinged. As a nurse, she has witnessed death and damaged bodies but never being left in the street to decompose on their own. Unsure what the world holds, she speaks without turning from the window.

"Jason, are you seeing all this? I knew it was bad but never imagined it like this. These people just died in-place with no one to even care about them. Friends will never know what happened to them and families will never have closure."

Mandy is asleep in my arms so I put her gently into the nest of blankets we fashioned in her cradle on the seat next to us. Taking Anna's hand, I reflect on the mayhem.

"It must have been terrifying. Everything is quiet now but only months ago this place was like a war zone. I can't help but think about Noah's time. People were warned to prepare but nobody listened... they ate, drank, married, and partied... until Noah entered into the ark, the rains came, and they all perished. Back then there were only eight souls to repopulate the earth. I'm not sure about the rest of the world but our little slice is a lot like ol' Noah faced. World events will follow their course but the U.S. is going to sit on the bench for the remainder of the game. Maybe we'll be able to live in peace while the rest of the planet slugs it out. We're not listed in end time Bible prophecy. Maybe all these events explain how a first world power completely evaporates from history in just a few weeks."

Anna turns to give me her full attention but she doesn't look comforted. "And this is supposed to give me a warm fuzzy feeling about bringing our daughter into the world and trying to raise her? There's a lot of 'maybe' in your explanation and I'm scared for Mandy's future. What kind of world is she expected to face? This is Ragnarök."

Nicky Chambers, riding in the seat behind us is curious at the new word.

"Anna, I don't mean to interrupt, but what's Ragnarök?" she asks.

"Not a problem," Anna says. "It's a Norse term. My family is Danish and we have a lot of Viking ancestry. In Norse mythology, Ragnarök describes an end time battle, leaving the gods dead and the world in shambles. The mortals are left to reconstruct civilization without help from their gods."

"So who were the gods?" Nicky asks.

I give her the answer. "Money, government, technology; these were the gods the world used to depend on. They're all gone now and we have to find ways to rebuild without them... Ragnarök."

"I get it," she says. "It describes it pretty well. I guess we have a lot of work to do."

"Nobody ever knows what the next day holds," I say.

"We make our best plans but God still holds all the cards. Living by faith is going to get real for all of us. We'll have to do the best we can with what comes our way and pray for protection and direction. When you think about it, how different is this from how we've lived up 'til now? I doubt the world played out like our parents thought it would and our grandparents could never have imagined the things we take for granted. Now it's our turn."

Long road trips tend to numb your senses along with your backside. There's no traffic except for occasional abandoned cars. You are compelled to look but at the same time you hope there won't be anyone left inside. When remains are there, it's best if the doors or windows are open. At least scavengers disperse things. Otherwise, the scene is even worse.

Anna returns her gaze out the window reflecting on past conversations.

"An office worker at the hospital thought all preppers were 'Doom and Gloomers.' Susan's take was that the government always cares for its people and would never let us down. She felt safe in the inner city and if hard times came she believed food distribution would begin there. I wonder how she made out? Then there was Tim and Gloria at church; they were holding on for the rapture to rescue them from anything bad that might happen. Repeat teaching that the church would be spared from God's wrath never took into account that trouble might come by other means. You can't blame this mess on God. I tried to explain that prepping wasn't a social escape but more like fire insurance but they wouldn't listen. Their minds were made up and facts couldn't change it. What bothers me most is all the people who listened to their twisted reasoning out of convenience. Some of them had children. It's sad that children have to suffer for their parent's bad choices."

"Anna, I saw the same thing at work. Dad promoted the monthly preparedness meetings and even hosted conferences each year. Some people laughed it off, saying it wasn't for them. Others attended and said it was interesting and they planned to get into it once they retired. A few saw the handwriting on the wall and made changes. Nearly a dozen families moved out of the city to where they could grow gardens and raise chickens. The Buyer's Co-op started with them and made bulk food purchase a lot easier. It's easy to get all sorry for those who didn't heed the warnings but look at how many did. Some of them are on the bus with us right now. I'd say we are part of a job well done."

'Hazel Creek city limits' sign is a welcome sight. Since we are expected, there are no warning shots fired or hostile greetings, like met the reconnaissance team. Stopping in front of the Church we disembark, stretch, and meet the new townsfolk.

Cold Reception:

I've experienced warmer welcomes in my forty years. It's not for the lack of care from the people of Hazel Creek. They bring a fine dinner to the Grange Hall and everyone shakes our hands and says they are glad we made it safe. It's the lack of genuine smiles and joy that catches my attention. The only person showing any depth to her smile is Emily Bennett.

"You must be Anna. I'm Emily Bennett, and this must be little Mandy. She's beautiful! I'm so glad you all have come. Hazel Creek has a lot to offer and we have room to share. We live on East Dower drive, on the edge of town. If there's anything I can do to help you settle in, please call..." Emily stops short and smiles as she realizes what she said. "On second thought, "calling" won't work, make that... send for me, and I'll be glad to help. We're going to have to adjust to the way things have changed."

Anna takes Emily's hand. "Thank you, Emily. I'm very glad to meet you. You are the first person I've met from outside our group since last August and it is good to meet another friendly face."

Emily's smile changes to a more serious look. "I can tell you, we could have done without some of the new faces we've met during that time but you folks are a welcome sight. I think this is a start of something good for both our groups. But enough girl-talk for now, I'd guess you're all hungry after a long drive. Let's walk to the Grange. Can I help carry anything?"

Vince Parker raises his hands as he makes an announcement. "EVERYONE! Dinner is ready. Let's move to the Grange Hall and treat our guests to some Kansas hospitality."

As we move to the Grange, clusters of people begin forming. Josh Bennett and Keith Reed join up with Randy and John. I guess it's a positive sign when former guards who were ready to shoot you are now drawn to join company for a meal.

Dinner, as they call the mid-day meal in Kansas, is quite a spread considering the difficult times. Roast chicken and venison sausage are accompanied by deviled eggs, home canned corn, pickles, mashed sweet potatoes, and pitchers of cold tea. A large basket of dinner rolls, called "potato rolls," are delicious. It's been a while since our group has eaten wheat bread and I've forgotten how light it is compared to our milo muffins.

Once everyone is seated at tables, Vince Parker stands and addresses the group.

"On behalf of Hazel Creek, I'd like to extend a welcome to our incoming friends. I won't mince words, we've gone through Hell over the past six-months and the days ahead are full of challenges. But I think we are better suited to meet those challenges as a unified group. With the Lord's help, I'm looking for a bright future."

A mixture of soft amen's and gentle applause stops Vince for a moment.

"Let's bow our heads and join in the Lord's Prayer before we eat."

I've not recited the Lord's Prayer as a table grace before but thinking about the words, it is appropriate and adds fresh meaning.

Dad and Mom sit at the head table with the town elders and the rest of our leadership group. Anna and I sit with Byron and Emily Bennett. Karin Bennett sits at the same table with us but seems distant and only answer briefly if she is asked a direct question. She is never rude or discourteous but does appear to live in the shadows; not willing to expose herself to personal interaction. Her smoky-gray eyes somehow remind me of a wolf. Not in a vicious way but like a loner, hauntingly quiet, and independent.

"I see you have a fine church," comments Anna. "Do you have a minister at Hazel Creek?"

Byron and Emily grow solemn as Byron explains. "We had a preacher who traveled between here and two small communities nearby. After the collapse, he took to a small motorbike to save fuel and we all paid him in gas and food for a few weeks. Then he missed a Sunday and we found him a few days later in a field between here and Elma. He'd been robbed of his motorbike and shot.   Folks in Elma recognized a refugee on the preacher's motorbike and when he lied about getting it last Christmas, they took care of business with him but it was too late for Pastor Mike. He left a wife and son in Elma. They're taking it pretty hard."

"I'm really sorry," says Anna. "How are Pastor Mike's wife and son getting by?"

Emily answered.   "Pastor Mike and Jeanie are well liked and both Jeanie and Mike Jr. are doing OK. She teaches school at her home so they won't lack for food or anything. Not having Mike around is still a big loss."

"I hear you have a preacher in your group," says Byron. "We met for services a few times after Pastor Mike died but now we only meet for town business. Would your preacher care to fill our pulpit? I could bring it up with the elders but I'm pretty sure they would be in favor of having services again."

"Allen Duncan is a good man," I reply, "and I'm fairly sure he would be honored to serve as pastor. I'll talk with him and introduce you."

After dinner, Dwight Woodard stands and taps his empty cup on the table for attention.

"Our ladies have been busy for the past few weeks, cleaning and making ready many vacant homes in Hazel Creek.   They have the list of families you provided and it appears there are places for everyone. Some homes were empty so we've pulled together furnishings from other places. Many homes were left suddenly by their owners with all their belongings still there. In a few cases, previous occupants perished and were properly cared for and buried. All the houses are clean and safe to live in. As for the affects in those homes, we have left the pictures and personal items where they are so you can gain an idea who the people were that lived there. You may pack them away respectfully. If a previous owner returns, we'll work out something proper when and if that time comes. For now, my wife Florence has the list of available homes, their description, and maps to show you how to get there. "

Dad stands and speaks next. "I'm Matthew Connors and this is my wife Cynthia, my son Jason, over there, and his wife Anna, and in her arms, my newborn granddaughter Mandy. Let me offer our humble thanks on behalf of our group; not only for this great meal but for opening your hearts and community to let us find a home with you. None of our group was born or raised here but I trust, in time, we might earn our place as friends and neighbors. Thank you."

Again, soft applause is offered but more of courtesy than heartfelt. I'm accustomed to better hospitality in Texas but I've visited Kansas before and found warmer reception at a competitive bid meeting.

Anna is taking care of Mandy so I make my way to the table where Florence Woodard has housing packets arranged. One is set aside with Anna's and my name on it and a note: 'Next Door to Dr. Whitaker.' The map shows it close to town. I pick it up, figuring one place is as good as another. We've lived on a small sailboat, in a mud hut, and in an oversized hotel room; it's hard to imagine too many houses failing to step up from that.

After dinner, we make the short walk to see what sort of house it is. I'm not sure what I was expecting but it must have been something other than what we found. The house is suitable enough but is a cottage made of limestone. I guess I expected a wood framed house. The previous owners were the Samuel's and were visiting family near Los Angeles when trouble started. They stopped contacting anyone a few days after the financial collapse and never returned since the power failed.

They must have left a key with someone because it was in our envelope with the address, description of the house, and details of this family who lived here. I went in first but Anna was first to say something.

"Jason, this is weird. It almost feels like we're breaking into someone's home. All the pictures, magazines, old mail, and just everything; it's all right where they left it."

"I know," I reply. "They likely never made it. If they did, they won't be coming back here. This is like taking over someone else's identity."

Anna begins opening the kitchen cabinets. "There's no food. Probably picked up by the town's people; but all the pots and pans, table settings, and cooking utensils are here, even dish rags and towels. The refrigerator is cleaned out with the doors propped open, someone has gone to a lot of detail to preserve this place."

"It would appear this is a very honor driven town." I say. "There is a pump shotgun in the hall closet with a box of shells on the shelf. No telling what else is here."

Anna has gone to the master bedroom where the bed has been stripped to the mattress with clean folded sheets, blanket, and bedspread laid at the foot. In the closet, she finds a dress that must have been Mrs. Samuel's. Holding it up for size, the dress flows to the floor almost six inches further. Mrs. Samuel was also much wider than Anna's small frame.

"Well, what do you think? My size?"

With a chuckle, I reply. "I don't know... you may have to hem it up just a little."

A knock at the door startles us both and a friendly voice follows, "Hello, anybody home?"

We had left the front door open with only the screen door between us and the figure of a man at the door.

"Hello, I'm Jason Connors and this is my wife Anna and our baby, Mandy."

I open the door and the man steps inside.

"Pleased to meet you," the man answers. "I'm your neighbor next door; Dr. Neal Whitaker. My wife Kristine would be with me but she's not feeling well, she'll stop by another day. I understand you might be a nurse. Is that right?"

A New Home:

Shifting Mandy to her left harm, Anna extends a hand to greet Dr. Whitaker.

"It's a pleasure to meet you. I've been an RN for almost seven years. I graduated from Pacific Lutheran University in Washington State and have been on staff at Texas Memorial, Hermann."

"I know of that hospital," remarks Dr. Whitaker. "What did you do there?"

"I was a wound care specialist in the Trauma Unit."

Anna's credentials seem to impress Dr. Whitaker.

"Well I do hope you won't mind helping me care for the good folks of Hazel Creek. They've been through a lot but you couldn't ask for better neighbors."

"Dr. Whitaker, I'm being a terrible hostess. Won't you please have a seat? I have some questions you might be able to help me with." Anna motions to the living room and we all three sit and talk.

"I'd love to offer you something to drink but we don't have things sorted out yet. I was hoping you could tell us something about the Samuel's?"

Dr. Whitaker sits in the camel back chair and begins to explain.

"Ron and Barb Samuels moved here about three years ago.   He was a good neighbor; retired from the railroad... BNSF, I think. Barb helped out at the store and worked the post office there too. Their children all moved to California. That's where Ron and Barb were visiting when the trouble was announced. Two days later, they called Kristine to say they would be staying until it was safe to travel. We were watching the house while they were gone. They never called again and the news reported a lot of rioting in the part of town they were in. After the blackout, we stopped getting any news and we expect the worst has happened. They were good people, I'm sure they would be pleased you are able to use their house."

"It helps to know something of the family that was here," I say.   "You mentioned the town has been through a lot. We've been isolated down in Big Bend. Can you tell us some of what went on here? Most of the people we've met seem withdrawn. I get the idea that some very bad things have happened."

Leaning forward in his chair, Dr. Whitaker continues.

"I've watched these people change from normal, happy, and close neighbors to broken and terrified. Then I watched them harden and grow cold. Not cold like they didn't care but cold in a way that emotions don't affect them any longer. It started when Meredith

Tousley; that's Elmer's wife; she wasn't well and needed several medications for blood pressure, cholesterol, and some for anxiety. When the collapse came, her prescriptions were due and she couldn't them refilled. She lasted three weeks. Elmer said she died from not having her medicine but I think she may have ended her life with the last of her meds. Elmer took it pretty hard. Meredith was the first death we had to deal with on our own. In the past, the county picked up the body and Macer's funeral home took care of the details. For Meredith, we had to make a coffin and dig the grave by ourselves. The funeral brought death a little closer to everyone. "

"That must have been hard on folks," I add. "We heard about the group that burned the Reed home. Was that soon after Mrs. Tousley's funeral?"

"No," replies Dr. Whitaker. "There were a few things between. Two days after the funeral, some folks got concerned for the Matthews family. They hadn't been heard from in several days and didn't make the funeral. Their farm is north of here, a ways up Route 2, so Louis Roth rode out to see that they weren't sick or in need of help. He came back all shaken up. He said they'd all been killed and their bodies spread out on the front yard. He had to chase the buzzards off and found some tarps to cover them with. A group of men went back to bury them but it shook the whole town up. Their house was ransacked but the worst was the way they just killed the family. There was no call for that. It just wasn't decent. That was about the time Pastor Pritchard turned up missing and the folks in Elma caught the man riding his motorcycle. Similar killings like the Matthews had been done in Elma and folks had just had enough of it. When he lied about how he came by the motorbike, they quit asking questions and just hanged him. Some say that harsh justice brings peace but I'm seeing darkness moving into the souls of otherwise good people. There have been other killings of 'refugees;' they call them. Mostly any stranger caught lying or stealing meets a short end. We haven't had any more killing of neighbors since the Reeds but it has cost us dearly. I'm not sure we can ever get back to where we once were but the healing our people need isn't going to come from my bag. We have our work cut out for us. I'm terribly sorry for spreading bad news as you just get here. Please excuse my lack of consideration."

"Not at all," I reply. "Anna and I need to know what has happened here and you've answered a lot of questions for us. Thank you for explaining what must be painful to share."

"Well, I must be going and check on Kristine. Please don't hesitate to call for anything you need. Supper is at six o'clock at the Grange Hall. The ladies will have some groceries for each family by then and we'll get more organized. There's a pitcher pump out back and a five-gallon bucket of water to prime it with. Just make sure you refill the bucket each time you use it."

Anna takes Dr. Whitaker's hand as she says, "I'll be looking forward to helping you the best I can. I'll call on you tomorrow and you can tell me more about Hazel Creek."

As Dr. Whitaker walks back to his house, Anna and I

reflect on what we've heard.

"Well, THAT was a dose of understanding," I say. "It sure explains the odd reception we've seen. I bet we're the first outsiders since the crash that haven't been shot."

I can always count on Anna to expand my perspective. Where I see behavior and action, she sees motive and feelings.

"We have a lot to do. These people have been abandoned and left to themselves for everything they once depended on. No county, state, or federal agencies. They have to be their own police, judges, and executioner. They have to tend their own dead and watch helplessly as some can't adjust. They have to exercise force and power in ways they never intended and at the same time they feel powerless to provide other things that some desperately need. It's starting to make sense. In some ways, they demonstrate great strength but at the cost of becoming vulnerable. This whole community is suffering from Post-Traumatic Stress Disorder. Only they didn't have to go overseas; this war came to them."

Supper:

The Grange Hall is a bit more festive this evening. Our hosts have prepared a pot-luck style meal with a real roasted pig for the main course. We've grown to accept Javelina as a pork-substitute so this is a treat.

Kristen Palmer finds a piano against the wall and gets permission to play it. Though she has several music pieces committed to memory, she captures hearts with 'The Entertainer.'

At a break in playing, Vince Parker addresses the crowd.

"We're blessed to have food enough to share and good ground to grow more. After supper, we have boxes of groceries for our new families to take to their respective houses. We will help you as we can and for those who may not be proficient at farming... well... you've landed among a mess of good farmers and we'll help you with what we know. I am aware that among our new friends is an ordained minister. Can we impose upon Pastor Allen Duncan to lead us in the blessing?"

Allen stands and replies, "I'd be glad to. Heavenly Father, we are truly grateful for your providence and protection during this time of great calamity. Help our two groups to become one community of your children. Bless this bounty, the many hands that prepared it, and each one as we partake. In Jesus' name, Amen."

Lines begin to form as Scott and Roxy meet another young couple; Eric and Elizabeth Stokes. Their two-year-old daughter is Mary. After introductions to George and Jackie, they become a solid group and share many things in common.

"Eric is this real pork I see?" asks Scott.

"It's the real deal," replies Eric.

"I'm in Heaven," declares Scott. "Porky Pig's last gig. It's swine divine. We're puttin' on the dog with hog!"

Eric and Elizabeth laugh at Scott's antics but so do others in line. Between the music and Scott's humor, something appears to be cracking the protective shell for at least some people of Hazel Creek.

I seat Anna with Mandy and get both our plates for dinner. Returning, she is engaged in conversation with an older man.

"Jason, this is Elmer Tousley. Elmer, this is my husband, Jason Connors. Elmer lives on the river side of Main, off Center St., and his farm is behind the store."

"I'm pleased to meet you, sir." Setting down our plates, I extend a hand and know instantly from his firm handshake that this older gentleman is no stranger to hard work.

Anna continues her conversation as I excuse myself to get our drinks.

"Mr. Tousley, how long have you lived here in Hazel Creek?"

"Please, call me Elmer. I've lived here most of my life. Dad moved us here when I was five, back in 1940. He went to war a year later and left me, my two older brothers, and Mom, to farm the land. Mom worked right with us and we did OK. Art is my oldest brother. He was fifteen then and my next oldest is Jay who was twelve. Art left to join the service two years later as a Marine fighter pilot. He flew F4U Corsairs and was lost in July of '44. He was eighteen years old and presumed to have been shot down. His plane and body were never found. Jay wanted to join the service but was only sixteen when the war ended. I'm not sure what I'd have done if he left me and Mom to farm this place by ourselves. Dad came home in '46 and Jay married in '48. They're all gone now. I inherited the farm in '54. Meredith and I were married the next year and she passed last November. There's a family plot on the farm. I expect I'll be taking my place next to Dad, Mom, Jay, his wife Marjory, and my wife Meredith."

"Anna, you two are still young and you have so much to live for. Your sweet little baby needs a lot of your care to learn about life, and one day she'll be able to face it on her own. I've done all that. Meredith and I have four children, six grandchildren, and fourteen great grandchildren. I've taught them about as much as I know and they have done their parent's proud. Now I'm looking at my full life being mostly on the other side. My children, grand-children, and great-grand-children can do fine without me. They'll miss me when I'm gone but that's expected. It's just that I'm growing tired of seeing loved ones pass on without me. They make us who we are and as I sit here, there's more of me on the other side than is left on this side. I have no regrets from this life but death holds no fear for me. I'm ready to meet it and go through that door. Am I making sense?"

Resting her hand on Elmer's, Anna answers, "Elmer, I do understand and you have expressed it beautifully. This life is only a doorstep and for now my place is here to be a wife and mother but one day, I will join you and Meredith for a grand reunion."

Seeing Anna's smile accompanied by a sparkle of tears in her lashes, speak volumes for her depth of soul. I return with two glasses of tea as we are joined by Dick Reed.

Elmer does introductions. "Dick, this is Jason and Anna Connors and their daughter Mandy; Jason and Anna, this is my friend Dick Reed."

Handshakes go around the table as we begin to eat.

Elmer continues the conversation. "I talked Dick and his son Keith into coming to live at my place. They're a real help and I enjoy their company."

Dick joins the conversation. "Well, Keith and I enjoy Elmer's company and I think we're getting the better end of the deal. I've been farming all my life and thought I knew dirt until I met this man. Elmer's uncanny about knowing what crop to plant. A few years back, we had a really good season for potatoes. Everybody planted potatoes and we saw a bumper crop. Then the bottom fell out of the market. Every farmer had bins full of potatoes and you couldn't sell 'em for what it cost to dig 'em up. That was one really bad year for dirt farmers. The next spring everyone got together and chewed the fat over what they were planting. Most went with corn but some said wheat or soy beans. When they got to Elmer, he said potatoes. You could hear the jaws drop. Everyone said it was foolish and that he would lose his shirt two years in a row. Well, we had another great year for potatoes but Elmer was the only one with a crop to sell and the market held high. It takes a good man to make money in dirt and Elmer is that man."

Arriving a bit late, I notice Dr. Whitaker come in with who I assume is his wife. Excusing myself I make my way to them.

"Dr. Whitaker, good to see you again. Is this your lovely wife, Kristine?" Offering my hand, she returns the courtesy as I continue. "We enjoyed meeting your husband this afternoon. I hope you are feeling better. Anna and I look forward to getting to know you in the days to come."

Kristine gives my hand a gentle squeeze in acknowledgment and replies. "Thank you for your concern. I am feeling a bit better after a rest and I'll try to get over to meet your wife in a day or so."

Establishing Roots:

Stephanie Sweeny hasn't decided on housing so she accepts an offer from Harry and Rachel Taylor to stay with them. The Taylor's new home has a rec-room converted to a 'mother-in-law' apartment with its own bathroom and small kitchen. For now, it's perfect for a single young lady who isn't thrilled by living alone and she can be a help to Harry and Rachel.

The Taylor's, Fred and Irene Livingston, and my Dad and Mom all live on Central Street, about a half mile north of the store. Their homes are made of brick and have cellars. Cellars are not common where we lived in Texas.

Walking is going to keep us in good health. Anna finds a sarong in the closet and fashions a sling to carry Mandy.

"That's really clever. How did you come up with that?" I ask.

"On one of our trips to Hawaii, while waiting for our

snorkeling trip to Molokai, a street vendor was demonstrating all the ways you can use a sarong. Did you know these can be used as a dress, a blouse, a skirt, or baby carrier? I left mine at the Ranch but was sure glad to find this one in a closet. The Samuel's must have vacationed in Hawaii. I wonder if they sat through the same street vendor show we did?"

"I'm glad you were listening; I don't even remember it."

"Of course you didn't," she says. "You were at the docks asking if we could spear fish in a game preserve."

Anna's sly smile doesn't need a reply.

We walk to see how my folks are settling in but they aren't at their house. They are at the Taylor's and Anna catches sight of them as we start to go back home.

"Hello neighbors!" she says, making our way up the driveway.

"Oh, look Matt," says Mom. "Mandy came to visit and brought Anna and Jason with her."

With hugs and handshakes all around, we go into the Taylor's living room to sit and relax.

After sharing descriptions of our respective houses and the families that used to live there, Irene Livingston voices an observation.

"Have you noticed the people of Hazel Creek being rather distant and hard to get close to? Emily Bennett will talk with me some and Vince Parker seems to be the spokesperson for the town but even they seem to exert a lot of effort when they do."

Rachel adds, "The younger couples don't seem affected as much. I saw our newlyweds connecting pretty well with a local couple but the missing 'welcome wagon' is pretty evident around here. I don't think it's resentment but there does seem to be something hanging over this town."

"Dr. Whitaker came over when we arrived," says Anna. "He's a nice man and we talked quite a bit but his wife wasn't with him. He said she wasn't feeling well but that could be for anything. He did tell us of some deaths and killings that have really shaken the community. He talked about the town changing and becoming cold with protective barriers. I think that's what we're seeing and I don't think they mean to be this way."

Dad says, "Fred, Harry, and I went to a seminar on hiring prior combat veterans. They described conditions of post-traumatic stress and they were a lot like what we're seeing from this whole town."

"I was just thinking about that," says Fred.

"Me too," adds Harry.

So typical of Mom to listen to everyone and speak last. She offers, "We may have two things at work here. I can understand the stress of having to face down evil men but they have also suffered the loss of not only friends killed but also those who have left and not come back. They were friends and neighbors, perhaps lifelong friends, and now we're living in their houses. I felt a little strange having personal affects still in place but after meditating about it, I think they either can't bring themselves to part with dear friends or they want us to know about them so their memory won't be lost... or both. I get the feeling these homes are like shrines to the memory of those friends. Becoming part of this new community may require us to become part of the old one. I know I'm not going to be moving any furniture for a while."

Irene suggests, "Maybe we need to visit our group members and share this. I think Cynthia has discovered a clue to helping these people and we don't need to create any unintentional offense."

Word passes from one to another and our group agrees to respect the homes we occupy as though we are guests of owners who will return someday.

The Spencer's, Chris, Becky, and Gina, are on the other side of town on West Dower Drive and a half mile north of Main St. Their house is one of the newer homes with fiber cement siding. Mom walks with Anna and Mandy back home while I walk to the store and find Chris riding a bicycle into town.

"Hey Chris. How are you and the family getting on?"

"Not too bad. The house is a lot like what we left in Lubbock. You know that couple that Scott and Roxanne met at supper last night? Well, we're next door to their parents, Steve and LouAnn Stokes. LouAnn seems to like Becky and Gina so I left them home while I rode into town on this bicycle I found in the garage. I think it's going to get a lot of use."

"Looks like you have a hot-rod there," I say. "Just don't get any speeding tickets." We chuckle as I shift subjects and share what we've observed and our possible plan for reaching the people of Hazel Creek.

Chris listens carefully and agrees the plan is a good one. "Yeah, I think this whole town has P.T.S.D." he says. "Becky and I sorta started working it already. We talked quite a while with LouAnn about the people who lived in our house. They were about our age. Rob and Ceal Simmons; LouAnn took to Ceal like a daughter. Rob was a computer analyst and worked from home mostly but regularly had to travel to fix systems at Banks and major industry. Ceal went with him on some of those trips and loved to shop the big cities. That's where they were when everything collapsed; Manhattan of all places. LouAnn said they called several times before the grid failed. The airlines grounded flights until the money could be figured out and they had been using taxis to get around so even if they could have found gas, they didn't have a rental car to drive back with. Nothing has been heard since and Steve suspects the worst but LouAnn isn't ready to quit hoping. She did say that Becky reminds her of Ceal and that she's glad to have us next door."

"It sounds like you two are making good headway," I say. "Keep at it. Maybe rescuing this town won't be as hard as we first thought."

Sunday arrives and church is nearly full. Allen Duncan is about to preach his first sermon to a combined assembly of both groups. There are signs of blending already. Scott and Roxanne sit by Eric and Liz Stokes with George and Jackie next to them. In the row behind are Chris and Becky with Gina and next to them, helping with Gina, are Steve and LouAnn Stokes. The Parkers sit with Fred and Irene Livingston and the

Bennett's share a pew with Mom, Dad, Anna and me. Karin doesn't join us though. She sits with her brother Josh on the back row.

Allen's message about 'healing the land' is spot on.

Farmers:

With no telephone and few people with CB or ham radio, news spreads by notices posted at the Grange Hall or store. A farmer's meeting is scheduled for seven o'clock this morning to discuss crops and planting methods in light of changes. A good crowd gathers.

Dwight Woodard opens the meeting. "Thanks everyone, for coming out and bringing your best ideas for a challenging planting season. Considerations we need to address are the lack of commercial fertilizer and pesticides. We have a small amount on hand but not nearly enough for what we normally use. Another issue is subsistence farming verses cash crop. A third issue is limited fuel to run machinery. I think we should start with the question of how much land can we till without fuel."

Elmer Tousley stands and is recognized. "It looks like my timing was good. As many of you know, I've been reading up and experimenting with this no-till wheat farming. As a trial, the Great Plains dealer lent me a small no-till planter to drill in my winter wheat and it's still in my barn. It's not big but could be pulled by a horse or two. It can adjust for corn or wheat so we should be able to plant a couple hundred acres. Our yield will be off because we don't have the nitrogen we need but we should be able to grow plenty more than our needs."

Daemon Eckerd speaks next. "Elmer, with no-till, isn't the grain interval smaller and how does that affect fertilizer demand and soil degradation?"

"The smaller interval actually helps," replies Elmer. "Weeds have less effect on no-till so there's less competition for nutrients. It's still going to be less than optimal but it'll save us the effort of tilling ground and it should produce better. "

Louis Roth moves to another point. "We're also going to need a lot of victory gardens or one great big one. How are we set for seed?"

Daemon answers, "Vicki said the store still has seed from last spring and Valley Coop has wheat and corn if we can work a deal with Fred to get it."

Byron Bennett offers a point. "Spreading out those produce gardens will limit insect loss. It also spreads the work out. We may have to look after the new gardeners but they'll learn."

Stephanie has been listening up to now but offers an idea. "I'm Stephanie Sweeny and we had some measured success with applying organic farming techniques down in the Big Bend area. We learned to plant shorter rows and intersperse insect repelling plants. We had some insect damage but it was isolated and easily controlled. Composting and livestock manure collection can also offset the lack of fertilizer."

If silence ever made a noise, the room grew loud with it. After a noticeable pause, Vince Parker replies.

"Thank you Ms. Sweeny, we'll take that into consideration."

As locals again begin discussing other ideas, Stephanie makes her way to the door and walks out. I follow her and we talk while walking back toward our houses.

"Can you believe that?" Stephanie had some venting to do. "I might as well have tried to promote devil worship. They didn't even listen to what I said. What's wrong with these guys? All they know is production farming with chemicals and machinery but they're not even willing to listen to other ideas. It's not like I want to tell them what to do. All I wanted was to join the discussion."

"That might be your problem." Stephanie stops walking and turns toward me as I continue. "You're a third their age and, pardon my saying it this way… just a woman. This is ultra conservative Kansas and women farmers are pretty rare out here. Besides that, you were right. There are two sides to every war and the enemy of chemicals is organic farming. A huge chemical industry has bought farmer loyalty with agricultural loans, Congressional lobbying, and a huge public relations effort to paint organic farmers as pot smoking hippies. You aren't going to win these guys with discussion."

"So what good is my major in botany and what I've

learned from Lisa at camp? I'm not interested in a sex change."

That gets me to laugh a little and Stephanie at least cracks a smile in return as I offer her some advice that Dad has given me on several occasions.

"When words fail, actions speak. Check on the cache of seed we brought from camp and see what will grow well here. If you can produce better crops with less insect loss, they'll have to listen. It's going to be a lot of hard work but what can you lose?"

"All right then," Stephanie is so competitive. "I'm building my team and we're going to kick some Kansas butt."

I think Stephanie missed a calling. If I ever need a recruiter, I know who to ask. In two days I notice Randy, Scott, and George searching the river banks for limestone. Roxanne, Jackie, and Nicky are hauling three garden carts filled with old livestock bedding, and Stephanie is organizing others to dig up a huge garden area in the field behind the Taylor's new place. So many people are helping and it seems everyone is motivated.

Dad finds me at home and asks me about it.

"I haven't seen this group so energetic since we started expanding the camp. What did you do? Stephanie tells me this was all your idea."

"Not me, Dad... I think YOU started all this." I'm sporting a huge smile.

"Me? How's that?" asks Dad.

"Stephanie tried to help out the farmers during a planting meeting in town and she got shot down," I explain. "It seems they gave her the impression that her ideas weren't welcome. We talked afterward and she was pretty upset about it. That's when I remembered and shared your advice to me back when I was starting out with O.S.I. (Oilfield Solutions Incorporated) You told me that 'When words fail, actions speak,' and I shared that with Stephanie. She's been a woman on a mission ever since. So, you see, it was YOUR words that started all this." I'm still grinning ear to ear.

"I never thought of myself as a motivational speaker, much less one in absentia," says Dad. "But if we're going to have some positive competition, growing food is about as good a focus as any."

We live on West Dower Drive, parallel to West Main St. with about half a mile between. Chris and Becky Spencer live another half mile to the west of us on the same road so we see each other often. It's no surprise that Chris shows up at our door one evening but the look on his face indicates trouble.

"Jason, can we talk? I need some help figuring something out."

"Sure Chris. Are you and Becky having trouble?" I ask.

"Yes but not like you think. Becky and I are fine but something's wrong between us and the Stokes next door. Becky asked LouAnn if she'd done something to offend them and they say no but the sudden coldness says different."

"You were doing so well, tell me what was going on

before and when all this happened. We may need some help from Anna and my Mom on this. They can read people better than most."

"It started yesterday. Becky was talking to Stephanie about gardens and since Steph had plenty of help at their garden, Becky decided to lay one in at our place. We didn't want to disturb anything but the Simmons already had a garden plot all worked up. Becky began turning the soil and found it easy work. Rob and Ceal had it mulched and the soil looks really good. She got it cleaned out and ready to plant about the time the Stokes came home and the glare from LouAnn was like a silent war cry. I don't know where they went or who they had talked with but we haven't spoken with them since. Becky's really upset."

"I don't know, Chris. I was at the meeting when Stephanie spoke up with the farmers. She didn't say anything offensive but it sure got a reaction. I'd hate to think it started something."

Many Hands:

Byron Bennett can't help but notice Randy's multiple trips with a wheelbarrow to bring back limestone from the river. "You're Randy, right?"

"Yes, hello." Randy stops and sets the wheelbarrow down to shake Byron's hand.

"I guess I'm a little curious what you are making with that soft rock. It's not very strong, you know." Byron's curiosity is killing him.

Somewhat laughing as he understands the odd appearance, Randy explains. "I guess it does look strange. This limestone has a lot of minerals in it and we learned back in Big Bend that crushing it up and adding it to the soil helps feed the plants. We're using hammers to crush the stone to powder and then working it into the garden plots."

"Was that one of Stephanie's ideas? I was at the meeting when she tried to share some of that. I don't think it was well received but I'd like to come see it, if you'd let me help some. I'm an old dog that can still learn new tricks."

"I'm sure you're welcome and we never turn down help," says Randy.

The Bennett's place is only a quarter mile from the Taylor's where Stephanie has 'Garden Central' in full swing. Byron finds Stephanie that next morning, and takes her aside for a word.

"Stephanie, I'm Byron Bennett and I would like to apologize for the way you were treated at the planting meeting. Farming has been a way of life for generations on this prairie and I'm afraid we don't take to new ideas very well. I've read about organic farming and see benefit to it, especially now that we don't have machinery or chemicals to work with. If you don't mind, I'd like to know more about what you're doing and how we can implement your ideas to solve some of our problems."

"Mr. Bennett, I'd be glad to show you what we're doing but I'm still learning about organic farming. The things I don't know would astound you." Both Stephanie and Byron get an opportunity to laugh together at something.

"Stephanie, we're looking into no-till planting because it makes best use of available nutrients but I see you're tilling deep. What's with that?"

She explains, "We're assuming that after generations of getting the most out of the land, there's little nutrients left in the soil. Most of what's grown depletes the top four inches of soil so we're turning the soil over from a foot down. We start by digging out the first row and saving the dirt aside. Then we turn the next row into the first row, turning it over in the process. When we're done the whole garden will be upside down with good soil on top. As we go, we're adding pulverized limestone for minerals, wood ash for potassium, and we're making manure tea for nitrogen."

"Manure tea?" he asks. "That's a new one. How do you do that?"

"Those plastic barrels over there are holding fresh manure." She points to a row of half dozen plastic barrels. "When they are two thirds full, we fill the barrels with water and let them sit for ten days. They need weights on top because as it decomposes, methane generates in the mat. After ten days we press out the liquid, dilute it with water and irrigate our garden with it."

"I'm impressed," he says. "How large of a garden are you planning?"

"We need to be planting soon but by using high density companion planting, we should get an impressive yield from thirty-five feet square," she says.

"OK," he asks. "Explain high density companion planting for me."

"Sure," she says. "In the wild, plants grow much closer than we let them in traditional gardens but that's because we need room for tractor tires. Since we'll be tending this by hand, we can plant mutually beneficial plants closer together and block out weeds at the same time. Using the same space, we'll grow pole beans, corn, and squash. The corn provides stalks for the beans to climb, the beans provide nitrogen to feed the corn, and the squash acts as a living mulch to block weeds and retain soil moisture for both the corn and beans. Other plants work that way too."

"I seem to remember some of this but it's been a long time," he says. "Aren't there some plants that repel pests?"

"There are," she says. "Marigolds are known for that and we'll use them around the edges but onions, basil, and collard greens work too and you can eat those. We're also planting short rows and breaking up any long runs of the same plant. Predator insects like to start on a row and follow it to the end. We stand a better chance of stopping an infestation with shorter rows."

As Byron and Stephanie work their way over to where the guys are pulverizing limestone, he picks up two pieces about the size of a potato and rubs them together. The rock is so soft from sitting in water that it sifts sand-like particles to the ground.

"You know; I've been fascinated with how soft this rock is since I was a boy but never thought it was good for the soil. I'm looking forward to seeing what this garden will do."

He tosses the small stones back on the pile and reaches for a much larger stone for Randy to begin breaking up. Yanking his hand back, he grasps one hand in the other as two red dots form in the web of his right hand between his thumb and forefinger. Byron has been snake-bit.

"Byron! What did that?" says Stephanie. "I didn't see it."

"I should have been more careful," he says. "Most likely a prairie rattler. That's what we have around here. Best get Doc. Whitaker. I might be in trouble here."

"I'll get the Doctor," Randy says. "Scott, George, be careful but take that pile apart and kill that snake. Doc. Whitaker will need to know what it is."

Stephanie drags over a lawn chair for Byron. "Sit down here and try to keep calm. Keep your hand lower than your heart. I'm going to find a rubber band."

She runs to the house as the men begin pulling the rock pile apart with shovels and rake handles.

Scott sees the snake first. "I see it, it's in there. Watch the back door, it may try to run."

A few minutes later, George jambs his rake into the pile. "I have it pinned. Its head is under this rock."

Scott pulls a few more rocks away and plunges his shovel into the snake, almost severing its head. "Got it!"

Not wanting to confirm the stories about dead snakes still biting, George extracts the viper with the rake and lays it out on the grass. It measures almost four feet long.

"It looks sorta like a diamond back," says Scott.

Byron can see the snake from the lawn chair and confirms what it is. "They look similar but that's a Prairie Rattler. The spots are a little different shape and the color isn't quite the same. It's a big one though."

Stephanie returns from the house and places a large

rubber band on Byron's arm above the bite to restrict venom migration as they wait for Dr. Whitaker.

News of the snakebite takes ten minutes to reach Dr. Whitaker. Anna hears Randy calling from the road as he runs past our house and leaves Mandy with me to see what she can do.

Dr. Whitaker may be retired but he sure knows how to handle emergencies.

"Did you get the snake?"

Randy replies, "It came out of a rock pile. Scott and George were looking for it when I left."

"I hope they're careful. We don't need more bites to deal with."

"Anna, I need you to go back with Randy and begin transport back here. I'll set up to receive him. Keep track of vitals; especially watch for shock and respiratory distress."

As Randy and Anna pass our house, she dashes in to grab her bag and tells me to take Mandy to Mom and Dad and then follow her to the Taylor's. I know better than to ask details, my Viking warrior is back.

"Hello, Byron. Do you remember me? My name's Anna. I'm an RN and helping Dr. Whitaker. We're going to take you to his house but I need to check a few things first."

Anna pulls out a pair of bandage scissors from her bag and cuts the rubber band from Byron's arm. "Is this the only bite?"

"Yes, he only got me once. Doesn't that band slow the

poison?" he asks.

"They used to think it did and a rubber band is better than using a tunicate. It doesn't help but at least it does no harm. I just need it out of the way so I can get good blood pressure readings."

Anna already has her blood pressure cuff on Byron and is listening to his heart and respiration. She pumps up the cuff and since the bite is on the right hand; she checks readings on each arm.

"Byron, how do you feel?"

"My hand is throbbing and I feel buzzing around my lips," he says.

"How about breathing?" she asks, "any shortness of breath?"

"No, I'm fine," he says.

Anna can see sweat beads on Byron's brow. "Are you feeling warm?"

"Well, I'm sweating a lot but I don't feel hot inside. I think it's the venom."

Byron's hand is starting to swell around the bite marks and slowly weeping blood from the two holes the fangs made.

I arrive with Dad and Fred Livingston as Anna completes her assessment. Byron looks pale.

"How can we help?" I ask.

Patient:

"Get me that cushion from the recliner. We'll use that in the wheel barrow to get him to Dr. Whitaker." Anna is barking orders but nobody minds.

"I think I can walk," he says. "You needn't go to all this trouble."

"Byron, we need you as calm as possible to slow the envenomation. Let us do the work and you try to stay calm. We'll try not to spill you out on the way. Pretend you're on the way back from an all-night bender." Anna's humor is uncharacteristic in her Viking mode but it does raise a smile from Byron.

With the cushion in place, Byron stands as his lawn chair is replaced with the wheelbarrow. Seated comfortably he says, "Drive on McDuff!"

Byron is trying to put on a good front but he's already showing signs of the venom's damage.

Dr. Whitaker has an exam room set up at his house since the small medical clinic up the road has no electricity and its treatment rooms have no windows. For a converted extra bedroom, it serves well. An exam table and manual hospital bed take up most of the room. He has a stool on wheels and two glass front cabinets holding various medical supplies. In the corner is an I.V. stand.

We help Byron in as Dr. Whitaker motions us to put him on the bed. Repeating B.P. measurements on both arms, he compares with Anna's notes and then turns to his patient.

"So, Byron, looks like you stuck your hand where it didn't belong. Did you at least kill it?"

"I didn't but the boys did. Prairie Rattler, about four feet long but with three inch fangs, I think." Byron's humor is intact.

Dr. Whitaker, turns to Anna, "Edema at the wound with subdural hematoma already present; I think we have a moderate envenomation. Have you any training for this?"

"We've seen half a dozen cases in the five years I was at Texas Memorial," she says. "I was generally called in after initial response to address wound issues."

"We may need that," he says. "These wounds can be nasty if we don't treat it right. Have you ever worked with Crotalidae antivenin?"

"I know it is administered I.V. and is equine sourced so it can have a strong reaction. Is it available?" she asks.

Dr. Whitaker opens a glass cabinet and removes a small box of vials. "I have exactly ten vials of Crotalidae. I took these from the clinic along with this medical furniture when we lost power. Once the power dropped, everyone went home at the clinic but as a local contributing doctor, I have a key to the E.R. entrance. Dick and Vince helped me haul everything here along with as much of the drugs and supplies I could use and store. This was all the antivenin they kept on hand. It's enough to treat minor to moderate envenomation and enough to stabilize a serious case before medevac to Wichita. It's going to have to be enough."

"What if he reacts to the Crotalidae?" Anna's concern is justified. On one occasion at Texas Memorial, a patient reacted so strongly to the equine based drug that the reaction became more problematic than the bite being treated.

"It's possible but we really don't have an alternative," he says. "We'll start with ten percent over five minutes and look for complication. If he reacts, we have epinephrine standing by. If he accepts it, we give him fifty ml. as fast as he can take it."

Anna starts an I.V. drip as Dr. Whitaker rehydrates the first vial of antivenin; setting it by a vial of epinephrine. Injecting the Crotalidae into a smaller I.V. bag and rocking it back and forth to mix, he hangs the bag on the pole a bit higher than the saline that Anna just started and connects it to a port. Adjusting the roller clamps, he monitors the drip rate of each I.V. bag and sets them perfectly.

Anna comments on Dr. Whitaker's handling of the I.V. "I haven't set a manual drip since clinicals. I can do it but not that fast. You're good."

Dr. Whitaker replies with a bit of 'old school' satisfaction. "When I started practice, there were no pumps. I'll grant you they make things easier but when you don't have all the toys, you have to fall back on training. It gets easier with practice."

As the minutes pass slowly, Byron shows no sign of reaction to the serum. After five minutes Dr. Whitaker asks Anna to hydrate four more vials of antivenin.

Emily Bennett arrives with a worried look. "I got here as soon as I heard. How bad is it?"

Emily goes to Byron's bedside and gently strokes his hair; Dr. Whitaker explains. "Sometimes these are dry bites with no venom but this one isn't. He got a pretty good dose. Thankfully, we got him here right away and he's taking the antivenin well. It's going to be a lengthy recovery but Byron's doing pretty good right now. The next twelve hours should show marked improvement."

"You're not rid of me yet." Byron appears weak but manages a smile. "It'll take more than an angry rope to take me down."

Karin and Josh enter the room but stay by the door.

"How'd it happen?" asks Josh.

"It was over at the Conway farm," Dr. Whitaker explains, "where the Taylor's are staying. He reached for a rock from a pile and the snake got his hand."

Byron tries to offer details but Dr. Whitaker ushers everyone out of the room to let the medicine work.

"Right now, Byron needs quiet to let the antivenin do

its job. We'll keep you posted if anything changes. Plan on seeing him in the morning; It will take that long. He's in good hands."

"Love you, Daddy," are the first words I hear from Karin. For the most part, she hardly speaks unless directly spoken to and then only in brief replies.

In Dr. Whitaker's living room, on the way to the door, I hear Josh asking Karin, "What was he doing over there with 'them' anyway?"

More Trouble:

Chris and Becky Spencer are waiting for me at the house. Becky is occupying their daughter Gina but I can tell she's upset.

"What's up, Chris?" After all the trouble today, I half don't want to know.

"More of the same," he says, "but I overheard some things in town that I thought you should know about. I rode up to the store and when I parked my bike on the side, I heard some of the farmers talking about Stephanie and the work going on at the Taylor's. They were calling her an 'eco-twink' and that her 'hippie-dippy organic farming junk' was just a waste of good seed. It didn't sound like the right time for me to walk in so I left and went home to find Becky in tears."

"LouAnn, again?" I ask.

"Yeah," says Chris. "Only this time she got after Gina and told her to go play in her own yard. There's no fence between us and while Becky was working in the garden, Gina played on the grass area. She's done it several times before with no complaint from LouAnn. I don't get what's happened but something went sour between our two groups. There's something else strange too. When Becky turned over the garden, she found some rose bushes buried in the dirt like someone deliberately buried them. They were barely alive. We don't know who buried them but Becky didn't want to make a fuss. She re-planted them on the far side of the house where LouAnn couldn't see; in case it was her that did that to the Simmons garden.

I try to encourage Chris and Becky to remain strong, keep working at it, and to be patient. "These folks are hurting and they appear pre-wired to be offended. I'll pass all this to Dad and see if he has some advice. I'll get back with you."

Anna sends word that she's staying at Dr. Whitaker's to care for Byron through the night. The antivenin is working but he needs close observation.

Dad and Mom come over to help with Mandy. Mom brings me some dinner.

After conveying to Dad all that has transpired with the Spenser's and the comment I heard from Josh Bennett as he left Dr. Whitaker's house, I was looking for answers.

"I think we have several things complicating our two groups and it's going to take a lot of prayer and patience to sort out. Nearly a third of the town was either caught away or lost to violence that came here. We're staying in the homes of many of those and it's hard for these neighbors to see us living where their friends used to live. Then there's the huge change forced on all of us. People are reluctant to change and that's generally good but when you're pressed to change, it brings conflict. I think that's where Stephanie's trouble lies. She's right to enrich the soil with organics. What other source is available anyway? But that's not the way these farmers have successfully farmed for generations and it rubs them the wrong way. She'll win them over when they see the yield and quality of her garden but it will take time. Byron's snake bite is another issue. It's being played politically against us. We're being blamed for something that was purely an accident but it happened from a rock pile we created and while he was at the Taylor's place. Emotions are just that and rarely shaped by reason. With all the stress this community is under, they're probably just a step away from a torchlight parade with pitchforks. I don't think we're in any danger but we need to walk carefully and let all this settle down. I'll talk with Vince, Daemon, and Dwight tomorrow. Maybe they can shed some light on things from the town's perspective.

Even though Anna is staying with Byron, Mandy has to go visit her for meals. Breast feeding is such a good excuse to let dads get a full night sleep. I tell Anna, "I'd love to help with some of the night feeding but I'm lacking the equipment." That's when I get 'the look' that I've seen Mom give Dad on occasion. I doubt Mom and Anna share notes or took classes to learn how to do that look. I think it's something all women are genetically predisposed to.

Dr. Whitaker's door is not locked but I knock anyway.

I hear Anna's voice and before I can say anything, Mandy starts her baby sounds and gets really active. She's hungry.

Anna steps out of the exam room where Byron is resting and sits with me in the living room taking Mandy from my arms to nurse her. Kristine Whitaker comes in from the kitchen where she has brewed a cup of herbal tea for Anna.

"I heard you come in as I poured this for your wife. Would you like a cup of tea? There's plenty."

"Thank you for the offer," I say, "but I'm fine."

Kristine hands Anna a cup and saucer. "Anna, you need to keep your fluids up for that precious baby of yours. This is an herbal tea we blend right here. It has blackberry, lemon grass, and mint. I hope you like it. Jason, are you sure you wouldn't like some?"

"It sounds really good but I'm OK for now," I reply. "Thanks again."

Anna leans over to sip the tea, being careful not to let the hot tea pass over Mandy. She sighs, "This is SO good. Thank you so much."

Kristine smiles, "I'm glad you like it. When you have the time, I'd be glad to show you where we pick the ingredients. I'll leave you three to visit. Anna, if you need anything, I'll be in the bedroom. Just knock. Dr. Whitaker will sleep right through unless I wake him. He's a good sleeper."

Kristine leaves the room and Anna, Mandy, and I are alone in the living room.

"Has she been any trouble?" Anna asks.

"She's been an angel, like her mother," I reply. "How've you been and how's Byron?"

"I'm OK.   Byron's pretty uncomfortable but the antivenin appears to be working. He got a pretty good bite. Dr. Whitaker was really thinking ahead when he stocked Crotalidae. I'd hate to think where we'd be without it. I'm tracking his vitals and we're scoping his urine for blood. There's some ecchymosis surrounding the bite but it's expected and not severe."

"OK, what's ecchymosis?" Anna sometimes forgets that she's speaking medical terms and we don't use those terms in the oil field. I do the same with her and have to back up to explain oil field terminology. Just as I don't apologize for stopping to explain an oil field term, Anna doesn't apologize for explaining medical terms.

"Ecchymosis looks like a bruise and is cause by escaped blood in the tissue but a bruise is from impact. In this case, the venom caused bleeding and the blood gets trapped under the skin in the tissues. Some is expected and as long as it doesn't get too large, his body will take care of itself. If it spreads fast or get's extensive, it means we didn't use enough antivenin."

"How long 'til he can go home?" I ask.

Anna's expression tells me she doesn't like the answer she's about to give. "I think he'll go home in a couple of days but I want to keep a close eye on him for at least ten days. As long as he stays quiet with low activity, he should do fine. The problem is that he can develop a reaction to the serum from five to ten days later. Mrs.

Bennett is going to have to keep a tight rein on him. You know how men are."

Mandy has finished feeding and fallen asleep. Passing her back to me, I kiss Anna as I tell her, "If Emily is anything like you; Byron doesn't have a chance."

 We chat about a few other things then change Mandy's diaper before I head back home. Anna checks on Byron before I leave then locks the door behind me. I feel better knowing the door is locked even though I'm only next door.

The moon is bright tonight so walking back with Mandy isn't challenging. A mouse crosses the road about twenty feet ahead of me but I can easily see it in the moonlight. I jump just the same. At this point, everything looks like a snake. It's quiet and a peaceful calm settles over Hazel Creek. I just pray that calm is felt by everyone and that the raw emotion of the past few days will fade.

After a second trip for Mandy to visit 'Anna's Diner,' Anna suggests I leave her there. Kristine made a place for Mandy in the living room and Anna isn't going to sleep tonight anyway. I tell her that I'll be back in the morning and gratefully head home for a few uninterrupted hours sleep but walking back without Mandy or Anna; I feel empty and alone. My shift will come when Dr. Whitaker relieves Anna in the morning and it's her turn to sleep.

Morning arrives too quickly and I meet Anna as she rounds the corner at our gate.

"You look beat," I say. "How's Byron this morning?"

"He had a little blood in his urine but it's clear now. The nausea is gone but he's still very weak. His system is working hard so that's expected. Dr. Whitaker thinks the next few days will tell."

I carry Mandy as we walk the short way to our house next door. Anna eats a small breakfast and heads to bed while I try to keep Mandy quiet. Except for feedings, Anna sleeps about six hours and gets up when she hears Mom coming over to bring lunch.

"Oh, I didn't mean to wake you, dear," she says.

"I don't think you did," replies Anna. "I was awake when you came to the door and decided to get up. It's hard to sleep during the day anyway. I smell something good. Did you bring lunch?"

Dad comes in and we all sit down for lunch or dinner as locals call it.

"I saw Byron and Dr. Whitaker," Dad says. "Emily and Karin were there but Josh left as I arrived. Doc says he might go home tomorrow but he wants to keep him for observation at least one more night."

"How are Mrs. Bennett and Karin taking all this," I ask.

"Emily is doing OK but I think Karin is struggling," Dad says. "I heard Emily reminding Karin that snakes were here long before the town and snake bites happen when it's nobody's fault. Dr. Whitaker had some concern over the wound though. He said it wasn't healing right and may have to be opened."

Getting her bag, Anna kisses Mandy and me as she makes her way to the door. "I need to get over there. Dr. Whitaker can use the help and I want to see that wound."

Division:

Allen Duncan delivers a moving sermon and Kristen Palmer plays hymns beautifully but Sunday's attendance is very one sided. Most of our group is there, except for Anna, who is still helping Dr. Whitaker with Byron, but most of the Hazel Creek residents are missing. Vince and Lois Parker, Dwight and Florence Woodard, and Emily Bennett are the only residents to show up. Scott and Roxanne sit with George and Jackie but their new friends, Eric and Elizabeth Stokes, are missing. Dad has a chance to talk with Vince about what might be driving this.

"Matt, I see attitudes feeding on nothing and I can't put an end to it. People are suddenly polarized and have an 'us' verses 'them' attitude. Something needs to pull this town together, ALL of us, or we'll break apart."

"We're seeing it too Vince. I don't have any answers but there's certainly a wedge between us. Both our groups have very different experiences but we're still similar people. I think, in time, this will iron out. I sure pray it does. We need each other. I know it's planting time and several of our men have volunteered to help but they're all told their help isn't needed."

Stress is obvious on Chris and Becky's face. Even little Gina doesn't run around with as much energy. The only smile Becky shows is when she shares with me some gardening news.

"Jason, remember those plants we found buried in the garden? I planted them on the far side of the house, against the foundation and they are taking off like crazy. I thought at first they might have been blackberry plants but it turns out they were roses. Tell Anna that I'll send her some when they bloom."

Chris adds, "You should see the garden coming up too. I never knew Becky had such a green thumb but it looks like we're going to be eating well. She's got beans climbing the corn; beets, broccoli and onions together; and carrots, tomatoes, and lettuce all mixed up. I've never seen a garden like hers but it does pack a lot in a small space."

I learn the Spencer's garden is not alone. Almost every garden planted by our group, looks very different than the neat straight rows of the local farmers. What also looks very different is that the gardens with improved soil and watered with doses of 'manure tea,' are sprouting early and growing much faster.

Byron is home now so Anna and Dr. Whitaker make daily trips to monitor his progress while I watch Mandy. It's about a half mile from our house to the Bennett's farm and they use that time to chat as they walk.

"How are you and Jason settling in? I know Mandy takes up a lot of time, are you two finding time for yourselves?"

"Thanks for asking," Anna replies. "Jason's Mom loves to keep Mandy for visits and we get short dates from time to time. I have to say, life is simpler since the collapse but it didn't get less busy."

"This is a lot like when I was a boy. We were one of the first farms to get electricity under the Rural Electrification Program. Poles carried the wire from the road to a post, mid-way between the barn, our house, and pump house. On that post was a single electric light and that was the extent of our electrification. Dad didn't trust electricity in the house and nobody let it in their barn. In time, trust eventually grew. Trust will grow in the same way between our two groups, if we can wait all this out."

Anna can't help but ask, "I've always been curious how you got along without refrigeration back then."

Dr. Whitaker continues. "We kept a root cellar for most things. It's not the same as your basement. A real root cellar is much cooler and more humid than a basement. I remember a neighbor who had the great idea to build a cement wall root cellar with a concrete floor. We had to help him through that next winter because all his stored food went to ruin. We kept eggs in what was called water glass. We bought it in the hardware store and it sealed the egg shells from air. We could keep eggs usable for as long as a year without refrigeration. They were good as fresh for the first three months. After that the yolks would usually break when fried.

You could scramble them until about nine months and use them to cook with the rest of the time. We hardly needed to keep them very long anyway; the chickens only stopped laying for about a month during molt."

"How did you keep meat without freezing or refrigeration?" asks Anna.

"We had a smoke house and cured our own hams, bacon, jerky, and dried beef. We also laid up salt pork. We didn't eat as much meat as we do today but what we ate was good. Jerky was never eaten like kids do today. Ours was thicker and Mom would cut it into chunks then soak it overnight to rehydrate it for soup or stew. During winter, fresh meat was usually chicken and when we butchered a cow we shared it with a neighbor. Between two families, we got fresh beef twice as often that way. We also ate fish, prairie chicken, ducks, geese, venison, and rabbit, but we ate those fresh."

Anna is impressed. "How did you find time for all that and manage the farm?"

"Dad and my older brothers rarely had time away from the field between planting and harvest but they got in a few good late fall hunts. The rest was up to me and my sister. Everybody learned to shoot by age twelve, and we were pretty good hunters. I had to work at it if I was to stay ahead of my sister. It made you feel good when the family sat down to a dinner you put on the table."

Arriving at the Bennett farm, Anna and Dr. Whitaker change their subject to Byron's hand.

Emily greets Dr. Whitaker and Anna at the door,

thanks them for coming and shows us to the room where Byron is laying on a bed. Karin promptly leaves the room without a word.

"Anna, I don't like the look of the bite area. Ecchymosis is acceptable but the edema isn't uniform and we have some abscess issues."

"How are you feeling today, my friend," Dr. Whitaker asks.

"I wish I could say better. I ache all over and have no energy. I just want to sleep all day," says Byron.

Anna continues to take his blood pressure and heart rate but waits to take his temperature until Dr. Whitaker's questions are done.

"Where does it ache? Is it muscle ache or in the joints?"

Byron puts his hand on his elbow. "Joints, I feel like an old man."

"You ARE an old man, but that's no reason to feel like one." Dr. Whitaker's dry humor brings a smile to Byron's face.

"Now let this pretty nurse take your temperature while I look at your bite." Dr. Whitaker presses a few places near the wound while looking for any indication of pain on Byron's face; there is none.

Anna puts a thermometer under Byron's tongue as Dr. Whitaker removes the loose dressing on the wound. Most of the discoloration is fading from purple to shades of green and yellow but there are two pronounced bulges. One is on the back of his hand between his thumb and forefinger and the other just above the wrist.

As Byron lays back and closes his eyes, Dr. Whitaker and Anna discuss the state of his wound. "These abscesses are creating pronounced paresthesia of the radial nerve. I'd like to drain them but lancing will open a new wound and coagulapathy could pose a problem."

Anna feels strange, offering suggestions to a doctor but she has years of applied wound care to draw from. "We could try two #16 or #18 needles; one to irrigate and the other to drain. That would create a smaller incision. I saw it done for a burn patient at Texas Memorial."

"I love good ideas young lady." From his bag, Dr. Whitaker removes a large bottle of sterile saline solution, two 60ml syringes and a package of five #18 needles. After loading the needles onto the syringes, he hands one to Anna and fills the other with saline solution.

"Byron, just lay back. You might feel two pokes but try to lay still. We're going to drain these abscesses on your hand."

Byron turns his head toward the window, looking away.

"You start, Anna." The large needle penetrates the skin without a flinch from Byron. Anna can feel the resistance fall off as she penetrates into the large cyst. She draws back on the syringe just enough to see dark fluid; confirming she has found the target area.

Dr. Whitaker places his needle into the cyst from the

other side as Anna begins to draw the fluid down. The cyst shrinks as fluid is drawn off, then grows again as Dr. Whitaker irrigates. After a couple irrigation and drain cycles, the draining fluid appears thin and nearly clear. After disposing of the fluid and attaching fresh needles, they repeat the process for the second cyst.

"All done, my friend; and you can thank Anna for bringing some clever wound care. What we did was relieve pressure from your radial nerve. It's going to wake up after a while and you're going to have some feeling back in that hand. I can't tell you the feeling will be good; in fact, it's probably going to hurt. Just remember, pain is reserved for those who heal. I'll leave you with something for it."

Anna looks up to see Karin standing in the door. Usually silent, she is surprised when Karin asks a question.

"Is my dad's hand going to be all right?"

Dr. Whitaker turns to Karin and speaks calmly. "Yes, Karin. Thanks to Anna's help, your dad's hand will be fine. He still needs to rest but I expect a full recovery."

"He can't feel anything in that hand, how long will it take for the feeling to return?" Karin isn't the stone faced girl that we've come to know. Right now, for the instant, she is passionately concerned for her dad. Buried under layers of grief and experiences that no sixteen-year-old should endure, is a girl struggling to find the surface and Anna sees it.

Sensing a need to break the Doctor/Nurse protocol where a nurse remains quiet allowing the Doctor to explain, Anna receives a non-verbal approval by an instantaneous glance as she speaks with Karin for the first time.

"Karin, have you ever sat for a long time, only to find your leg has gone to sleep and you can hardly get up?"

Karin answers while nodding her head slightly, "Several times."

"Well that happens because our position and weight has compressed a nerve and the signals can't connect with our brain to tell us what's going on. Your dad's hand had two pockets of fluid that were compressing the radial nerve and it went to sleep. We just drained the fluid so that nerve will start waking up pretty soon. It's going to tingle at first, just like when your leg or arm starts waking up. He's going to need you here with him when it wakes up. I'm sure you remember how crazy it feels."

For an instant, Anna sees what can almost be described as a smile on Karin's face.

"I can do that. I hate that buzzy feeling."

Looking over Karin's shoulder, Anna can see Emily's shadow in the hall. Dr. Whitaker and Anna gather up their things and pass Emily as Karin stays with her dad.

"I want to thank you both for coming to check on Byron but you need to know; those are the most words I've heard from Karin in six months. She's always been very close to her daddy. If anything were to happen to him, I just couldn't imagine it."

"I noticed that too," Dr. Whitaker comments. "I think Anna may be building a connection with Karin. That's a good thing."

"You're both very kind," says Anna, "but I think it's Karin that's making the move to come out. I think she wants back what has been denied her by circumstance and I can't take credit for that."

On the walk home, Anna makes apology to Dr. Whitaker. "I didn't mean to be out of place in explaining nerve recovery from paresthesia....."

Before she can continue, Dr. Whitaker interrupts. "In that room were two victims; one with a wounded hand and the other with a wounded soul. I delivered Karin sixteen years ago. Seems like yesterday but she's not the little girl I watched grow up. She appears to connect with you so I was glad to let you reach out to her. You called that one right and you were not out of place."

Gremlins:

George and Jackie join the crew helping Stephanie with the big garden at the Taylor's. The garden is a lush island of vegetation centered in a wide area of cleared ground. Summer's heat calls for additional mulch to contain moisture and keep soil temperature down. Stephanie explains that when the soil reaches seventy-five degrees, plants will stop setting fruit. Already many tomato plants in traditional gardens are setting less fruit but this garden is still going full on.

George walks over to speak with Stephanie; in hand are several leaves.

"Steph, I think we have a problem. Look at this."

Stephanie examines the withered leaves. "I'm not sure what this is. Something's attacking the plants but it's not anything I've dealt with. There are so many insects and plant diseases to choose from. Have you seen any bugs?"

"None that I've seen," he says. "Could they be coming

out at night?"

Stephanie looks at the leaves again. "Possible but I don't think we have time to guess at this. I'm going to go pay a visit. Wish me luck."

The Tousley farm is nearly two miles walk but walking has become a common mode of transportation these days. It gives time to think and sometimes, problems can be worked out on a good walk. The wheat and corn look good from a distance but a closer look reveals a low yield without fertilizer.

Rounding the fence and turning down the drive to the Tousley place, Stephanie sees Dick and Keith Reed with Josh Bennett, standing next to Elmer. As she approaches it would be difficult not to hear Keith saying, "Here she comes." Josh follows with, "Bet she's here to tell you how to farm again."

Elmer appears a little annoyed at his guest's comments and tips his hat to acknowledge and welcome Stephanie.

"Hello Stephanie. What brings you out here on this fine day?"

"Hello Mr. Tousley, Mr. Reed, Keith, Josh." As she finishes her greetings, Elmer interjects.

"Call me Elmer, it's a lot easier and prevents me from looking for my father."

Stephanie smiles. "Thank you, Elmer. I've come to ask your help."

Surprise hardly does justice to the look on all faces but Elmer's.

"What's your problem and how can I be of assistance?" he asks.

Stephanie explains and Elmer agrees to come see her garden in the morning. She thanks him and turns back for home.

"Well don't that beat all," says Dick. "When she said she had a pest or disease she didn't know how to handle; I about fell out. I thought she knew everything."

Josh adds, "Watch yourself up there, Elmer. They like snakes and keep 'em around the garden."

"I think you boys are being a bit rough on these folks," replies Elmer.

Dick asks, "What do you think is their problem?"

"Won't know 'till I get a look at it," Elmer says, "but my guess is they're trying to raise too much on poor soil. Without fertilizer, that soil can't raise but so much. Look at this field. Five years ago, I'd disc it for the insurance. Weak plants invite disease and pests so it's any guess until I look at it."

Becky Spencer tries to keep Gina out of trouble with their neighbor but it can prove challenging for a newly four-year-old. After supper she shares an idea with Chris.

"My Grandma had a gardening custom where she gave away the first pick. She called it the 'first fruits' and said the rest of the garden produced better when the first fruits were given as a gift. I want to do that for LouAnn. Our garden has already been producing well so it's too late for the first fruits but we've had a good crop of green beans and tomatoes with a few heads of broccoli. I'd like to take some next door. What do you think?"

Chris thinks hard on Becky's idea. "I think it's a great idea but why not add a bouquet of those beautiful roses you've been hiding behind the house. The sun against the back wall really made them take off and I think it would be a kind gesture."

Becky looks scared. "But what if it was LouAnn that buried Ceal's roses? She's been so upset, what if that sets her off completely?"

"What can you lose?" he says. "I don't know why but I just think it's the right thing to do. If it fails, it fails. At least you tried."

Dawn comes early on the Kansas prairie and it's usually Becky's favorite part of a day but not this day. Today, she would have rather slept in. Chris is already off to work and Gina will be up soon. For now, she is alone with a mission overflowing with uncertainty. An appropriate size wicker basket with a handle across the middle sits on the counter. Becky arranges two large broccoli nested on a mat of green beans. Half a dozen dark red tomatoes and a border of green onions trim the edge. It does look beautiful but she's worried at how the roses will be accepted. There's only one way to find out. Pouring a cup of tea, she waits for Gina, prays, and looks for any excuse to delay the unforeseen. Lifting her cup to take another sip of tea; it's already empty. Afraid of what might happen, she doesn't even remember drinking her tea. Pouring a second cup, Becky tries to keep her thoughts in order.

Anna is up with the roosters and visiting the Whitaker's where Kristine is quite taken with Mandy. She's holding her when Karin comes hurriedly to the door.

"Is Dr. Whitaker here, Dad's real sick."

Dr. Whitaker was resting in the bedroom but begins to stir as Anna asks questions.

"What happened? How is he sick?"

"He has a fever that came up real fast and a rash on his stomach and chest," she says. "His bones hurt really bad too. Mom's with him but sent me to get you. Can you come?"

Dr. Whitaker comes from the bedroom and walks to the exam room, talking over his shoulder as he grabs two bottles of pills from the glass cabinet and a tube of cream salve.

"Serum Sickness. It was coming on this morning but we stopped the serum already so it should pass quickly. Anna, you can go back with Karin and handle this. Run vitals, look for urticarial rash. Benadryl and Tylenol should be adequate, use the Benadryl cream if he's too uncomfortable. Karin, you did good to come. Would you walk back with Anna? She's a good nurse and knows how to help your dad."

"I'll watch Mandy for you," Kristine offers. "I'm sure you won't be long but if you are, I'll walk her over to Jason."

Anna quickly inventories her bag and adds the two pill bottles, the salve, and goes with Karin.

"Is my daddy going to be OK?" There's fear in Karin's voice. For a young girl forced to grow up so quickly, right now she appears vulnerable and open.

Maybe Anna learned it from Rita or out of habit has copied Mom's practice but instinctively she reaches out and takes Karin's hand as they walk.

"Your dad is doing well and this is not a serious complication. His body is reacting to the antivenin we gave him for the snakebite but it should pass soon and he will be fine. I have some medicine that will help him feel better and I'm going to check his other signs to make sure he's all right."

With a squeeze, Anna releases Karin's hand and they walk together toward the Bennett farm.

"Your baby is cute." Karin's unexpected comment suggests a breach in the wall she shelters behind. Anna carefully responds.

"Thank you. That's sweet of you to say. Maybe you could come by some time and see her. She loves company."

"Maybe," is the last word Karin shares but somehow, Anna knows Karin's soul is healing.

Byron's fever drops as fast as it came. His rash is limited to his stomach and chest but the Benadryl helps and Tylenol relieves his aching joints.

Swelling in his hand is subsiding, feeling is returning, and Bryon is complaining, so all is well at the Bennett place.

"I can't say as I thank you for fixing my hand this

morning. Before, I had no feeling but now it hurts."
Byron gripes with a smile.

"Hurts is good. That means it's alive and alive is good," says Anna. "If you feel up to it, you can get up and walk around the house tomorrow. No strenuous work and be careful. Snake venom affects the blood's ability to clot for a while. Cuts will be slow to stop bleeding."

Turning to Emily, Byron says, "She sounds just like Doc. Whitaker."

The fever doesn't return and the joint pain is manageable with Tylenol. Byron is recovering and though Emily claims he was more manageable, confined to his bed, she is glad to have her husband back.

Joining Forces:

Morning finds Elmer making his way to the old Conway farm where Stephanie stays with the Taylors. Dawn's light is just overcoming the last hint of darkness as roosters welcome the sun. For Elmer, this is the best time of day. Air is cool as the world quietly awakes.

Stephanie is finishing a breakfast of biscuits, eggs, and tea, as she sees a figure making his way up their drive.

"Hello, Elmer. I'm glad you could come."

Elmer tips his hat. His old school manners don't allow for shaking hands with women but a tip of the hat suits fine.

"Let's have a look at that garden of yours. I have a few ideas but can't know without a close look."

She guides him around the kitchen into the back yard. The garden comes into view and Elmer just stops to let out a whistle.

"Will you look at that? How did you pack all that into one space and get it all to look so healthy? But there's no order to it.   You have no rows and things are climbing all over everything."

Understanding his confusion, she explains. "I thought the same thing the first time I saw this type of gardening. The idea duplicates how things grow in the wild. You never see wild plants in rows and different plants all grow together. In this space, green beans use the corn for poles but draw nitrogen from deep in the soil and deliver it to the corn to help it grow. The squash acts as living mulch, protecting the ground from the sun's heat and trapping moisture for both the corn and beans. It's called companion planting. Over here, collard greens repel bugs while preventing evaporation loss for the tomatoes. "

"I half expected opportunistic insects were preying on weak plants but these are healthy," he says. "How are you doing this without fertilizer?"

"We anticipated that generations of farming have depleted the soil so we began pulverizing limestone and tilling it in to raise mineral content," she says. "Calcium stops blossom-end-rot on the tomatoes and helps other plants too. We gathered wood ash from stoves in town for pot ash. Finally, we make manure tea and water once a day for more nitrogen."

"Manure tea?" he asks. "How do you make that?"

"Over here." She leads him to four big drums set on pallets. "We collect fresh manure, which is too hot to put on the garden directly, and load it into these drums. Next, we fill the barrels with water and weigh down the manure with a wood disc and cinder block. The manure mat will generate gas and try to float up without the weight. After ten days of fermenting, we draw off the liquid from the bottom tap and dilute it with water. We use it for everything except root crops and it works pretty well.... Except for whatever is attacking our plants right now. Organics from the drums are composted and tilled in for next year's garden."

"Stephanie, I think you're onto something we can use," he says. "Let me look at your plants and see what's bothering them."

Making his way into the mass of vegetation, Elmer looks closely at several leaves.

"Stephanie, you got Thrips. See here." Turning a leaf over, Elmer points to what looks like a small dark line wiggling next to a leaf vein. "These suck moisture from the leaves and are causing your trouble. They generally prefer the weeds but I see you've cleared them too far back and now they're after your plants."

"Is there something we can do to get rid of them?" Stephanie asks.

"I know an old trick that's supposed to work and it's one that you would approve of," he says. "We'll tobacco juice 'em."

"Whaaat?" Her face looks very confused and Elmer is amused as he continues.

"Tobacco juice. We could collect cigarette butts from butt cans but that resource is long gone. I planted a tobacco patch behind my barn because I've been curious about this for some time, and I'm tired of the rising cost of chemicals. Tobacco is a natural insecticide with many healthy uses as long as you don't eat it, smoke it, or chew it. When you dry and soak it, the tea makes an effective insecticide... or so I'm told. We can add dish soap to help it cling to the plants."

Concerned at how long this might take, she asks, "How long does the tobacco have to dry?"

With a sly smile, he says, "Longer than we have.... BUT we don't have to wait because I began experimenting last year and have plenty all dried and ready to go. This will be my first bug infestation to test my home-brew on. Do you have another of these barrels we can use?"

Pointing to a barrel, "We can drain the last from that barrel and use it. How much dish soap are we going to need? It's not a renewable resource but we can ask for donations. We'll have fewer dishes to wash if the garden fails so I'd expect generous support."

"A cup should do it," he says. "If you go get the detergent, I'll get the tobacco and meet you back here. My Dad talked about doing this when things were tight during the depression. Dad said it works on everything except potatoes, tomatoes, and egg plant. Can't tell you why I still remember that but it stuck with me. If we kill the thrips on the other plants, it should help the plants we can't spray. If this works like he said, we may need to expand our operation."

Elmer heads home for tobacco while Stephanie rounds up runners to ask for donations of dish soap.

Across town, Gina has awakened and Becky Spencer is

carefully selecting the best rose blooms to top her garden-gift-basket. As she selects and cuts each stem she prays that they will be well received and that LouAnn won't become even more unfriendly. Gina is at her feet and toddling from bush to bush, smelling each flower.

"Don't touch, these flowers have stickers and they make owies."

Becky's warning isn't heeded and she must stop to console her. As she bends down to kiss Gina's sore finger, her eye catches one single rose with a distinguishing color. It's in the back row of bushes against the wall and it's blue. This rose isn't lavender or any shade of purple; it's blue. Carefully cutting it from the bush, Becky admires it and then rests it on top of the six other red, orange, and yellow roses.

"What a beautiful basket!" she says to Gina. "Let's go make a delivery and hope this works. Come Gina."

Gina follows until they reach the side yard between their house and the Stokes. She stops and looks up at her mom.

"It's OK. Take my hand."

With the basket on her left arm and Gina in her right hand, they continue to the kitchen door of the Stokes house. Becky knocks at the side of the screen door and calls out.

"LouAnn! It's Becky, are you home? I have something for you."

LouAnn comes to the door and as soon as she sees the basket on Becky's arm she buries her face in her hands, sobbing.

Becky steps back a bit. "LouAnn, I'm sorry! I didn't mean to make you sad. I thought these would cheer you up. Please forgive me."

LouAnn reaches out to unlock the screen door and holds it with one hand.

"No, it's not that at all. Please come in, both of you. Please."

Becky and Gina come into the kitchen and join LouAnn at the table. LouAnn accepts the gift-basket and sets it on the table next to them as they sit across from each other.

"Becky, I'm so sorry. I've misjudged you and I've been terrible to both you and Gina. That garden behind your house was Ceal's rose garden. She had been trying desperately to grow them and had hoped this was the year they would do well. Kansas winters are so harsh, she decided to try what she called 'digging them in' until spring. I don't know about roses but had been hoping against hope that Ceal would return in time to wake up her roses and finally have the beautiful blooms she always hoped for. I could never bring myself to dig in her garden and when I came home and saw you had tilled the whole garden, I thought Ceal's treasure was gone."

Realizing what she had done, Becky leans forward to LouAnn.

"LouAnn, I'm so sorry. I should have asked you about it first. I thought that was where the Simmons kitchen garden was. I've never seen buried roses before and when I found them, I replanted them against the southeast wall of the house to catch the morning sun, like my grandma used to do. I can't imagine what you thought."

LouAnn carefully removes the blue rose and holds it as she tells more.

"Ceal grew up in California's Napa Valley where her mother tended a large rose garden at their vineyard. She and her mother have been working for years to perfect a blue rose and the year before last, her mother sent her the second of only two such plants. There are other blue roses but this one was the product of their work together and has won prestigious awards out west. Ceal was desperate to see it thrive but it never did."

LouAnn's tears return as she thinks of her friend.

"I was afraid that Ceal's prize rose was gone and I would never see it or her again. When I saw this rose on top of your basket, it was like Ceal had sent it to me herself. It's a part of her, like part of her spirit, and perhaps Ceal was working through you to save her rose and let me know that things are OK. I know this sounds silly, but somehow I know Ceal is OK and this rose is special. You have no idea what this means to me."

Standing, she reaches for Becky and hugs her neck.

"You've done more for me than you know."

That evening when Chris comes home from working the group garden and helping tend livestock, Becky tells the whole story through tears as they sit on the couch.

"We gabbed the rest of the afternoon away. What a change one rose can make."

Chris replies, "And what a disaster if that blue rose hadn't made it. I think God sent some gardening angels to assist my own angel of a wife."

As Chris turns to kiss Becky, Gina steps over and sits on Becky's lap to assume the full attention of both parents.

Old Dogs:

Josh looks up to see Elmer turn the corner on the driveway to his barn and house.

"Glad to see you back in one piece. Did ya have to dodge any snakes?" Josh isn't hiding his cynicism.

Dick and Keith step from the barn. Dick is wiping his hands on a rag as he comments.

"What was the trouble at 'Greenhorn Acres'? Can't they grow a batch of tomatoes without help?"

Elmer stops under the shade of his walnut tree between the house and barn as the four men talk.

"You won't believe what they're doing up there?

Dick, Keith, and Josh exchange looks and begin laughing.

"Bet it was hard deciding whether to laugh or cry," Dick says.

"Book smart but dirt stupid," adds Keith. "You'd think

when it comes to farming, those who've been doing it all their life might know how it's done."

Josh adds, "Maybe we can let them help us harvest in trade for feeding them through the winter."

Dick, Keith, and Josh are entertained by poking fun at Stephanie's efforts at the Conway farm until Elmer begins to speak in a quiet calm tone.

"I expected the same as you but it's not what I found."

The momentum of Dick and Josh's rancor suddenly stops as they look at Elmer, not believing what they've just heard.

Elmer doesn't wait for them to find words.

"She's getting higher yield than I've seen in this county and from dirt that's been farmed out years ago. The girl's no dummy."

Dick finds words first. "What's her problem then? Why did she ask your help?"

"Thrips," says Elmer. "She's never seen any and couldn't identify what is common here but unknown where she's from. We're going to treat with tobacco tea and see if my insecticide experiment pays off. Maybe, if WE help THEM, we'll get to share some of their harvest. I'm tellin' ya, I learned a few things today."

Elmer makes his way to the back of his barn where neat rows of tobacco has been hanging in bundles since last fall. Stringing several bunches on a pole makes them easy to carry but he looks like an old hobo. Parking his small load and turning to his friends, he remarks.

"Let's have dinner and I'll take you back with me to see

for yourselves."

During a meal of biscuits and sausage gravy, Elmer explains what he saw that morning and how the creative manufacture of home grown fertilizer could help their wheat.

"Smart men never stop learning. We've farmed one way for generations and it's always worked for us but now things have changed and we need some new ideas. The chemical dealers have left and taken their 'easy payment plans' with them... and good riddance. Our soil is tired but I think we can improve things if we learn from each other and experiment some."

Discussion continues with plenty of questions and explanation but Josh remains quiet. After dishes are washed and put away, they make toward the road back to the Conway farm, carrying tobacco with them. Reaching East Dower Drive, Josh speaks up.

"You guys go on ahead. I'm going to go see how Dad's doing." Josh turns right and heads to his house.

Pat Wagoner makes his way to the Taylor's with some exciting news for Nicky.

"Nicky, I got a message back from your folks in Montana. It was relayed to me from another local ham about an hour ago."

Handing her the neatly folded paper, Nicky's hands tremble as she unfolds the note and reads:

GENERAL MESSAGE

TO: N5OSI for Nicky and Jackie Chambers; Location, Terlingua, TX DL89

FROM: K6OIL for Ron Chambers; Location, Philipsburg, MT, grid square DN36

MESSAGE: We are well. Thrilled at wedding news. So glad you found us and that you are OK. Our prayers are answered! Please keep in contact. We love you. Dad and Jen.

DATE: 5/15 23:10

Nicky can hardly contain her excitement and throws a hug around Pat's neck.

"Thank you, Pat. I've got to find Jackie. Thank you, thank you, THANK YOU!!!!"

Jackie isn't far. She is helping harvest broccoli, kale, and cabbage so the ground can be tilled for planting cucumber, potatoes and carrots. When Nicky shares the message, the excitement is heard across the entire field of workers.

Nicky and Jackie quickly pen a return message and begin a rugged correspondence.

At the Bennett farm, Emily and Karin are sitting with Byron and talking as they haven't done in many months. Something about Bryon's brush with death has brought them closer together.

"Daddy, you gave us a scare," says Karin. "Didn't Grams ever tell you to leave snakes alone?"

Byron is delighted to hear his daughter's voice in so many words. Since she began as a shooter in the town's perimeter defense, she had stopped speaking on a personal level.

"I guess I've always wondered what it's like to be snake-bit. If you're ever tempted to experience it, I'd suggest you try something else. I sure don't plan on going back for seconds."

Emily is comforted that Byron will be OK but an equal bonus is the subtle change coming over Karin. In that bedroom they are talking and sharing. Emily has hoped and prayed for this but secretly, even hidden from her prayers, she had almost given up that her daughter would ever be the same.

Josh comes in the house and Karin goes to meet him in the living-room.

"What brings you home so soon?"

Not showing any pleasure that his sister just spoke a complete sentence to him, Josh fires back.

"What got into you?"

Karin answers, "I'm just glad that Dad's better."

"Nothing's going to be better as long as THEY are here." Josh walks down the hall to his room and leaves Karin standing.

They have always been close. Even when she joined others to guard the town, Josh was always there for her. Now he's grown cold and shut her out. The hurt is real but she knows it intimately. Her sorrow is equally for the loss between her and Josh and a sympathetic remorse that her brother is now victim of the dark anguish that consumed her for the past half year.

That evening, Josh leaves with a pack on his back. He leaves no word where he plans to go or when he may return. Perhaps he doesn't know himself. Karin goes to the walnut tree in the yard and climbs silently as she has done so many times in other trees with a shooter's bag and rifle. This time she just watches her brother make his way to the highway where she finally loses sight of him heading east. Telling her mom will only begin the sorrow earlier. For now, her mother seems to have found a reason to put away her blues. It doesn't seem right to take that peace away when there is no remedy.

New Tricks:

Elmer's tobacco tea kills the Thrips. Stephanie is quick to correct those who credit her ownership of the garden, insisting it is a community project but Elmer, Dick, and Keith still call it 'Stephanie's Garden.'

Many hands help spray, especially the underside of all plants except for the potatoes, tomatoes, eggplant, and squash.

Dick and Keith lend a hand and are amazed at how lush and productive the small garden is.

Dick comments, "If we got this result from a field of wheat, we wouldn't have to plant half what we do."

In two days the Thrips are gone and Elmer takes Stephanie on a walk over to where they stopped clearing the grass and brush.

"This is what Thrips prefer," he says. "If you let the grass grow right up to your garden, the Thrips will feed there and not on your plants."

Elmer picks some of the grass and shows Stephanie the same Thrips feasting away.

"I guess I didn't recognize grass as a bait plant," Stephanie responds.   "I wonder if it also harbors beneficial insects."

"It might," remarks Elmer, "especially with a nice bunch of Thrips to feed on."

Dick asks about the liquid fertilizer.   "Elmer, do you think we could saturate the pulverized limestone with the manure tea, then dry it for spreading?   We might have something easier to spread."

Elmer is pleased.   "You might be onto something, Dick. We can sure give it a try.   We might try several things and make a research field with different ideas working on separate areas for comparison.   I think we need to start with another meeting and have the rest of the guys see what's going on here.   Stephanie, would you mind hosting a show?"

There is a healing that begins to draw our groups into one.   It doesn't happen all at once and for some it takes longer than others.   At best it's a move in a good direction.   None of us can completely return to where our lives were before the collapse but we can get to a better place than where we've been thrown by it.   Just as you can't un-ring a bell or turn time back, lives are changed by events that we can't avoid.   What we can do is determine our attitude in dealing with it.

Byron is recovering from the snake bite though he's still working to regain strength in his hand.   He has full range of motion but tissue damage will likely leave marks.   Karin communicates more freely and has volunteered to watch Mandy on several occasions. She acts like an adult with no sign of the adolescence that she's been robbed of. Josh hasn't returned though Jeanie Pritchard visits from Elma and says she has seen him there twice.

The gardens have been harvested and we hold a Harvest Dinner after canning is done. It is a lot like Thanksgiving. Community canning is an amazing process at the Grange Hall. Ladies bring their canning jars and pressure canners along with produce from the gardens. Wagons bring half a dozen wood burning cook stoves and tables are brought out of the hall. Right here in the street, food is prepared, packed in jars, processed and canned. When everyone helps there is an enormous amount of food put away for winter. Shocks of wheat come from the field and are spread out on a swept area of the street. Using home-made flails, the men beat the wheat in preparation for winnowing. A grain flail is like a long nunchaku. One end of a four-foot handle has a short chain attached to a two-foot section of a thick wooden stick. Flipping the long handle sends the short end crashing down to break up the heads of wheat and free the grain from the husks. With the wheat all separated, the straw is raked aside to be used for bedding with the remaining wheat and chaff gathered onto blankets. With a person on each end of a blanket, they toss the wheat into the air and catch it again. Fall's light breeze carries the chaff down-wind while the heavier wheat falls back to the blanket. It's a lot of work but that's where we get wheat for making bread. It takes two days but everyone working together brings more emotional healing to what we thought was already done.... I guess recovery will be ongoing.

Jackie and Nicky find time to talk with Pat Wagoner and the subject always surrounds messages to or from Montana.

"No word still?" Jackie asks. "Is there trouble up there? It's not like Dad and Jen to go silent."

"The last message was returned with 'Unable to Locate' and I took liberty to contact the operator at the far end," he says. "I asked him for an update or if he could find out if they were alright. He sent me word that the cabin was in order but closed up and that their canoe was gone. He said they may be on a hunting trek. Philipsburg Montana isn't an agricultural area so packing in meat for winter is pretty important. They need to bag a moose or several deer along with fish and other game. It could take some time and they can't return empty handed. That message was six weeks ago so I'd expect they are back and you should hear from them soon."

"I hope so," says Nicky.

The big dinner at the Grange Hall gives opportunity for discussion of the challenges we face. After the meal, Dad, Fred, and Harry join Vince, Daemon, and Dwight at their table while all the ladies admire and visit over the mountain of canned food, dried food, smoked meats, and sacks of grain that is gathered for display. It looks like we have plenty of food to get us through winter.

Dwight begins the list of challenges. "Winter's coming and propane is running low. I doubt we have enough for heat 'til spring."

Daemon Eckerd always has good ideas but comes up dry on this one. "A few houses have wood stoves but they're mostly for occasional fires since firewood isn't abundant enough around here to keep a fire going. Some folks have pellet stoves but you can't get pellets anymore. I heard of a stove that was converted to burn corn but we don't have enough of that either and if we did, there's no electricity to run the auger or the blower."

Harry comments, "Furnaces won't run without power either so the LP is only good for cooking but we need to impress on everyone not to heat with their stove or they'll be cooking over a campfire in the dead of winter."

"But when people get cold," adds Vince, "getting warm is going to override other priorities. Folks won't reserve their propane if they can't get warm."

"Solar hot water works for now," says Fred, "but when the cold hits, those collectors are going to freeze solid. What we need is a heat source that burns junk wood."

Dad replies, "We may all be standing around barrel burners if we don't come up with something."

There's a chuckle raised but it's a sober one. Had there been less truth to the comment, we all could laugh more freely.

Karin is taking part in community gatherings. No longer hiding in the shadows she participates but is rarely far from her Mom, Dad, or Anna and Mandy. Mandy likes her and appears to have claimed a big sister. Anna and I have grown close to Byron and Emily. After Byron's snake bite and the time Anna spent caring for it, a good friendship has grown between our families. That also helps draw Karin from her shell.

Resting after dinner and admiring the massive food resource, the women's small talk gives way to conversation.

"Have you heard any word about Josh?" asks Anna.

Emily takes a deep breath to answer but Karin speaks first. "He's been in and out of Elma a few times. They think he's staying in a fish shack near the river."

Pleased anytime Karin joins a conversation, Emily adds, "He can't call or write and email is gone but we still hear word through Jeanie now and then."

"How's she doing?... and Mike Jr.?" Anna asks.

"They're doing OK," she says, "It's hard but they have a lot of support from their church in Elma. She might be here for services this Sunday. I invited her to stay with us and she said she'd like that. I plan to send her home with some groceries. Dick said he'd drive Elmer's team with the wagon to pick her up. My... how things have changed."

"I remember Papa telling me about life on the farm without telephones, computers, or 'motor buggies' as he called them," Karin says. "I never thought I'd actually live it."

The ladies can't help but laugh a bit.

"Grand-parents always said it was better times back then," says Emily. "I guess we get to find out."

Mandy begins to squirm in Karin's arms. Anna reaches

instinctively for her shawl and baby; it's feeding time again.

"What's it like to nurse your baby?" asks Karin.

Emily instantly interrupts. "Oh, Karin, that's personal. You shouldn't ask."

"It's alright." Anna replies. "It's just us girls and I don't mind at all. To answer your question, I have to say that it's comforting; not only to Mandy but for me too. Mandy stops fussing and settles down to her own rhythm of nursing and breathing, her eyes look up at mine. We bond as she nurses. Then for me it's relief too. I get pretty full and Mandy takes a load off me in a real way." Emily and Karin both chuckle. "I enjoy the special time and I can only imagine how much I would miss it if I went to a bottle and formula but I think there's another part that might be even more important. Peace has been taken from us by all that's happened over the past year. Nursing Mandy is a peace that we both can enjoy and no matter what the world does, I don't have to give that up."

"Did you nurse me, Mom?" Karin asks.

Emily is a bit more comfortable with the subject but not entirely. "I nursed both you two... right up 'til you got your first tooth."

"Ow! I bet that put a stop to bonding. Did I ever bite you?" Karin is full of questions.

"Both of you did. Now let's change the subject." Emily says.

"I'm sorry for biting you, Mom. I didn't mean it." Karin is serious.

"Sweetheart, it's a part of growing up and I love you just the same. Your time may come and we'll laugh about it then. Now, how about this weather?"

Strangers:

Jeanie Pritchard's visit is perfect timing. She learns of our heating issue and shares what they are doing in Elma.

"They're called 'rocket mass heaters.' A couple came to town about a week ago and showed us how to make a furnace out of a metal drum and a bunch of clay. It burns any old trash wood and can heat a whole house for days on just a box of sticks. Only the top part of the drum sticks up from the clay and you can cook on that. The rest of the smoke-pipe runs through what looks like a sitting bench, then out a side wall. When the clay gets warm, it heats the house for days. We only run it once on these fall days and maybe twice a day, come winter. It hardly makes any smoke."

"That sounds like something we need to look into," says Emily. "Would you mind sharing this with our men after church?"

"I'd be glad to but I've told you about all I know," says

Jeanie. "The two from up-river are the real experts."

"Up-river?" asks Emily. "Aren't we up-river from Elma?"

"Well... yes," Jeanie explains. "But these two came down the Missouri before they branched off to come up the Kansas. They've been traveling quite a way to get here. They're heading west."

Anna, Mandy, and I, join the Bennett's for Saturday supper. I'm still getting used to calling lunch, dinner and dinner, supper. Jeanie is a strong woman and is dealing with the loss of her husband better than most would be expected to. She's learned to manage their home and raise her son without Mike and that takes a lot of woman and a faithful God.

"I see Mike in Mike Jr. all the time," she says. "It helps to know that he's not gone in a permanent sense and that we'll see him again. Until then, we'll get by a day at a time."

"You have our prayers and you're on the prayer chain at church," I say. "Everyone's going to be glad to see you and Mike Jr. at church tomorrow."

Byron and I excuse ourselves to the rec-room after supper while the ladies continue to visit. Mike Jr. joins us. For such a young boy, Mike Jr. seems very mature.

"How old are you now, Mike?" asks Byron.

"I'm going to be nine this November 11th," he says.

"You're growing up fast," Byron says. "What are you doing about school?"

"Mom teaches me and six other boys from town. The

other families pay Mom with food and Mrs. Allen sews us clothes."

"Are there any girls in your class?" I ask.

"Not in our class," he says. "There's some in the other school but they're older and learn on their own at the library. Mom just tells them what to learn and grades their papers."

"Do you like school?" Byron asks.

"It's OK. I don't miss riding the bus and school doesn't take as long," he says.

"It sounds like you boys are lucky to have a good teacher," says Byron. "Jason, what do you think about this 'rocket mass heater' that Jeanie tells of?"

"It sounds like what we could use," I say. "We might send some guys back with Jeanie and Mike to learn more. I'd like to see one up close."

Byron stretches as his supper settles in. "I was thinking the same. I'd like to meet these travelers too. We might hear some news about what's going on up north. I think we'd learn more than what we can get from short wave."

"Pat says with everyone conserving battery time, they pretty much stick to business and don't talk as much as they used to." I say.

Nicky, Jackie and George, are having supper with Scott and Roxanne just a half mile up Dower Drive. After the meal, their conversation shifts to long term plans.

"I'm worried about Dad and Jen. We haven't heard from them for nine weeks and I'm ready to pack up and go find where they went," says Nicky.

Nicky has always been the voice of reason but this time, Jackie has the clear head.

"We wouldn't know where to look. All we have is the town they live in and we already know their cabin is vacant. Getting there would take us into winter and I doubt we're ready to face a Montana winter. I think we have to wait this one out and pray they make it to where they can get word to us again."

"Jackie's right," says George. "Parts of Montana are probably getting snow already and Philipsburg is in the mountains. I know you two need to see your folks again, just like I need to see my Aunt Dee and Uncle Ed. We can plan a trip in the spring."

"You guys have the same split as me and Rocky," Scott says. "Her folks are in east California and mine are way up at Trout Lake, where MY Uncle Ed lives. We could get to the California high country in the spring but northern Alberta has a narrow window of opportunity. Sometimes the snow doesn't fully melt until after May and it starts again as early as September. It would take us five months to get there if we could travel fifteen miles every day and two months of that are after we cross into Canada."

"We could all go together to Montana and Scott and I could go from there to Alberta," says Roxanne. "As much as I want to see my folks; crossing the Rockies and three deserts on foot probably isn't realistic. We haven't heard from them either so there's no telling what we'd find when we got there. At least we know Scott's family is a safe place to go."

"Until we hear from Dad and Jen," Nicky says. "We don't know that Montana is a safe place to go. I've always heard it's great for prepared people. Dad and Jen love their cabin but now I'm not so sure. What could have happened to cause them to just go like that?"

Nicky isn't expecting an answer and it's a good thing because no one can offer one. They will have to wait and hope for some kind of word from up north.

There is something refreshing and healthy about a full church in a small community. Members are growing in their faith and knowledge of the Bible under Allen's teaching. His messages are practical and apply to daily needs. Bible teaching always has value but when the message speaks to you all week, that's practical and especially useful.

Attendance is growing and we are working more as community with less distinction between our two groups.

Sunday School classes now cover two youth age groups, a young adult class, and 'Duffer Disciples.' A title they took for themselves.

Jeanie Pritchard's visit is welcomed by standing applause and rounds of hugs from dear friends. Her eyes well up as she addresses the church.

"I only wish Mike could see how this church is growing. It was always his passion to watch a body of believers grow as you are doing here. I'm sure he would be honored to see you all here today."

Applause fills the room as Jeanie is seated and Louis

Roth stands to speak a word.

"My grand-dad once told me why farmers were people of faith. He helped build this church when he was a young man just starting to farm his own place. He said it was the land that made people faithful. If a man worked very hard, planted well, got blessed with good rains and a dry harvest, he stood a fair chance of surviving winter to do it all over again.   They depended on help from neighbors and giving the same, but after it all, success in farming rests in the hands of God's grace. Farmers learned to take their needs to God and trust His plan. We've drifted away from that over the years. Between crop insurance and warehouse grocery stores that ship in food from all over the world, we got so we don't feel the need to ask God for things. The church was left to women and children while farmers continue working their cash crops. Now things are different and I can't say as it's not better from God's point of view. We never stopped needing God's hand in our lives but with everything falling apart like it has, we realize it more…. and that's all I have to say."

"Amen!" comes from many

Allen asks everyone to stand and join hands as one long chain weaving through the church. Together, we pray for one another and for God's provision and protection in the days to come. One thing is noticeably missing. No one watches a clock or complains if the service runs past the hour.

Elma:

It's quite a sight to see us taking Jeanie and Mike Jr. back to Elma on Elmer's wagon. I think I know why springs were developed for cars and trucks. Dick Reed is driving the team, Jeanie and Mike Jr. are seated with him on the ONLY spring assisted bench seat while Fred, Harry, and I try to get comfortable on the cargo deck of the buckboard. Elmer said he restored the wagon for parades but it has proved its worth these past months. It is a bit light on creature comfort.

The twelve miles to Elma feel longer than they are and takes us two and a half hours to make the trip. Once in town, we are greeted warmly as everyone recognizes Mrs. Pritchard and Mike Jr. Some recognize Dick Reed but Fred, Harry, and I need introduction.

With the team unharnessed, watered, and fed, it's time for lunch.... or should I say 'dinner.' Mrs. Pritchard and Mike Jr. have headed home but we are invited to eat at the home of Gordon and Rachel Lewis. They are the happy owners of the first rocket mass heater built in

Elma.   The man and wife travelers are staying with them and we can talk over design details as we eat.

The team is tied out in the city park next to the trading post; it used to be called a store but since currency doesn't mean anything anymore, they trade for goods. It's working pretty well.   You can trade eggs for milk while supply and demand determines value.   You could own the world for a case of 'AA' batteries. Anyway, the store-keep says he'll watch over the team and we head out with Gordon to his farm for something to eat.

Elma is a little larger than Hazel Creek and not as defined by the small stream that connects us. Here, the land has less roll to it and the stream doesn't turn and twist.   Roads are straight and the city covers only two blocks off either side of the county highway, making Elma a stretched out, long city.   An advantage is the short proximity of farms to downtown and the fact that the county maintains their principle street, leaving fewer side streets for the city to maintain.   The drawback is that once in town, you may have some travel to find the business you are looking for and with no county roads department they now have to maintain everything.

The Roth's farm is only a short walk of half a mile.   I remember when I thought a half mile was a much longer walk but these days, we walk almost everywhere.   Fields extend behind the house but the front yard is green with flower beds and a short white picket fence.

"I'm home!" says Gordon.   "Rachel, I have some guests

for you to meet."

Emerging from the kitchen is a slender woman who doesn't show half her years. Wiping her hands on her apron, she smiles and greets us.

"Welcome! I was told you were coming. I'm glad you could visit and have some lunch."

"Lunch," I say. "I haven't heard that in a while."

Almost laughing, Rachel explains. "I grew up in Tacoma Washington and met Gordon when he was in the Army at Fort Lewis. I never got used to saying dinner when I meant lunch. It's just the way I was raised."

"Me too," I say. "In Texas they use both but I always stuck with lunch. Tacoma?... my wife, Anna, is an RN and graduated from P.L.U. Isn't that close to Tacoma?"

"It sure is!" says Rachel. "Parkland to be specific but it's all in the Tacoma area. When did she attend there?"

"She graduated eight years ago but we've lived outside Houston ever since then."

"That's after my time," she says. "Gordon and I were married fifty-two years ago and I've only been back to visit four times. It's beautiful country but it sure rains a lot. Kansas suits me just fine."

"No doubt, this is good land," I say. "Texas is beautiful but has no hold over Kansas."

She turns to where Harry, Fred, and Dick are standing. "I'm sorry. I'm being neglectful. I'm Rachel Lewis, and your names are?"

Introductions complete as another couple knocks and comes through the kitchen door.

"Just in time!" says Gordon. "Gentlemen, I'd like you to meet our two distinguished travelers, Ron and Jennifer Chambers."

All four of our mouths drop as we each stare in disbelief. The couple look at each other and then back at us, wondering what has taken us by such surprise. I finally compose my thoughts enough to speak first.

"Ron and Jennifer Chambers? Do you happen to be from Montana and have two daughters... Nicky and Jackie?"

Jennifer explodes with emotion and shouts.... "YES!!! Do you know them? Are they OK? Do you know where they are?"

"I think we made the right turn at the Kansas River," Ron says.

Lunch is good and our chatter is non-stop. Gordon and Rachel don't get in a lot of words in but Rachel said they had already heard one side of the story and listening to us fill in the blanks was fine by her. Conversation is all about the girls and how they are doing. The rocket mass heaters will wait for now.

Rather than spend a lot of time looking over the heaters, it's decided for the sake of travel time that we load up and head back with our new friends, Ron and Jen Chambers. The folks at Elma are building their own heaters from how Ron has shown them so there is little holding them from coming with us to see their daughters.

We load up belongings on the wagon but leave their seventeen-foot canoe in the Lewis' barn, intending to retrieve it on a later trip. The wagon is very full.

With no way to get word to Hazel Creek, we are bringing a huge surprise back with us.

It is four-thirty before we reach Hazel Creek but on the long ride home, we hatch a plan.

Ron keeps us entertained with his harmonica on the ride from Elma and he's an accomplished musician. Our plan is set. Upon arriving at Hazel Creek we quickly load the Chambers and their things into the Grange Hall. Seeing Chris' bike at the store I walk over and enlist his help. He rides over to George and Jackie's to tell them we brought something for them from Elma and they both need to come pick it up at the Grange, then he rides over to Nicky's and delivers a message that a new girl came back with us from Elma and could she come to the Grange to meet her and see if she might room with her in her extra bedroom. It's a good thing Chris is in good shape because that bike ride loop is a little over two miles.

George and Jackie have further to walk but get their message first. They get to the Grange just ahead of Nicky, whose coming down Center St. about a hundred and fifty yards away, they wait for her as they talk with us.

"How was the trip?" asks George.

Trying to act as normal as I know how, I reply. "Bumpy and long. Next time, I'm bringing a pillow. Elma is a nice town though, good people and good neighbors."

"What's the package we need to pick up?" Jackie asks.

"Oh, it's in the Grange Hall. You might wait for Nicky though; it's sorta for both of you." I say.

As Nicky joins us, Ron can see them through the open window from inside the Grange Hall. He and Jen remain just out of sight as he begins to softly play Amazing Grace on his harmonica. Instantly, both Jackie and Nicky look at each other and nearly fall over each other getting into the hall. Their only word is, "DAD!!"

Hugs, kisses, tears, and laughter fill the Grange Hall for the better part of half an hour. Hardly any of them can talk for joyful tears. For now, the girls need only to hold their Dad and Jen, knowing they are safe and right here with them.

Bug-out:

Ron and Jen move their things to Nicky's house and plan to stay with her. Settling down for the evening after washing off miles of road dust, they begin their story of traveling from Montana to Kansas. Jackie and George stay to visit.

"We didn't have time to let you know we were coming," Ron begins. "Everything came apart quickly and we had to bug-out."

"It started when our friend Dillon stopped by the cabin," Jen says. "He's a fire fighter with the forestry department. He'd been working a growing fire on the federal reservation next to us. He said things weren't looking good and that we had best prepare to leave as soon as we could."

"But it wasn't for the fire," Ron says. "He said the fire wasn't out of hand but he'd worked a lot of fires and this one looked like it was deliberately set. Then his crew was shot at by 'survivalist snipers' according to the feds.   We all know both the preppers and survivalists living up there and none of them would shoot at fire fighters."

Jen continues.   "Dillon came by because he and his crew were sent home and replaced by National Guard but not from Montana. 'Federal Fire Fighters' they were called. The thing is they had guns but no shovels. They weren't geared to fight a forest fire and showed no understanding of even basic fire suppression skills."

Ron says, "Peculiar to Dillon was that as soon as they were sent out, the shooting stopped. A rifle shot can be heard for a mile and they never heard another shot after crews were switched. Dillon hid to watch what would happen next and he couldn't believe what he saw. They were using accelerants to spread the fires up the valleys and canyons. There were people living up there and they were burning them out. He saw plenty of DHS, FEMA, and BATF&E insignia but they all had weapons and none carried fire equipment. Helicopters dropped something into the tops of the ravines and it looked like retardant if you didn't know better. Retardant is red but this wasn't retardant or water. Dillon tried to radio out but all channels were blocked. We tried to contact our local ham operator, the one we got your first message from, but he said something about all propagation was down and that it may be from a solar flair. After the fires were out, the feds restricted entry to the whole area. Their explanation was they suspected survivalists may have left explosives similar to what they claimed started the fire. Dillon snuck in anyway and what he saw was sickening.   Land held by preppers was selectively burned and every cabin was cleared of food and supplies. The fires came later because there were no shade marks from cans sitting on shelves; supplies were removed before the fire got there. "

"What about the people?" Nicky asked.

"Dead," says Ron. "All dead. Convoys of trucks hauled out case after case of these people's food stores and they just killed them to get it. He found one site that made it clear we all had to get out. A four-member family was laying dead on their cleaned out property. All their stores were gone and none of the family had been shot. He found accelerant set to carry the fire into their homestead but the fire petered out just before it reached the fresh fuel. In their rush to the next cache of supplies, they missed covering their tracks with a convenient fire. Dillon knew this family and they had gas masks. Whatever killed them was quick and gave no warning until it was too late. He thinks it was military grade gas of some kind."

"The next day," says Jen. "Dillon came to our cabin with a forestry service truck loaded with diesel. He picked us up with our canoe, bug out bags, and whatever we could pack to get out."

"He drove us as far as Bismarck and we paddled down the Missouri to Kansas City. From there I took a gamble on the Kansas River and ended up at Elma. We had no idea you two were this close."

George takes all this in and comments. "I've heard a lot about Montana, Idaho, and Wyoming being the great American prepper paradise. It always bothered me to have so many people with so much resource concentrated together. It would appear they became an irresistible target for someone's greed. Do you think this was a federally organized raid?"

"Probably not," says Ron. "The federal structure fell apart months ago but pockets of organizations with previous federal resource, appear to have teamed up and become monster guerrilla armies. They must be running low on supplies to pull a stunt like this. We need to keep our wits about us."

Chris and Becky Spencer are enjoying an evening with their daughter, Gina. The past difficulty with neighbors is behind them and you would think life is good but Chris is restless.

"Becky, what would you say to a trip up to Iowa in the spring?"

"That's a long way," she says. "How would we get there? It's not like we can just pack the truck and go. Gina needs so many things... we need a bigger truck."

Becky's quip from the movie 'Jaws' brings a smile to both of them.

Chris continues. "It's about five hundred miles but we could make it with a horse pulled trailer."

"A what?" she says. "Where would we get either a trailer or horse to pull it? Besides, we don't even know if the route is safe to travel and we'd be all alone."

"I've been talking with Elmer," he says. "He has gas welding equipment. It wouldn't take much to cut the back off one of the old pickups and make it so a horse could pull it. Two horses would be better but one could do it if we scrap the box and replace it with a lighter structure to lash cargo to."

Becky is following but still not keen on leaving the safety of the group for regions unknown.

"Where would we sit on something like that? Gina is a pretty active four-year-old."

With Becky asking more detail, Chris feels confident he might actually sell her on the idea.

"On a buckboard bench seat under a parasol sun shade, and we can stop regularly for Gina to burn off energy. If we only made twenty-five miles a day, we would be there in about three weeks."

"But what kind of trouble could we run into?" she asks. "Us two and a baby are hardly a match for a gang and you can't outrun much on a loaded down horse drawn wagon."

"I've been thinking on that," he says. "I wanted to pass this by you first and if you're interested, I'll start talking up the idea in town to see if others would join us. Are you in?"

"I think so," she says, "at least to find out more and if others want to join us. It's scary though. We'd be like pioneers crossing the prairie in a covered wagon but it would be good to see your brother and be close to family again."

Heat:

"So with not much more than adobe mud, a fifty-five-gallon barrel, and flue pipe, you make a wood gasifier stove with a secondary burn chamber."

Ron Chambers is explaining to Fred and Harry how a rocket mass heater works so efficiently.

Harry needs some detail explained. "I get the idea of secondary burn and using adobe mass to store heat but how does it draft with no stack?"

Ron explains. "It's all in the barrel. The small burn box feeds the riser inside the inverted barrel. That's where the draft comes from. As exhaust from the riser enters the barrel, it meets oxygenated air and burns the second time, then cools, becomes denser, and falls. The spent gas can't keep up with the riser so it gets pushed out the horizontal flue pipe buried in the adobe mass. By the time the exhaust reaches the outside, it's just warm and smokeless. Even twelve hours after a burn the adobe mass will still radiate heat into the house.

The best part is that it will burn almost any dry wood."

"This I gotta see," says Fred. "Where are we going to build the first one?"

The most appropriate place to begin is chosen and the Whitaker's home comes up on top. Their home has stone walls and they don't have a wood stove. No one thought it good to have someone die of frostbite in the waiting room. While men construct the working parts, Nicky Chambers and Beverly Roth team up to make a 'Blob of Clay' into an artistic expression that's both functional and attractive. When complete it looks nothing like a woodstove. Kristine Whitaker gives it a new name.

"It looks like it came from a child's storybook. It's a Who-Heater but I like it."

The Whitaker's home becomes open house for the town. Everyone enjoys the warmth and how efficiently the "Who-stoves' run. New ideas and improvements come with each unique design and some later versions even have bread ovens.

With few critical parts, stoves are built in place all over town. Ron and Harry join forces with Elmer and Dick to produce the firebox and riser as a single unit. Having that part done assures that without a major departure, the stoves will keep our homes warm through the winter months. It's a good thing too because nights are already noticeably cooler.

The last two stoves constructed are the largest; one at the church and the last at the Grange Hall. The last is magnificent. It has two ovens built in. Elmer cut up two matching electric ovens to insert into the adobe near the barrel. From experience we have learned where to get just the right heat and the oven temperature stays at 350 degrees.

"Well, gentlemen, I think we've beat ol' man winter," says Dad. "It was close but thanks to Ron's expertise...."

"Wait a minute, Matt," says Ron. "All I did was show you a design that's been around for decades. It was your town that got nearly eighty built in three weeks. I've never seen anything like it."

"I think our Kansas winters might have provided some inspiration," says Vince. "However the price of busted pallets has gone up considerably."

Everybody laughs but at least for some, it's partly relief that we've surmounted another obstacle.

Mandy has been crawling for several months now and getting more difficult to catch. With our house comfortably warmer, thanks to our new 'Who-Heater,' Mandy likes to pull herself up on the warming bench. She can't get up onto the bench but she can get standing and she walks as long as she can stabilize herself with one hand. It won't be long before she's really walking.

Anna enjoys the slow time at the clinic. "Dr. Whitaker is a great teacher and I'm learning a lot of what he calls 'old school ways' like setting up a manual I.V. drip without pump control."

After dinner we spend time with Mandy in the living room. She cruises the room for hand holds while Anna and I sit on the warming bench.

"Jason, you can't believe how much we've grown dependent on new technology. The manual skills I'm learning from Dr. Whitaker are just as good as the modern methodology and they don't require expensive equipment. All that stuff has to be a part of why medical costs were so high. I'm not sure why we ever needed it. It has to be one of two reasons. Either the medical equipment industry has good lobbyists to influence standards or insurance companies pushed it to limit liability. Strange thing is, there are plenty of malpractice cases from I.V. pumps set wrong. They didn't fix much and it may even dull a nurse's training. Having to set things manually makes me think about what I'm doing in the first place. I'm more attentive and I feel more competent."

"I know what you mean," I reply. "I don't know about nursing but we became better sailors when the GPS failed on Intrepid. We knew how to use map and sextant but we became better at it by the time we reached Sitka. It's the difference between book learning and experience. New engineers in the oil field thought they knew their job. Given time they all ran into a problem they had no idea how to handle. Then a roughneck, who may never have finished high school, would step in and fix it for them. I think we've all been served a slice of humble pie now and then. It makes you appreciate others and keeps you aware of how much we need everyone."

Mandy starts to fuss. She's made her way to the other side of the living room and used an end table to get to her feet, but her tank has run dry and she wants to eat.

Anna pats her hands together twice and says, "Well,

come on."

Holding her hands out to see what she'll do, Mandy just let go and walked four unassisted steps to reach Anna.

"Well, look at that," I say. "Mandy's now a two legged terror."

"YEA!!!" says Anna. "You did it! Wait 'til I tell Mom."

Mandy isn't all that thrilled with our excitement. She just wants to nurse and keeps fussing.

Visit:

Karin still struggles from her experiences as a shooter and may never regain the youth robbed from her but losing her brother Josh hasn't made things better. As a shooter, she has grown accustomed to long hours perched among the branches of a tree. Now it has become her quiet spot; alone with her thoughts. Josh was her confidant during bad times, when the pain of what she had to do outweighed the safety of reclusiveness. Anna has helped bring her out and she interacts with others now, even laughs at times, but the months of duty lie buried; never shared. The one who understood was Josh. He knows all the struggles; the feelings; and the nightmares. She could share her heart with him because he too lived behind those terrible crosshairs.

Nights growing cooler; fall is surrendering to winter and her perch in the walnut tree will soon go vacant 'til spring, but for now; it's comfortable. In her jacket and toboggan cap, Karin drifts into the soft unconsciousness of sleep.

Awakened, perhaps by a sound, her eyes open as she methodically scans the fence line and yard for anything out of place.

"You're getting lazy, girl. I had you cold."

It's Josh! Right there at the base of the tree, looking up at her.

Without a word, Karin scrambles from the tree and throws her arms around her big brother.

"I've missed you so much!" she says. "Where've you been?"

"Mostly around Elma but I've been in and out of Hazel Creek a time or two," he says. "There're several old fish cabins along the water. One had food and supplies cached in. I'm guessing it was a bug-out location for someone who never made it. I'm doing OK. How's Mom and Dad?"

"Dad's hand is getting better but it's going to take time to get full use of it," she says. "Mom is pretty upset that you left and worries about you all the time. Josh, it really wasn't their fault that Dad got bit. It just happened."

"I know that. From what I've seen, they seem to be good neighbors," he says. "They'll fit in."

Karin's heart is aching as she asks, "Josh, please come home. I really need you. Nobody understands me like you."

"I don't know who I am anymore," he says. "I don't know who to trust or who will turn on me down the road. There was a man following the creek and he stayed with me a couple days. He didn't have any place to go but didn't stay anywhere for long. He said something that stuck. He said some folks wander because they find peace anywhere they are. Others wander, searching for peace they can't find anywhere they go. I'm still searching, I guess."

"Can I come with you?" she asks.

"No, it isn't safe. Besides, I came to warn you about something." Josh's voice takes a serious tone, reminiscent of the dark times.

"You have incoming, but it's not something you can see," he says. "Don't let any new people enter town for the next few months. They are carriers of bad sickness. Another thing, this is a bad time to travel. The sickness is all over. Now, I have to go. Tell Mom and Dad that I love them and never meant to hurt anyone.... especially you."

Karin gives Josh a long hug. To think they ever fought as kids. Right now, all she wants is for her brother to come home, and be close again.

A Mockingbird greets the sun and wakes Karin, still perched in the walnut tree. Climbing down, she examines the ground around the trunk for boot marks. The sod is too dense to tell. Was it really Josh? It was too real for a dream but she couldn't remember him leaving. All she can do right now is cry softly.

There is a board at the Grange Hall door with notices and listings of things wanted or needed. Prices always depend on what you have to trade. A new post reads:

Wanted:
Persons interested in travel to IOWA.
Please see Chris Spencer

The store still does a fair trade on barter. It's run by Vicki Eckerd who does the buying and selling on most days. It makes a modest profit but is also a center for sharing the news and gossip that keeps a town alive. If the store ever closed, I'm not sure which would be missed more.

George meets Chris as he leaves the store.

"Chris!" he says. "Are you serious about leaving us?"

"We're thinking about it," he says. "Becky's folks are passed and her sister is too far away in Alaska. That leaves my family up in Iowa. My parents are there and my brother and his wife."

"Funny how things play out," George continues. "Jackie had family in Montana but they're here now. I grew up in Iowa and graduated from Iowa State. I was originally from Tampa but my folks died when I was in middle school and my aunt Dee and Uncle Ed took me in. I'm sure they could use the help on their farm outside Monteith."

"Monteith!" says Chris. "In Guthrie County? That's where I want to go. My folks have a farm near there and my brother Dan lives next-door. He was farming both places, last I heard."

"Dan Spencer!" says George. "Why didn't I make the connection? Dan's been my best friend since middle school. We graduated together."

"You're the George he got into a fight with on your first

day of school!   Dan has written me about that a hundred times when I was deployed.   He was a bit of a bully up to then but felt so bad about that fight; it changed him for the good.   He says you are the best friend he ever had.   You know, I think you may have won that fight after all.   It looks like you beat the bully out of Dan, even if you got bruised for it."

Chris and George share some epic stories before they get back to business.   "Well, we have us a situation," says George.   "I think we need our wives and Nicky and her folks if this can be hashed out.   As much as I want to see Iowa again, it wouldn't be right to take Jackie away from her parents or Nicky after they just got back together.   Let's do pot-luck at our house this Sunday after church.   I'll ask Nicky and her folks to join us and we can talk it out."

"Sounds good to me," Chris says.   "I'll ask Becky."

Jeanie Pritchard and Mike Jr. arrive Friday afternoon.   They caught a ride from Elma on a neighbor's wagon as they were coming this way.   Emily is always glad to see her best friend and the Bennett's keep a room ready for her and Mike Jr. but Jeanie can tell something is bothering her.

"Emily, what's wrong?" she asks.

Nearly in tears, Emily hugs her friend.   "You couldn't have come at a better time for me.   I think God sent you.   This morning I went to Karin's room to see if she was up and she wasn't there.   She sometimes sleeps outside but her pack's gone.   I'm afraid she's gone looking for Josh."

"Karin's a strong kid and can take care of herself," says

Jeanie. "You raised her right and we'll pray for her safety. I know your upset but it's not like her to leave without saying unless she plans to be back soon. Did she leave a note or anything?"

"There wasn't one on her bed or on the stove. She doesn't generally leave notes so we don't have any set place to put one. There's one last place she knows I'd look...." Emily walks out the kitchen door to the walnut tree.

There on the tree trunk is a note pulled from a pad with Karin's writing.

Mom and Dad,
Please don't worry. I'll be fine.
Josh is in trouble and needs me to find him.
I'll be back when I know he's OK.
Love, Karin.

Emily is a strong person but losing both her children is more than she can bear. Jeanie sees the look in her eyes and the note in her hand. Sometimes words can't comfort an aching heart but a hug from a close friend does. Fellowship at church is another powerful support.

Kristen Palmer gets better at playing hymns every week. This Sunday she and her sister Kellie play a medley of hymns as a piano duet to everyone's delight.

Formality at church is replaced by attention to the changing needs of its members. Today, Allen Duncan senses a need to ask for prayer requests and Emily shares the need to pray for Karin. The service changes to a prayer meeting as a peace settles among them with fresh energy. Allen's message about trusting God couldn't have been better planned.

Sam Elliott arranges to borrow Elmer's wagon and team to take Jeanie back to Elma after church. Sam has been helping Elmer on his farm along with Dick Reed and his son Keith. He won't have time to return before dark so he'll stay the night in Elma and return Monday.

At the Hardin's home, the pot-luck gets down to business after dinner. Jackie cooks two roasting chickens with onions, garlic, carrots & potatoes. Nicky and Jennifer bring fresh bread and a vegetable-rice casserole while Becky surprises everyone with blackberry pie. She found a secret stash of berry bushes near the water.

After dinner the subject of Iowa comes up.

"I guess everyone has seen our post about going to Iowa," says Chris.

"We've been talking about it already," George adds. "I think we have a lot of interest."

Nicky is next, "I'm deferring to Dad and Jen. I can settle anywhere but that 'anywhere' needs to include family."

"I guess that's our cue," says Ron. "Jen and I have been talking it over since George shared your plans with us. We're fine with Kansas but Iowa is just as fine as long as the kids are there. If you want to move to Iowa, count us in as long as we stick together. I only ask that we travel some other way than by canoe. That seat left a terrible mark on my backside."

As smiles and laughter subside, it's Jackie's turn. "I

know the emptiness Nicky and I felt when we couldn't reach Dad and Jen. Right now, we have them back but George has that emptiness for his family. We have an opportunity to keep our family and find his at the same time. Let's go see Iowa."

Becky casts the last vote. "Count me in. Gina and I would be pretty lonely without you all. Besides, who would I fix pie for?"

The ladies gather to talk moving plans while the men discuss how to get to Iowa. Winter will be busy tending to the details of a workable strategy. It's not like you can call the movers and meet the truck at the other end.

Sickness:

On the way to Elma, Sam and Jeanie Pritchard talk of where Josh may be staying.

"I can search from daybreak to about three and still make it back to Hazel Creek before dark," he says. "I'll try to follow the creek, there's usually a fishing trail along the bank."

"Be careful," she says. "There's no telling who you might run into."

Arriving in Elma as the sun is setting; Sam drops Jeanie and Mike Jr. to their house and continues to the Lewis'. Gordon and Rachel said they would always have their barn available to their Hazel Creek neighbors who needed lodging. Their house is small with little room for visitors but the barn is clean and they've made a tack room into guest accommodations complete with bed, sink, table and lamp. It's sparse but perfect.

Sam has only been to Elma once before but made quick friends with the Lewis'.

Gordon meets him as he makes his way to the barn. "Rachel guessed we'd have visitors bringing Jeanie back home. Glad it's you, Sam. How was the ride?"

"It's never long with someone to talk with but the empty ride home won't be fun," he says. "At least I get a good visit with you fine folks. How's Rachel?"

"She's good. Supper's waiting for you. Let me help you with the team. They're looking better every time you visit. Drafting a wagon suits them."

With the horses out of their harness, brushed, fed, watered, and in their stall, Sam and Gordon go to the house but not before Sam brings out a blackberry pie from Becky Spenser.

"Chris and Becky send their love and a blessing."

Joking, Gordon says, "That looks good, maybe we ought to keep this safe out here in the barn. Rachel might not have room to store it, you know?"

Both men continue to the house, chuckling as they go.

Rachel's voice is strong and steady for a woman in her seventies. She claims it's from singing in the choir every Sunday. "Hello Sam. Glad you could stop by. Was the trip all right?"

"It was good," he says, handing her the pie. "Thinking about your cooking made the ride all worth it. This is from Becky Spenser; she sends her love."

Sam gives Rachel a kiss on her cheek and turns to Gordon. "Good thing you married this woman and took her off the market. She wouldn't last long today."

"Oh, sit down and eat," she says. "You'll make this old

woman blush. My! This will be good. Please send Becky our thanks. What a sweet girl."

Supper is homemade biscuits and beef stew. Rachel cans beef in stew size cubes to have ready for meals at any time. It tastes like it was made fresh.

Conversation turns to my task of finding Josh and Karin. Gordon thinks he may know where he's camped.

"I've seen smoke and believe I know the shack he's found," he says. "It's one of the better ones. Most are shacks in the worst sense but this one is more like a cabin and can stand up to weather. I'll show you how to get to it come morning."

Back in Hazel Creek, hog killing is a community activity requiring lots of participation. Long forgotten skills are needed, but thankfully, we have members of previous generations to show us how it's done.

We're gathering at the Tousley farm where Elmer has collected six fattened hogs. Two were caught wild as piglets and penned at the Parker place. Two are Elmer's and the last two came from the Eckerd's. The hogs each weigh between 180 to 275 pounds.

It's easy to see who's experienced in this tradition and who's seeing it for the first time. A pig is isolated to a narrow pen and Elmer approaches with a .22 rifle. Aiming about 2 to three inches above the eyes and center between the ears, a single shot drops the hog without even a squeal. Several ladies and a few men have to look away but the shock on their face as they realize how pork gets to the grocery store is unforgettable. Our remoteness from the farm has allowed us to live protected lives. Seldom do we consider the work and sacrifice necessary to fill grocery carts.

Dick and Keith quickly open the pen and drag the pig out. While Keith hooks a gambrel to the hog's hind legs, Dick connects a block and tackle from a thick branch of the shade tree and begins hoisting the hog by its hind legs. Once off the ground, a cutoff barrel is placed under the snout and Dick cuts the jugular vein to bleed the pig. This initiates a second round of looking away for the squeamish.

While the first hog is bleeding out, a second is put into the kill pen and dropped. It is hoisted up next to the first and bled the same.

The process continues to the scalding vat, scrapping, gutting, butchering, and salting for curing hams and bacon. We are all amazed at the precision and 'knowing what to do' demonstrated by the senior residents of our communities. Many overcome shock and begin learning each step of this age old process that sacrifices the life of our animals to sustain the life of our families. One is dependent on the other and it's the way of life.

By day's end, we have nearly 700 pounds of processed meat, curing hams, and smoking bacon that will help feed this town through the winter. Most are new to this and expected more meat for the work we did. One thing is sure; all of us have a greater respect for the food on our plate.

Gordon Lewis walks to his barn at daylight. Surprised to find Sam already awake, shaved, and dressed, he calls him to breakfast.

"You're too good to me, Gordon. Don't tell me Rachel is up this early."

"She gets up before me, most days," he says. "She's got eggs, bacon, and hotcakes on the table already."

"What? No coffee?" Sam replies.

"If we had any, she'd have made it for you," says Gordon. "I think she's sweet on you for some reason. After breakfast, I'll take you over to that cabin where I think Josh may be staying. He may not be there anymore. I didn't see him at all last week."

"Do you see him often?" asks Sam.

"Regular enough," he replies. "He doesn't stop to talk but we see him come and go. He keeps to himself."

Full of breakfast and ready for the day, Gordon leads the way across town toward the water. Brush and tree cover is thick, making it easy to conceal a small cabin. If this doesn't turn out to be where Josh is staying, Sam's work to find other cabins is cut out for him.

The cabin looks deserted from outside. There's a window in the door but it's covered with a towel that looks to have been hung years ago. The cabin is built on pier and beam, about two feet off the ground. Cautious of what to expect, Sam stands to the left of the small porch and remains low as he knocks on the door; softly at first, then more firmly as he calls out, "Anyone here? It's me, Sam Elliott."

There is movement in the cabin; not as much footsteps as boards creaking. The door lock clicks and the knob turns. Without caution, the door swings open. It's Karin.

"Sam, Josh needs help," leaving the door open she goes back into the room.

With no time for questions; Sam and Gordon follow Karin to the couch in the one-bedroom cabin. On it, Josh is resting but he doesn't look good.

"I don't know what he's got but he's getting weaker," she says. "He didn't want me to get anyone but he needs help."

"Gordon, is there a doctor in Elma?" Sam asks.

"The only one we had, left when the power failed," he says. "Doc Whitaker is closest."

"Karin, stay here with Josh and I'll get the team hitched and bring the wagon back. We need to get Josh to Hazel Creek," Sam says. "Are you good with that?"

Karin nods yes. Sam and Gordon head back to the barn for the horses and wagon.

Calling the floor of a farm wagon 'bumpy' is an understatement but Gordon has an old bed spring frame that we set a mattress on. With pillows between the mattress and springs, it bolsters a trough shaped bed keeping Josh from bouncing out on the long ride back to Hazel Creek.

Karin starts at Josh's side but moves to the buckboard seat after Josh falls asleep.

"Will he be OK?" she asks.

"I don't know," he says. "I'm not sure what he has.

How long has he been this way?"

"I found him yesterday morning," she says. "He was really dehydrated and barely alive. I got water in him and later found some broth. He started to come around and I thought he was getting better but today he quit talking and loses consciousness. I'm really worried."

"Did he say when he first got sick?" he asks.

"About two weeks ago," she says. "He thought it was flu but it didn't go away. He's got a rash all over. I didn't see it at first. It's not on his face or hands but it's all over his chest, back, arms and legs. I've never seen anyone sick like this."

"He's lucky you found him," he says. "How did you know to come look for him?"

Karin shares what must have been a dream at the walnut tree and Sam is amazed.

"I guess it makes me look crazy but I couldn't get Josh out of my head," she says. "I had to find him. I knew he needed help.

"It's not crazy at all," he says. "Chris Spencer told me about a deployment in Afghanistan, he and his fire team were hunkered down for the night in the remains of an old building. It was the only good cover he could find. About two o'clock they were awakened by a lone Navy SEAL who told them the site they were on was targeted and would be shelled at daybreak. They left and dug in near a small berm, away from that good cover. As advertised, shelling began at first light. Round one hit dead center and they never would have survived it. When he got back to base, Chris ran intel on their guardian SEAL and learned that he was KIA when that building was first hit about six months prior. Now THAT's crazy but it's not an isolated story. I've heard plenty others and quit trying to figure them out. God works in strange ways and may have given you a vision to get your brother some help."

Karin and Sam continue talking for most of the trip back to Hazel Creek.

Cooties:

Arriving at Doc Whitaker's house with Josh in the wagon, Anna and I hear the activity and go next door to see how we can help. It's a relief to see Karin with them.

Doc Whitaker examines Josh and then starts barking orders. Perhaps my Viking wife is rubbing off on him.

"Jason, don't come any closer! Keep back," he says. "Anna, I'm going to need you but this is going to be quarantine. Jason will have to tend Mandy for a time. Sam, start a fire to burn this mattress. Jason, Sam and Karin will need fresh clothes; can you get them and bring them to our gate but no further? We'll also need some signs to keep folks away. This looks like Typhus."

"Typhus!" says Anna. "I thought that was only in the history books."

"Well, it's back now," he says. "Typhus is a bacterial infection passed by body lice. Josh looks to have had it some time now so he's probably covered with infected lice. We need to get him out of these clothes and de-loused. Then he needs some antibiotics but this has gone untreated for a long time. Anna, get me a sheet from inside."

Stripping Josh of his clothes reveals the extent of his rash before they cover him with a sheet.

"This is really bad," Doc says. "Three; four weeks maybe. Even delirious, he shuns the light. Could be Meningoencephalitis."

Sam helps carry Josh inside to the hospital bed while Karin burns his clothes on a fire that Sam started for the mattress.

Karin turns to Anna. "Will we have to burn our clothes too?"

"Probably not," she says. "Lice can't stand hot water so we'll boil yours. We cut Josh's clothes off so there's no sense saving them."

Anna and Karin go indoors as Sam comes out to tend the fire.

"Anna," says Doc. "Get me the box marked ceftriaxone 2g. It's in the cabinet on the right wall. Hydrate it for infusion, I'll start an IV."

Anna passes the hydrated ceftriaxone to Dr. Whitaker along with a syringe and needle. He transfers the antibiotic to the IV solution and rocks the bag to distribute the medicine. After hanging the bag and setting the drip, he gives the next instructions.

"In the kitchen, over the stove," he says. "We need one

cup of white vinegar mixed with one cup of cooking oil."

"I can do that," says Kristine. She has come from the kitchen and is standing at the door to the exam room.

In a few moments, she returns with the solution in a quart size measuring cup.

Anna doesn't have to ask what it's for because Dr. Whitaker always explains what things are for and how to administer each. He is a great teacher.

After running Mandy over to the Wagoner's, I return with fresh clothes for Karin and Sam.

Kristine takes Karin to where she can shower and change.

"It's a bit cool to use the outside shower so I've put a five-gallon pale of warm water in the inside tub for you. There's some shampoo for your hair in the corner. Put your old clothes into this bucket and I'll get the laundry started," she says.

As Doc takes the vinegar and oil to the bed he says, "This is for the cooties."

"Cooties?" asks Anna. "I thought that was a child's game we played. Don't boys come with those?"

"Little girls too," he says. "According to the little boys, that is. The term cootie actually refers to body lice. Typhus is spread by body lice and this rash is from them. DDT is the best at de-lousing but no longer used since they blamed it for causing harm to wild bird eggs. Third world countries never stopped using DDT and they have plenty of healthy eagles and falcons.

Something else caused the trouble but they blamed the best mosquito and louse remedy ever discovered. We're using a country remedy. It's messy but works. We'll make a Joshua salad with vinegar and oil. This salve will kill the lice and the eggs too. It needs to go on all the rash."

For the next ten minutes Anna and Dr. Whitaker apply the oily salve to Josh. Unconsciousness may be the only thing saving him from death by embarrassment.

Karin returns looking refreshed from her indoor bath. How times have changed that inside plumbing is again a luxury.

"How are you feeling?" asks Anna.

"I'm a bit sore from the trip but should be OK after I get some sleep," she says. "How's Josh? Is he going to be alright?"

Doc has a serious tone as he answers Karin.

"Josh probably wouldn't have survived another night if you hadn't found him," he says. "You did the right thing at the right time but he is still very sick. The infection has spread to the membrane that encloses his brain. That's why he's sensitive to light and for now, is unconscious. I've never lied to you and won't start now. We're doing all we can but it may not be enough. In the early stages, Typhus is not difficult to treat but this is very advanced. He needs a lot of prayer."

Tears fill Karin's eyes but she maintains her composure. She's a very strong young lady.

Morning finds Karin feeling poorly with flu-like symptoms. Dr. Whitaker starts her on a series of azithromycin as these are the beginning symptoms of Typhus.   In the absence of others sharing similar symptoms, it's a good move to assume this is not flu.

With great sadness, Josh doesn't make it through the next day.   Dr. Whitaker says his kidneys failed but he never regained consciousness.   He's buried in the family plot at the cemetery.   Karin was unable to break quarantine to attend but said she saw him when he was still conscious and knows he isn't there at the cemetery anyway.   She'll see him in heaven.

Two days later, Sam shows symptoms and is also put on antibiotics.

Mandy and I are missing Anna.   It's been a week since the quarantine was declared.   Emily Bennett is eager to see Karin but no one is allowed past the gate.

Kristine is a workhorse.   Though her strength is low, she is constantly boiling and washing clothes, towels, linens, and blankets.   Anything that can't be washed in a tub is getting misted with white vinegar to kill both lice and eggs.   It seems to be working.

I'm told life is never fair but death is.   Death claims a hundred percent.   The last to come down with Typhus is Kristine but her body can't take the antibiotic needed to heal her.   She dies from acute kidney failure after two weeks and is buried not far from where we placed Josh.

After the funeral Anna asks Dr. Whitaker how he is doing and he offers an insightful reply that I plan to remember.

"I'll be OK in time.   It's a funny thing.   Time only

moves in one direction. Forward, always forward. No matter how fast you run, you can never catch it and all we have in the end are the memories of how we spent the time we've been given.

Without additional victims, the quarantine is lifted but not the heaviness in our hearts. Kristine was a hardworking and compassionate soul who lived her life for others. Dr. Whitaker is openly affected. He has lost the love of his life.

"Jason, remember when we lost Carlos at camp and you helped me stop double guessing everything I did?" Anna says.

"You're always hard on yourself," I reply. "Doing the best you can sometimes isn't enough. All I did was remind you."

"It's different when you work under a good doctor," she says. "Dr. Whitaker is a great practitioner with more experience and intuitive medical insight than any doctor I've been privileged to work under. But now, he's going through the same doubts that I felt. I started to tell him those two rules you shared about life; that everybody dies and some die young, and the second where nothing you do can change rule #1. He knew them already but I think the reminder still helped. I just wish I could help him more."

Taking Anna's hands in mine, "He needs to grieve. If I could add a third rule it would be, time is sometimes the best medicine."

Settling:

Sam stays at Elmer Tousley's farm with Dick and Keith Reed.   The four work well together and are good company besides helping Elmer.

Sam and Stephanie spend more time together these days.   She was very concerned when Sam took sick with Typhus and perhaps it has prompted them to focus on matters of the heart.

Karin drops in on Sam fairly often too.   It seems she's found another person who understands her and they talk at length.

"Sam," says Elmer.   "You're courting a cat fight with two attractive women vying for your attention."

"You're trying to be funny," Sam says.   "Steph and I go back a long way and Karin is just a kid."

"That's what YOU say but that youngster is now seventeen," he says.   "Meredith was only sixteen when we married and Karin has blossomed fast in these tough times.   Watch yourself or that kitten will catch herself a mouse."

Pat Wagoner has been upgrading his radio equipment and manages to find several Kansas Department of Transportation solar panels that no longer have purpose. Remote flashing road signs also contain rechargeable batteries. Pat now has enough reserve power to effectively work the airwaves every other night and transmit twice the time he was previously limited to. He provides news once a week before church and would offer it more often but few sites have power reserves to transmit regularly. He has to collect bits and pieces as he can and a week of listening can be summed up in about ten minutes.

"I'm getting very little from the east coast," he says. "That's where population was heaviest and suffered more from violence, sickness, and food shortages. Survivors of the initial months have been hit by Cholera and other opportunistic diseases. Topping all that, nuclear power plants are polluting nearly everything east of the Mississippi River. The good news is that west of the Mississippi, Typhus seems to be under control again and communities are getting more organized. Trade is starting and there are many survivors in rural areas like us."

George asks. "How well are messages getting through? Could we reach my family in Iowa, like Nicky reached her folks in Montana?"

"We can always try," he says. "We got lucky in Montana and found a local ham who could handle messages for us. Maybe we can find one in Iowa who lives near your family."

Questions continue but no one is concerned that church start on time or that it ends on time. If any good can come from our radically changed way of life, it has to be that we conduct things according to the seasons and by the relative position of the sun. Daylight starts our day and we work as long as there's light.

On Tuesday we hear an almost forgotten sound. Driving into town under its own power comes a two-ton box truck, pulling a large trailer. Hand painted on the side of the trailer and truck, are the words:

Stan's Trading Post
Supplies You Need
Trades Welcome!

Attached to the front bumper of the truck are two barrels with tubing running into the grill.

"HELLO ladies and gentlemen! I'm Stan Richter, owner and operator of Stan's Trading Post. I have supplies and hard to find items you may have been looking for. Would it be alright for me to set up my store for you to browse what I have to offer? Everything is for trade and I have a list of items and their relative values."

"Pleased to make your acquaintance, Stan. I'm Jason Connors. I just live here but I see Vince Parker walking this way, he's our mayor and can speak for the town."

Vince was at the store and started our way when he heard the truck. Extending a handshake, he greets Stan.

"Vince Parker." They shake hands. "No problem setting up your store. We haven't seen vehicle traffic in quite some time. Gas has gone stale and any diesel was used up months ago. How do you run your rig?"

"That's my most frequent question. I'd be glad to show you." Stan reaches into his cab and pulls a notebook from his dash. "Here are some diagrams of what's inside these two barrels. The stack here, is where I put sawdust or wood chips. It burns from the bottom as the fire drafts air down through it. There isn't as much flame as there is heat and it generates wood gas that's collected in the rest of the barrel and fed to run the engine. Acceleration isn't great but she runs and with two of these gasifiers, I can run my truck and pull the trailer. By the way; one of the items I take in trade is pulverized organic material to fuel my truck but it has to be real dry."

"I am most impressed," says Vince. "Could some of our men have a close look at it so we could make one to run some things around here?"

"Sure, I'd be glad to show them the insides but it will have to wait 'till it cools down. Perhaps tomorrow morning; if I can stay the night."

"That would be fine," Vince says. "Let's have a look at what you're selling and what you need."

Stan goes to work setting up his wagon/trading post. First he shuts down one gasifier and diverts the other output to run a generator, mounted on truck's back bumper. He's devised a bellows to pull the wood-gas down the pipe to the generator but once started, the generator draws the wood-gas on its own. With the generator supplying power, he turns on lights, circulation fans, and then says, "Watch this" as he loads a CD into a small player. From loudspeakers on the roof of his trailer comes the unmistakable 'Ice-Cream Truck' tune… 'Turkey-In-The-Straw'.

"That attracts customers," he says.

The music works as it carries a long way in the absence of other sounds and people come from all corners of Hazel Creek.

Stan knows marketing. His trailer is set up like a little store with at least one of everything he has to offer.

"Folks, here's how everything works. My business is selling and trading. Prices change based on supply and demand. I buy whatever I can sell and try to stock what folks need and want. I like what I do and like the people I deal with. This is my run; I work from Kingman to Fowler but I meet up with other operators who trade in Oklahoma and other parts. On the wall behind the counter is the list of things I'm buying and the price I'll give you for it. Prices are in trade-credits and are firm at the time each sale is made. Now you don't know me very well but in time I hope we get to trust each other. I plan to do regular business here and I need your business as much as you need mine. When you're comfortable, I'll keep an account for you so you won't have to spend all your credits every time I show up. If you let me know something you want, I'll do my best to get it for you. Another service we're trying to set up among us operators is a kind of mail system. It'll be slow and some mail might get lost but it's free and just something we do to help folks."

Most popular items are butane lighters, matches, fish hooks, cigarettes, and various types and caliber of ammunition. Demand is what determines price but one of the luxury items at very high cost is toilet paper.

"Where did you find toilet paper?" I ask.

"I was able to trade two gallons of 'gentleman blended sippin' stock,' also known as moonshine, for one package of twelve rolls. I can't afford to use it myself but I get pestered more for this than any other item. Had I known what times were upon us, I'd have stocked a warehouse of toilet paper."

Everyone in the crowded trailer gets a chuckle with Stan's humor and perspective. He's already working his way in favor with the folks of Hazel Creek.

Sam finds his way to the Trading Post. "Have you been over to Elma?" he asks.

"Just came from there," Stan says. "Good folks. Is there an Emily here?"

Vicki Eckerd comes in from the store. "Not yet but she should be soon," she says.

"OK, there's a Jeanie Pritchard who sends her regards from Elma," he says.

Sam continues. "We had a round of typhus come through here. Did the sickness hit them very hard?"

"It was there but they got through it OK. No one died but they used up all their antibiotics. They just about cleaned me out to restock their supply. If you have any to sell, I'm buying and the price is good."

"Doc Whitaker might spare some. He keeps all that stuff," Sam says.

"You're lucky to have him.   Doctoring is scarce everywhere," he says. "I just took in several cases of honey, preserves, and canned goods. I'm also in the market for ladies who can sew shirts, pants, undergarments, and dresses, per order. I take orders in one town, get them filled in another, and carry that order back to those who need it. I have several bolts of fine fabric in stock. It's slow but faster than waiting for the malls to reopen."

Smiles erupt as we settle into a new way of business. This cooperative barter and trade stands a good chance of catching on. Stan brings us things we need and can't find while we provide goods and services that others need and can't find. He is a mediator between people along his route and we all get something out of it.

He stays another day before heading west.   Fred, Harry, and Elmer get a good look at the gasifier and believe they can make one to at least run some small equipment. Byron and Emily invite Stan for dinner and offer him a room for the night but he prefers to sleep in his trailer.   With it being his livelihood; they understand. He does OK with us but will do better now that we know what he has and what he wants. We no longer produce only what we need and may not have to suffer without the things we can't get. Stan's Trading Post opens the possibility for us to market what we produce to get items we couldn't find before. The Trading Post gives us a connection with towns along his route. Stan is another contact with a world beyond Hazel Creek. Without government, regulation, and taxes, an economy is being birthed before us.

Thanksgiving:

Fall runs right into Thanksgiving and Hazel Creek holds another community dinner. The rocket mass heater and double cook stoves provide a warm and fragrant atmosphere to the Grange Hall. Different from previous dinners, food is now prepared here, cooked here, and served right from the oven. Even the menu changes with a working kitchen on site. Fred Elkhart supplies three large turkeys from his farm. He said they are partly Elmer's gift because he's been supplying the feed to grow them since spring.

Anna, Becky, Nicky, Jackie, and Emily are all busy tending to various parts of the feast. Karin joins them and is more interactive than anyone has seen for some time.

Anna finds a moment with Emily while Karin is out of earshot. "Wow, Karin is sure coming out."

"Anna, it's an answer to lots of prayer. She's like her old self again. She's happy, talks with me, and goes to see friends. I was afraid she was going to close in after Josh died but she shared a dream she had just before he died and it seems to have changed her."

"Ya know," Anna says. "I wonder if we may have missed this from the beginning. I'm really glad for whatever reason that she's coming out again but what if Karin's been going through an awkward late adolescence and now emerging as a grown woman? What she's been through; I wouldn't wish on anyone but maybe she is growing out of this on her own."

"I'm too happy with the results to worry about the cause," Emily says. "It's just good to have my baby back."

Emily's eyes sparkle from joyful tears. Anna gives her a quick hug and they return to basting turkeys and checking bread rolls.

Elmer and Harry are busy out back of the Grange Hall. They won't share their secret but they're pleased about something. As people collect inside, a serving line is prepared with sliced turkey, casseroles, stuffing, bread rolls, and both hot and cold tea.

As Allen is about to say the blessing the sputtering of an engine interrupts. The motor smooths out followed by the clunk of the building's electrical disconnect and the room fills with light, dims again, the sputtering resumes, and then both the motor smooths out and the lights burn steadily. Elmer, Harry, and Fred have been building a wood gas generator from the design Stan showed them and it's now feeding a generator.

Applause follows in appreciation that the inventors can't miss. Entering the building the applause only intensifies and each take a deserved bow.

"Elmer, how did you guys do it?" asks Vince.

"I'll let Fred tell it," he says.

Fred speaks up. "We copied the design from Stan's example and tinkered with it to get a gen-set going. We pulled the power meter and wired it to the panel but had to adjust the air-fuel mix to handle the load. This is going to change things. We now have wood fired electricity."

Allen Duncan gets everyone's attention and says, "We have a great deal to be thankful for today. Let's ask the Lord's blessing."

His prayer is moving and genuine. Trade with other towns, electric lights, a bounty of food, and a working community are but a few things to be thankful for. Soon after the serving line gets going, Kristen and Kelly Palmer take turns providing background music on the piano. It's hard to remember things better than this.

With fall upon us and winter approaching, workloads turn from outdoors to indoors and extra time lends itself to more social activities. Elmer shares stories of bon fires they used to have and we decide to burn the pile of old stumps and roots that weren't safe to burn when we dug them up during the dry summer. Everyone is invited.

"It's too bad we don't have marshmallows," says Stephanie.

"We never needed marshmallows," Elmer says. "We have better things to cook at this bon fire. I have a box of sweet potatoes here and a big pan of cored apples with cinnamon and sugared honey. The ground becomes your oven when you bury these and pile coals over top."

Elmer explains as he digs a hole and places the covered pans on the bottom. With several inches of dirt covering the pans, he tops the hole with live coals from the fire.

"They'll be done by the hour," he says.

Stephanie and Sam sit together on a log connected to a tree trunk. Someone suggests they play charades but instead of teams, the last performer picks the next and gives them the word or phrase they are to act out. It's a lot of fun and laughs.

Singing follows with Fred Elkhart playing guitar and Daemon Eckerd on mandolin. They have obviously been playing together for some time. Once everyone is sung out, soft music continues. Karin sits watching just across the fire from Sam and Stephanie. Nicky's attention is drawn to Karin's expression as she sees Sam give a long kiss to Stephanie. Few besides Nicky notice as Karin slowly backs away from the fire and disappears to the darkness.

Winter coming doesn't lessen the chores but it does change their nature. Work in the field moves to gathering heating fuel from the river's edge. Tillable land is already cleared except for wind breaks but the abundance of water near the river feeds a lot of trees and brush. Snakes are gone to their holes so clearing out dead trees is safe and productive. Rocket mass heaters make use of small wood that's typically ignored by firewood hunters and the wagon loads of dry sticks and branches is turning this area into a new park-like setting.

Elmer and Dick secure the loads on the wagon and haul the wood to the old grain barn on East Main, just across Central Street from the church. It's centrally located for easy distribution through the store.

"Elmer," says Dick. "We need a system to replace what money did for us. The dollar was a good tool to measure the value of work and let each person control their own budget. Stan Richter has his credits system and it works for him but we could use a standard currency for Hazel Creek."

"I've been thinking about that," says Elmer. "It would head off bad feelings that rise from not seeing what people do. Everybody sees what we do because they eat the grain we grow but others work as hard without being noticed. A money standard would also eliminate some horse trading. I pay grain for chickens but they can only use so much grain and I might need more chickens. Vicki was working on some sort of trade standard at the store. What say we get some heads together for a meeting and try to work something out?"

"Good by me," he says.

The load is tied down and Elmer runs it to the grain barn where Vicki is already binding the previous load into smaller 'three day bundles.'

"Thanks Elmer," she says. "How many more loads do you expect today?"

"We'll probably get three more with the daylight we have left," he says.

"That's good," she says. "We'll make it about eight weeks with this but when the bottom drops out of the thermometer we'll need more. We probably need five more days like this. Is there that much more to bring in?"

Elmer takes a moment to assess the need. "We have plenty for this season. What I'm thinking is, can we grow what we need as fast as we burn it? We may need to start growing white poplar. It's the only tree I know that grows fast enough."

Consensus:

December brings colder weather but it's the best time of year to bring people together for a town meeting at church.

Dwight Woodard calls the meeting to order.

"Thanks everyone for taking time to come and help us work through coming challenges. We're doing pretty well thus far, largely due to your cooperative spirit and willingness to pitch in. Let me be first to say thanks."

A gentle applause rises.

"I have a small list of items for discussion before entertaining new business. First, we would like input regarding the establishment of some form of universal trade currency to make our store barter system more manageable. Second, our scavenging of firewood is going to run out unless we cultivate and begin farming our own crop of trees. Third, and lastly, we need to hold an election of officers to represent Hazel Creek for the next two years. Now for item one; the need for a universal currency. Vicky Eckerd will present some background before we open discussion."

"Thank you Dwight," she says. "At the store, we see a need for standard currency every day. We've almost defaulted to a wheat standard because everyone needs it and we judge the value of Becky's blackberry jam by how much wheat we would trade for it."

Chuckling fills the room.

"We thought about using the old US currency but there's so much of it out there, we run the risk of outside money ruining our system," she says.

Louis Roth raises his hand to speak. "Yes, Louis," she says.

"With our system being so small," he says. "Why do we need hard currency? Can't we develop a virtual currency and let the store keep record of each person's credits? For the little we deal outside the store, we can use promissory notes like bank checks."

"You know?" says Vicky. "That's a great idea and it might work."

Elmer stands and is recognized. "During the depression, hardly anyone had real money but we got on well enough with just what we're talkin' about. The store kept account of what you bought and credited you with what you brought. Everything was priced in dollars and cents but paid by credit. It's a friendly way to do business and the store-keep serves as a banker."

Dwight looks over the audience and asks, "Is there any further discussion or comments?"

Brent Palmer stands and is recognized.

"Thank you Dwight.   How will prices be set to establish the value of the virtual currency?"

Dwight turns to Vicky for an answer.

"America became a great nation because of a free market," she says.   "Supply and demand set prices. When prices rose, opportunity presented itself for hard work to increase supply.   That system worked well until the government stepped in.   I think it's worth trying again."

Chuckling and smiles fill the room.

"Brent; to answer your question with more detail, the store operates on a five percent profit margin. Currently, everything is based on store credits and the new currency will simply formalize that.   Since we have no tax burden, operating costs are low and we keep the profit margin low.   There's still some haggling when we purchase items but the store price is based on what we pay for an item.   The virtual currency will probably continue to follow the wheat standard so I guess you can say it's our new gold standard."

"Sounds like a good plan," says Brent.

Dwight asks again, "Is there any further discussion before I call for a motion?"

"With discussion ended, do I hear a motion?" he says.

Brent says, "I motion that the store function as our bank and establish a unit of credit that can be exchanged either at the store or between us by means of promissory notes."

The motion is seconded and passes with none opposed. The second item, regarding firewood is addressed simply because it was presented. Some plan to raise a poplar grove to meet their own needs while others plan much larger stands of poplar as a cash crop. The third item starts an election cycle and candidates will be voted on at a January election.

New business is entertained and Lois Parker takes the floor.

"It has been the custom at Hazel Creek to hold a Christmas formal dinner. We have few opportunities to dress up and I'm afraid if we neglect this custom, our husband's will forget how to dance. I motion that we hold December 18th for our formal Christmas dinner and dance at the Grange Hall."

The motion is carried unanimously and for lack of additional business, our meeting is adjourned. The dinner/dance is now our chief topic of conversation.

"Nicky," says Stephanie. "Can I bother you to trim my hair? I'm guessing you're going to get pretty busy between now and the 18th."

"Sure," she says. "I'm free tonight, if that works for you."

"That will work," says Stephanie. "I'll stop by about sunset."

As Nicky heads to the foyer, Karin stands in the back of the room by herself.

"You've been keeping to yourself lately," she asks. "I don't think I've seen you since the bonfire."

Nicky catches slight recoil from Karin at the mention of the bonfire. Taking a risk, she cuts to the chase.

"I've noticed you looking at Sam. Do you like him?" she asks.

Karin makes eye contact with Nicky. "He doesn't even see me," she replies. "We talk but it's like he doesn't know me."

Nicky reaches softly to hold Karin's arm. "Girl, I can help you change that. If you want a man's attention, you have to reach out and take it. Why don't you stop over at my place tomorrow night? I think I have just what you need."

Nicky doesn't need a verbal reply; Karin's subtle smile lets her know she is up for the hunt.

That evening, Anna is frustrated.

"What's wrong?" I ask.

"We will be," she says. "In a little over two weeks, we are to attend a formal dinner and the best we have is dress casual. THAT's what's wrong."

"I thought that might be a problem," I say. "Stan is due through tomorrow and has always said he can get near anything. I guess I'll put him to the test for a petite formal dress in size ten"

Anna's eyes shoot back at me as I realize my life might be in danger. "Size FOUR, mister."

"What was I thinking?" I reply. "Size four, I knew that."

My smirk exposes the tease and Anna tackles me onto

the bed. "You are so mean!" she says. "It better be a good dress."

Across West Dower Dr. at Nicky's house, Stephanie knocks at the door.

Nicky's parents, Ron and Jen, meet her at the door on their way out for a walk.

"Hi Stephanie, we're heading out for the moonlight. The stars are amazing tonight. Nicky is in the kitchen, expecting you."

Stephanie walks in and calls, "Hi Nicky! It's me."

"In the kitchen!" she says. "We're all set up. What did you have in mind?"

They exchange ideas for a new hair design and Nicky starts to work while they chat.

"I've noticed you and Sam getting close," she says. "Are there any announcements coming?"

"Funny you should ask," she says. "We dated in Houston and really enjoyed each other's company. I guess it was always assumed we would be together but somehow, nothing ever came of it. I care for Sam and was worried sick when he went on that recon trip from Terlingua but each time we try to push our relationship closer, there's no magic."

"What about that kiss at the bonfire?" Nicky asks. "That looked promising."

"You saw that?" she says. "That's what got me rethinking things. I know Sam meant well and it wasn't 'bad'… it just wasn't magic. No fireworks."

"Does every kiss have to be magic?" Nicky asks.

"I don't expect magic every time," she says. "But that was the first real kiss I've had from Sam since Houston. Back then it was only a goodnight kiss after a fun date, nothing serious. I'd have expected SOMETHING more out of it. Sam and I are really good friends but it may never become more than that."

"For a girl who hasn't discovered her own Prince Charming, I'm no one to give advice," says Nicky. "Maybe you two are meant to remain great friends."

Nicky continues working on Stephanie's hair design and they talk about dresses, shoes, and men in general. After nearly an hour, Stephanie's hair looks fabulous. It has grown longer since Camp at Big Bend and is now a little past shoulder length. Nicky has feathered the sides and added some curl but the change is dramatic. Stephanie will be turning heads at the Christmas Dinner.

Dresses:

Stan Richter motors into town right on time the next morning. He's never on a tight schedule but today he arrives in perfect time. Waiting for him are Jason, Scott, George, and Eric, each with a tall order concerning their wives need of dresses.

"Formal attire," says Stan. "I think I know where I can lay hands on that. Would you care to buy or rent? I can give you a better deal if you rent."

"How's that?" asks Scott

"I figure there will be more formal events in other towns along my route and you boys just gave me an idea for another service line," he says. "I can start into clothing rental for weddings and such. And because you gave me the idea, I'll cut you a big discount for this inaugural event."

"Can you give us prices for both buying and renting and let us keep the option until after the Christmas Dinner?" I ask. "Our wives might change our minds and want to keep the dresses."

"Deal!" says Stan. "I yield to your understanding of the changing ways of the softer gender."

"I'm not so sure of the 'softer' gender," I say. "But I'm sure she'll scrap hard if she likes the dress."

All five of us get a smile over that.

"I'll hustle over to where I think those clothes are and should be back here in two weeks," he says. "Will that be enough time before your party?"

Stan finishes up his trading this morning and heads off toward Elma. I'm thinking he has his sights on an outlying suburb of Wichita but I could be wrong. It would take him about that long to make all his stops and return from there.

Days growing shorter brings sunset more toward late afternoon. As it arrives there is a soft knock at Nicky's door.

"Karin, I'm glad you came. Come on in. We have a lot to talk about and I have some beautiful things for you."

The door closes and the girls begin preparation for the Christmas Dinner/Dance.

Busier than usual; the crowd at the corner store is all talk with preparations for the big event.

"I'm not trying to impress anybody," says Elmer. "I believe I'll wear my tux shirt, a bowtie, and my best bib overalls."

With a laugh from the group. "This, I gotta see," says Vince. "I'm sure you will make a great impression with that."

"There's a problem with most of the Texas crowd," says Chris. "We all came without a lot of baggage and I'll guess few thought to pack formal attire."

"Stan said he's working on that," I say. "He seemed to know where a lot of good clothes were stored and is coming back with a bunch of dresses for rent. What size dress do you wear, Chris?"

Among another roar of laughs, Dick has an idea. "Before we have to see poor Chris in a dress, we might all check the closets of the vacant houses. I'm sure there are some suits and fancier clothes to be had. Let's get the sizes of all the men who need suits and try to match them up. Not a word to the women though. They always think we can't do anything without their help. Let's keep this our secret."

"Where can we stash the goods where the women won't find out?" asks Daemon. "AND VICKI ECKERD, you are sworn to secrecy."

Vicky laughs as she answers. "What's said here stays here. Your secret is safe with me, though I must say I'm impressed."

Sam offers to quietly collect sizes from all those who need a suit. "There could be some local guys who've outgrown their suits as well."

Byron and Emily sit down to another supper by themselves. Noticing only two places set at the table again, Byron partly asks and partly just comments.

"Karin's out again?"

"Yes, she's at Nicky's. They're doing something that I think has to do with the Christmas Dinner but they aren't telling," Emily says. "After the bonfire, I thought she was regressing but whatever happened; she's more alive now than ever. Nicky is proving to be a good influence."

"Does Anna know anything about what they're doing?" he says.

"Nicky only told Anna that it was going to be good but nothing more," she says. "Anna is as curious about it as I am. There's only ten days to go but I'm not sure I can stand it."

"Emily, you're as bad as a high school girl," he says. "Have you decided what you're going to wear?"

"I plan to wear the gray dress I wore for Marsha Elliott's wedding," she says. "Nobody's seen me wear that here so it will look like a new dress. I saw you taking a bundle of suits out the other day. Are you having them altered?"

"That; and having Beverly Roth freshen them up a bit," he says. They aren't soiled but have hung in the closet a long time. She said she would look them all over, tighten up the buttons and fix any loose seams for me. She hasn't had a lot of work lately so I brought her several suits to do."

"That's nice," she says. "Beverly does good work too."

The sun has been up less than four hours as the unmistakable sound of 'Turkey in the Straw' begins just outside town. Stan drives slowly through town, turns around at the far end and drives back, all the time playing his music at full volume. Stopping in front of the Grange Hall, he is in exceptional mood.

"You look like a man with a plan, Stan," I say. "Do you have something special for us?"

"Do I ever!" he says. "None of the big cities are worth going to. Everything's burned-out or empty anyway. But the suburbs and smaller towns weren't hit as bad. Don't get me wrong, most things you need are gone. Shoes, hardware, building materials... all gone; but formal wear; who's going to steal that? I found a completely intact bridal store... well, mostly intact. The cash registers were gone and the displays were bad because the windows were busted out, but they had a back room where they stored their freshly cleaned and bagged dresses and tuxedos. I hit the mother lode! They even had shoes in nearly every size, complete with socks!"

Stan talks as he sets up his store but he's anxious for the crowd to gather.

"Stan, before the ladies get here," I say. "What are you asking for a tux in 44 long, complete with shirt, shoes and socks?"

"Rent or buy?" he asks.

"Let's start with buy," I say. "I figure life is going to continue and that means weddings and more special events."

"I'll make you a deal," he says. "I'm not getting any younger and there's no health plans or hospitals to run to. If your wife will see me twice a year and keep track of my health, I'll count that for store credit with the first check-up paying for that tux and your misses a dress of her choosing."

"I'll check with Anna as soon as she gets here but I'm sure it's a deal." I say.

The next two hours are pure chaos in that trailer. Stan has packed away all but the most requested items to make room for racks and piles of dresses and tuxedos. A flurry of deals keeps him very busy and if he lives through the day, Anna has agreed to be his nurse.

"I'd have looked after Stan just for asking," Anna says. "But a deal is a deal, as Stan would say. And this emerald green dress is lovely!"

"I didn't see Karin or Nicky there, did you?" I ask.

"No, but they have SOMETHING planned but aren't telling," she says. "It's driving me nuts. Even Jackie and Emily don't have a clue. Jen knows something but she won't tell either."

The Post Office boxes are still in use at the store. Mail delivery is mostly local but Stan has bags marked with the cities he stops at and letters get delivered eventually. Emily and Jeanie correspond regularly and Jen writes to Rachel Lewis from time to time.

Stephanie's discovers a square envelope in her mailbox with a handmade card.

Stephanie,
Would you do me the honor
of allowing me to escort you
to the upcoming Christmas Dinner?

Sam

Vicki keeps small cards and envelopes available at the store and Stephanie buys one to return an answer.

Sam,
I would be most honored
to be escorted by you
to the upcoming Christmas Dinner.

Stephanie.

Vision:

Finally, the Christmas Dinner and Dance comes and lives up to everyone's expectations.

The atmosphere entices grand expectation while hams finish baking, punch-bowls are filled, decorations completed, and the room brightly lit by both electric and oil lamps. The ambiance is festive and romantic as couples arrive in their best formal attire. Tuxedo's and brown suits mix with formal gowns and regular dresses. Everyone is having a wonderful time. Kristen Palmer's piano playing is joined by Fred Elkhart on guitar and Daemon Eckerd on mandolin. They sound like a chamber orchestra.

Sam and Stephanie arrive, arm in arm. Stephanie has a wrist corsage of silk flowers as fresh ones are long past. Sam looks tall and dashing in his tuxedo and Stephanie is beautiful in an off white, floor length gown. They cross center floor to the punch-bowl and visit with others as remaining guests arrive.

Elmer does indeed impress everyone. Arriving, not in his promised best bib overalls but in a tuxedo with tails, complete with silk top hat, white gloves, and walking staff. It's a vintage tuxedo that perfectly fits him and steals the show. He enters to a rousing applause and takes a bow in response.

Silently raising his hands to pause the response, he exits again and returns with Nicky Chambers gracing his arm. She is stunning in a floor length light pink satin evening gown. The room erupts again in applause but I'm not sure if it's for her or the fact that Elmer managed to escort one of the prettiest eligible young women in town. There is something suspiciously coy about each of them. They have a secret and the mystery is about to be known.

With all eyes still on the entrance, Elmer and Nicky separate to each side of the doors. They open them once more as a breathtakingly beautiful lady enters the room.

Her floor length A-line dress rises to meet what Anna describes as a portrait neckline. It's a wide, soft scooping neckline reaching from the tip of one shoulder to the tip of the other. Dark royal blue satin is contrasted by a white lace shawl that is nearly concealed by curled and flowing dark brunette hair reaching from shoulder to shoulder. This is not the tree climbing young lady we've learned to call Karin.

Her smoky gray eyes are captivating and not at all compromised by the beautiful red that Nicky helped select for her lips.

As she stands, motionless, the room falls deathly silent.

Nicky is beaming with pride for the young girl now blossomed into a powerful woman.

Standing there, unaware of the silence, she sees only one other. Sam stands motionless by Stephanie. He doesn't notice her release his arm. He has no words, no consciousness, and no recollection of time. Before him is a rose in bloom for the first time and he can't move.

There is no trembling with her. She lost the trembles long ago sitting in a stand and glassing targets through a rifle scope. She controls her breathing just the same, relaxes the muscles across her shoulders, and waits, watches, observes.

With comfortable understanding that finally fits pieces together, Stephanie puts her hand on the small of Sam's back as she softly commands.

"If you don't go to her and take her hand, you'll kick yourself in the morning but not before I kick you now."

With a soft push, Sam slowly crosses the room and takes Karin's hand.

Daemon whispers to Fred and Kristen and they start playing the Kansas Waltz. Karin in his arms, they begin to dance. Her smile is radiant but Sam is lost in her eyes. Everyone watches them command the room initially but soon, others join and couples fill the floor.

Karin floats effortlessly in Sam's arms. He is awestruck by his sudden realization of Karin's beauty and grace. This hardened young girl in tactical gear with hair pulled back has emerged as a refined and enchanting woman; elegant and warm.

As they dance, Sam struggles for words. "I never knew

you danced so well."

Apprehending his conflict; drawing confidence from the effect she holds over him "There are a lot of things you don't know about me."

"I look forward to an opportunity to remedy that," he says.

Couples continue filling the floor and move to the music but all eyes follow the undistracted Cinderella and her prince. Few seem aware of anyone else in the room.

Elmer Tousley asks Nicky for a dance and she graciously accepts.

"Elmer, I had no idea you were such a good dancer," she says.

Smiling, he says "No one knew I owned a tux either but that's because nobody ever asked. Meredith and I used to go dancing every Friday night. She loved ballroom dancing and that's why I bought the penguin suit. You dance very well yourself."

Nicky's smile exposes more than acceptance of a compliment. "I've had a lot of practice over the past few weeks."

Elmer, privy to the work leading up to Karin's presentation, reflects an understanding grin.

Emily and Anna watch breathlessly from their spot near the stoves.

"I've never seen Karin so beautiful," Emily says. "And I never knew she could dance either."

"I guess that explains what Nicky and she have been up to all this time," says Anna. "Your baby is no little girl anymore, Emily. She sure cleans up well. It looks like she's cleaned up with Sam too. I don't think he even knows what hit him."

The ladies are laughing as I approach and ask Emily if she would watch Mandy while I dance with my wife.

Taking Anna in my arms, "Get a load of what happened with Karin, would ya?" Nicky's done a fantastic job."

"Nicky only frosted the cake," Anna says. "She had a lot to work with. Karin is a beautiful girl; she just needed a little help getting attention."

"I'll say," I reply. "There's not a guy in here who's taken his eye off her."

"Jason Connors! You keep your eyes on ME where they belong!" she says.

Digging my way out of the hole I just dug, "You know you're the only one for me. Karin is a pretty girl but she's not the one I married and not the one I plan to spend the rest of my life with."

I hold Anna closer and she seems to melt into my embrace but looking over her shoulder, I'm thinking... 'Man! she is quite a stunner.'

Stephanie finds Nicky by the punch-bowl after the first dance.

"Nicky, you've outdone yourself with Karin. She's beautiful!"

"Steph, are you OK with it? After we talked about you

and Sam, I helped Karin get noticed but..."

"Not to worry." Stephanie motions to the chairs against the wall. As they sit, Stephanie continues.

"I hope Sam and I will always be great friends and I owe him a lot. He saved my life by taking me with him to Camp but nothing ever grew from that. I'm meant for someone else who's still out there... somewhere. When I saw Sam totally spaced after one look at the new Karin, it all made sense. He's talked about her ever since they brought Josh back from Elma but I don't think he realizes that he's fallen in love with her. I guess at first, I didn't want to admit it either. I started testing the waters but it only confirmed that my love for him wasn't the right kind for building a life together. I wish the best for both of them... and for me."

Nicky gives Stephanie a hug and both girls are drawn closer together.

The first dance ends and Daemon taps his cup against the seat of his wooden chair to get the crowd's attention. Everyone quiets as he makes an announcement.

"We're glad for everyone here and we started tonight with the 'Kansas Waltz' but we would like to honor the other half of our community by now playing for you, Waltz Across Texas."

As the music begins, Keith Reed approaches and asks Stephanie if he might have the next dance.

"I'd be delighted," she says. "Nicky, wish me luck."

Nicky laughs as she catches her subtle humor. "She's a

good one."

Dancing only lasts for six numbers because that's all the music that was prepared. More will come in the future but six is a lot for a first time music group. Sam and Karin would have stayed together for all six but Byron cuts in to dance with his daughter for the last call.

Regaining conscious thought for perhaps the first time tonight, Sam finds Stephanie and asks for a spot on her dance card. They talk as they move to the slow music.

"I've been a terrible escort tonight," he says. "I really owe you an apology."

"Now that you mention it..." she says. "Yes, you've been an awful escort but no, you owe me no apology. I'm the one who shoved you over there, remember? Sam, we're good friends and I hope that never ends but the stuff you need to build a life together never grew. It's not your fault or mine, it just didn't happen. I see that magic starting with you and Karin and I hope for the both of you that it becomes more. You're in love with her and everybody sees it but you. I just hope she realizes what a great catch she's landed."

"You know something?" he says. "You're a pretty good catch yourself. I'm sorry the magic never developed between us. You're everything a guy could ask for."

As the music ends, Stephanie gives Sam a sincere kiss on his cheek and wishes him good luck. They will remain friends and continue to talk but their paths have reached a place that is less change and more of an altered awareness.

Buzz:

With Christmas a week away, Hazel Creek is filled with secrets and unusual activity. This is a season to tolerate some undocumented time, lending to Christmas giving.

Mom sits across the table from Dad as they finish their breakfast tea.

"Do you remember where we were last Christmas?" she says. "It's hard to believe all the change and how far we've come."

"How about the year before?" he says. "We went to Jason and Anna's and spent a week at the ranch. Then it was just a house... a nice house, but by comparison, it wasn't much different than our own. Six months later, we were hiding at Camp and six months after that we were calling indoor plumbing a luxury."

"I'm still waiting for indoor plumbing again," she says. "But aside from beds, blankets, and indoor plumbing; the country fell but the people are recovering and building again. Little ones, like Mandy, are coming along to fill the awful void from those we've lost, couples are finding love and getting married, and our two communities have joined to heal and become one."

"Don't forget a fledgling commerce with Stan's trading post and wood-gas generators to fuel some of what we thought we'd lost," he says.

"I wonder how the rest of the country is doing," she says. "Pat's radio provides some world news but not much local. At best the news is spotty. Do you think we'll ever get back to where we were before?"

"Cynthia, I hope not," he says. "I think the real beginning of the end was when the media changed from journalism to thought control. It was the same for our schools. They taught students what to think instead of how to think while the media stopped reporting facts and replaced it with manipulation that only fueled emotions. No wonder the country imploded so fast. It didn't last long. Progress led to corruption and I, for one, don't want it back. And you know something? I haven't met a liberal or a politician since."

"Well, in that regard," she says. "Some of our liberal friends saw the deception and made changes while some of our conservative friends failed to prepare and perished with those waiting for government rescue. In the end, we're all in this together and I doubt any of us will ever support big government in our lifetime. I guess life IS better now but I would like to find just one Macy's still open."

No matter what, Mom and Dad always find something

to laugh about. It's a strength I admire.

The Dinner/Dance provides abundant stories for gossip. The guys still meet at the store each morning for hot tea and 'discussion.'

"Elmer, I still want to know where you got that tux," Keith asks. "I know Stan didn't have anything like it."

"Like I told you, it's mine," he says. "I've had it for years. It wasn't an old style when Meredith and I bought it and I've worn it dancing with her on many occasion."

"Well, you did a whole lot better than a bow-tie and bib overalls," Dick says. "And your escort turned a few heads too. You two cut-a-rug pretty good."

Elmer chuckles as he explains. "Nicky's a sweet kid. I ran into her the day before the Dinner and asked her who had asked her out. Figuring she was sure to have been asked, I was surprised to find she didn't have a date. There's an advantage to age and she accepted my offer to escort her. We guessed our entrance would attract some attention so she let me in on her and Karin's shenanigans. We sort of set the stage for Karin's grand entrance. Worked too."

"Speaking of which…" says Dick. "Where's Sam this morning? He generally never misses the morning meeting."

"He's got something up his sleeve," says Elmer. "Probably has to do with the season and I'll bet it involves Karin."

"She sure was something," says Dick. "Keith, why didn't you ever pay her any interest? You two went to school together."

Keith changes posture like he's uncomfortable. "Before everything went bad, she was kinda normal but never interested in guys. After things fell apart, she turned scary. She quit talking and when she looked at you it made you feel like some wild animal's prey. Karin can look clean through you but if you look back you don't get past her eyelashes. Scares me half to death."

"That appears to be behind her after last night," says Elmer. "Sam was looking pretty deep into those gray eyes of hers."

Dick's big smile lets on that he is onto something. "Keith, it appears you saw something of interest in a long white dress. She looked mighty fine dancing with you."

"She looked lonely and I thought it was the right thing to do," he replies.

Now Elmer is all smiles. "Lonely? She was visiting with Nicky and you asked her before the second dance. I'd say you saw a good opportunity and did yourself proud."

Keith's red face and smile doesn't need a response.

There's a knock at Nicky's door. "Nicky! It's me, Karin. Can I come in?"

Jen opens the door. "Hi Karin. Nicky is in the kitchen. Go right on in."

Nicky looks up from the egg salad she's making. "Hello Princess, how was the ball?"

"It was wonderful!" she says. "But now I'm not sure

what's next. It's over; I'm back home, and Sam's back at the Tousley farm. Where do I go from here?"

Nicky stops to give undivided attention. Karin looks confused, almost frightened. This is an aspect of Karin she hasn't seen before. Always ready for any challenge; now she appears unsure and off guard. Last night's curl and fullness lingers in her hair with the telltale evidence of rouge that refused to wash away completely. Even without make-up, and Karin back in tactical gear, she is a beautiful woman to behold.

"Karin, you accomplished your goal to the max last night. You turned heads and most importantly, you turned Sam's head. He NOTICED you, big time. Now you have to do the hardest part. You have to wait."

"Wait?" she says. "Wait for what?"

"You wait for Sam to come for you," says Nicky. "Last night, he saw you as a woman, not a kid. He's going to chew on that and realize he wants more. That's when he'll come for you. It's his move now."

"I guess I've been a hunter too long. I don't wait well," she says.

Nicky tries to contain a laugh. "I don't think any of us wait very well. I'm not laughing at you but you just perfectly put words to how every woman feels at times."

Stan's Trading Post rolls into town again but his signature tune is hardly needed. Half the town is waiting for him. He collects rented gowns and tuxes but his store is configured to showcase gifts of all kinds. In place of disposable lighters, soaps, lotions, and towels are jewelry, books, shawls, and scarves. Stan knows what sells and today, his store is a gift shop.

He keeps an eye on what each person admires and when their spouse or parent comes by; he offers suggestions for appropriate gifts. It would be an opportune time for a slick salesman to unload merchandise but Stan has earned the trust of the people he serves and won't betray that trust for sales. It works for him AND us. Today, however, is a rainy day and among other things, Stan can't stock enough umbrellas.

Becky Spenser coos over an antique broach that reminds her of one her mother once had. Later, Chris passes through and they make a deal for Stan to have it missing on the next visit, one day before Christmas Eve. Stan is to spend Christmas with the Parkers and has agreed to carry Jeanie Pritchard and Mike Jr. from Elma to spend Christmas with the Bennett's. When he returns, if Becky notices the broach missing, the plan is to explain that someone bought it after he left. Christmas remains an opportunity for sneakiness.

Live Christmas trees aren't abundant in Kansas but most homes have at least one artificial tree tucked away. A large tree is assembled at the Grange Hall and adorned with favorite ornaments from each home. Even without lights, the tree is beautiful and we decide to combine a Christmas service and community dinner in the Grange hall. It saves wood to heat both buildings. Firewood is donated from each home to run the heater for these events. Dinners together are more efficient and we all enjoy the extra company.

Allen Duncan preaches as well behind a pulpit as he

does standing by a campfire. Today's message on God's gift at Christmas touches each heart and we're grateful for his care.

Dinner is followed by testimonies of what we are thankful for this Christmas. Most tell of family and the grace of God to have survived terrible times but Emily Bennett sums up a lot of feeling in her testimony.

"I'm, of course grateful for my family and that Bryon's snake bite is near fully recovered. I'm also grateful for my son coming to know God at an early age and for a daughter whose heart was open to follow God's leading to find Josh before he passed. God's goodness to us is amazing but it came in the form of a group of strangers that found their way into our hearts. The door to our heart was closed and behind walls of hurt from acts of human depravity not even imagination can describe. We didn't know how much we needed them until, through God's intervention, our hearts began to heal. Unselfish compassion rescued us from ourselves and it reminds me of that first Christmas when the world thought they were fine without a Messiah. They couldn't see their bitterness and hurt but God did. He sent a baby to rescue us from ourselves and for that I'm eternally grateful."

As Emily sits down, silence floods the room. Allen whispers to Kristen Palmer who moves to the piano. As she plays, we all join in singing 'The First Noel' and many sing with teary eyes.

Gift giving is not like it used to be; or at least as we used to do it. Christmas is not about the gifts you get but more about the gift you give. There aren't enough resources to give everyone you know a gift so they are reserved for the one closest to you. If you get just one gift, it's counted a blessing but if you don't get a gift, it's still a blessed Christmas.

Planning:

"It could cut a month long trip to under a week but we'd have to plan everything really tight," says Chris. "There aren't any repair shops along the way."

Chris and George are working through George's idea to convert a truck to run on wood-gas and drive to Iowa.

"There are plenty of trucks blocking the back roads around town," says George. "I'm sure at least one of them will run."

"That might be the problem," Chris says. "Hazel Creek can't be the only town with roadblocks and alternate routes could also be blocked.   A horse and wagon might be easier to get around an obstruction but then we have to figure on feed for the horses. Maybe Stan can get us some information on a route. He seems pretty connected with some of the other traders."

"In the meantime," says George. "I'll see Fred, Harry, and Elmer, about designing a gasifier for a truck, and try to match it to one we have near town. We can decide which to use after Stan's field report."

Days grow colder. Daytime temperatures have dropped another ten degrees but it feels colder still. Karin's perch in the walnut tree is abandoned in favor of a regular bed and pillows. She is also present at meals and showing more interest in cooking. At dinner today, Byron captures her complete attention.

"I saw Sam Elliott today. He appeared rather nervous about something." Byron stops talking as he ladles a bowl of Navy Bean soup with pork, and two buttermilk biscuits.

Emily can hardly contain her curiosity. "Well, what was he nervous about? Don't stop."

"Oh," he says. "He wanted to ask me if it would be acceptable with me if he called on Karin. He being twenty-seven and she only seventeen, he didn't want to cause any offense. I thought it said a lot for his character that he came to ask in the first place."

Karin can't keep silent any longer. "So, what did you tell him?"

Byron is toying with Karin and enjoying every minute. "I thought we should talk it over as a family and discuss the possibilities. You know you aren't thirty yet. This might be a bit early to entertain such things."

"Daddy!" Karin begs.

"Byron, please." Emily pleads to stop Karin's torment.

"I told him he may call on you and that your mother and I have already discussed this possibility. You've been raised with good values and I shouldn't have to remind you that keeping those values is your responsibility. I gave him our blessing."

Karin settles back in her chair. "Thank you, Daddy."

Emily smiles approval as she gives Byron an understanding wink.

Jeanie and Mike stay through the Christmas break but need to return to Elma for school after the first. Today, Jeanie spends time with Melinda Wagoner to standardize their curriculums as Melinda has begun teaching school in Hazel Creek. They hope to establish a structured educational system again. For now, they concentrate on their two cities and share whatever they can. Jeanie's High School study plan is useful for Melinda's two oldest boys. Robert is now seventeen and Brendon, thirteen. She offers to grade their work along with the group in Elma. They can correspond as Stan carries the mail or by anyone else making the trip. It will save Melinda some work and allow her to focus more on her younger students.

Pat Wagoner enjoys a break in a long stretch of poor radio reception. With radio bands opening up, he makes two coveted contacts in the same day.

This is K5OSI... CQ, CQ, CQ... this is K5OSI... CQ, CQ, CQ.

Copy K5OSI, this is XF1-K5FNF, I read you loud and clear. Is that you, Pat?

Roger that. Jim, it is so good to hear you again. Give my regards to Rita. How are you both?

We are well. Business is booming for us down here as US traffic is replaced by anyone who can fly cargo.

We've been given three additional aircraft by the Mexican government in exchange for providing air cargo service. It seems our spot in the sun isn't interesting to the cartels and they like the kind of work we do.

Glad to hear it, Jim. How's Rita?

Oh, you know; ornery as ever.

Jim's response is typical. Always the tease but he loves Rita passionately.

None of us believe that for a second. Give her our love. Have you heard much from Travis and the boys? How about Lucas and Adelaide?

Will do. Travis and his sons had a round of sickness but they all pulled through fine. Lucas and Adelaide insisted they stay with them so she could take care of them while they recuperated. I think she wants to adopt Willie. Some of their workers found their way back and they're making a go of running a trading post. They don't get a lot of business but they're getting by. How's little Mandy doing?

She's walking already, Jim. You'd have a hard time keeping up with her. We had a round of Typhus come through. Lost two from Hazel Creek and Sam Elliott got sick but recovered. Everyone else is healthy. We'll make it through the winter just fine.

Pat and Jim continue sharing updates and Pat takes notes so he can relay everything to the group.

Later that evening, Pat makes another very special contact by digital text with Anna and Scott's Uncle Ed, up in Trout Lake, Alberta.

Anna meets him at Scott and Roxanne's house to hear the news.

"Aside from general shortages of just about everything; they're doing pretty well," Pat says. "Ed says it's just like when he was growing up. No electricity, wood heat, and living off the land. He did say to remind Anna of the bear that ate your berries. They shot another one at that same spot last week and put him in the freezer."

"How's Mom?" Scott asks.

"She sends her love," he says. "Ed said they were all in good health and waiting to have you join them. They have space for you all, but I think they understand the difficulty getting there."

"Is Parliament still able to function?" Anna asks.

"Ed said they don't see or hear much but the store is still accepting currency," he says. "As far as they are from populated areas, there's not much of a government presence anyway. He said it was what attracted him to the area in the first place."

"That sounds just like Uncle Ed," says Scott.

Pat shares the rest of the news, including his contact with Jim and Rita. The updates are welcomed.

At the Tousley farm, George is talking over his idea of fitting a wood gasifier to one of the abandoned pickup trucks and driving to Iowa. Harry brings up a few obstacles.

"That conversion works best on older vehicles. Stan's truck predates electronic ignition and fuel injection.

When you run an engine differently than how it was designed, all those sensors and controls get in the way. What you need is a truck from before the seventies. These newer rigs will be nothing but trouble and require too much battery to run stuff you don't need but the engine won't run without."

"George, how big of a truck were you looking for?" asks Elmer.

"I was thinking of a pickup or Suburban that we could pull a trailer with," he says.

"Why not a single axel grain truck and forget the trailer?" Elmer asks. "I know where several of those are and I think the newest one is from the seventies. Most grain farmers around here have gone to full combine services that provide transport but they've kept their old trucks. You can't sell 'em for much but they're too useful to throw away. Most are still sitting in barns out there."

"I guess that would work," says George. "We could put our stuff in the box and add seats for riders. There's no Highway Patrol to give tickets and we won't be going that fast anyway."

"You sure WON'T be going that fast," says Elmer. "These old grain trucks are geared for racing turtles downhill."

Sam walks in and stops all conversation. It's not because Sam isn't welcome to join in, it's that he's all cleaned up like going to church. Something's up.

Elmer is first to notice. "Well, will you looky there. Sam, where might you be headed, all spiffed up? Did the kitten catch a mouse?"

Sam is all smiles; Elmer has him cold. "No comment. And yes, she has gray eyes."

"What kitten? What mouse?" George is confused.

Elmer smiles as he says, "It's a private joke between Sam and me; a good one, but private."

Sam hasn't been this nervous since High School. He asked Karin if he might stop by tonight and mentioned it to Byron. He can't understand why he has butterflies. The long walk only makes it worse. With clear skies and a full moon, the pale blue of moonlight adds a softness to trees and houses as he walks. The closer he gets; the more nervous he feels.

Turning up the walk from the street, he is startled by a voice.

"Hello stranger, where've you been?"

It's Karin, sitting on the glider swing in the yard next to the walk. Sam looks up and even in the moonlight, Karin's gray eyes light up. She's wearing a dress too but it's covered by her winter coat.

Sam normally has no trouble making conversation but right now, he struggles.

"You look very nice tonight. That's a pretty dress."

Karin giggles softly. "You can't see much of it for the coat but I actually do have dresses. I'm glad you like this one," she says. "Would you like to sit?"

"It's such a pretty night and the moon is bright, I thought we'd walk a bit," he says. "Care to?"

Karin starts to get up and Sam offers his hand to her. She takes his hand but keeps it as they walk. Her hand is warm and comfortable as they walk under the stars and share stories of childhood adventures. They talk about Josh but one area continues unshared; her time as a shooter. Perhaps one day, but for now; that part of her life is closed.

Economy:

Stan begins a business venture with Marge Wagoner. She agrees to some sewing and Stan delivers thread, buttons, and fabric, for three men's shirts. A worn shirt will serve as a pattern. Marge says it will do and takes the job.

Another opportunity takes him to the Tousley farm for a deal with Harry, Fred, and Elmer.

"I have two customers that would like gasifiers to run generators like you set up. I can offer a hundred-fifty credits per unit, if you're interested."

Elmer looks down and rubs his chin a bit. He's in a haggling mode.

"I was thinking a working gasifier, tuned to run a generator, would be worth a bit more than that."

"How much more?" asks Stan.

"About a hundred more," he says. "We can do it for two hundred-fifty credits."

"That's a bit steep, Elmer," says Stan. "I need some meat left for me. How about two hundred and I have some six-inch stainless tubing that I'll throw in with the deal?"

"That'll do." Elmer reaches his hand and they shake on it. Written contracts are for those who don't trust each other. This is between friends and honor lets a handshake seal the deal.

Chris waits for Stan at the wagon.

"Stan, do you have any contacts between here and Iowa?" he asks.

The next twenty minutes are spent tracing various routes from Hazel Creek to Monteith. Stan agrees to ask details of his other contacts and get back with Chris.

I meet Chris as he and Stan complete their business.

"How's the move coming?" I ask.

"We're not ready to pack anything yet but we're learning things and solving problems," he says. "Stan's going to check with other traders to help us find the best route and Elmer is helping us locate a truck to run on wood-gas. There's still a lot to do but we have plenty of time."

"We'll be sorry to see you go but I understand. Any word from Iowa, by radio?" I ask.

"Pat made contact outside of Jefferson but that's a long way from Monteith. We haven't heard anything back. My family is pretty self-reliant and they are in a good place. I'm pretty sure they're doing OK."

"Have you thought about making a recon trip?" I ask. "I'd be glad to join you."

"Thanks. I appreciate the support," he says. "I thought of that but our group won't be much larger than a recon unit anyway and if we get good intel from Stan, we might as well save the extra trip."

"You're probably right," I say. "It's still uncharted ground. We don't need the extra radio you picked up from that bunker. Pat's set will serve us fine. Why not see if Pat can set you up to maintain contact along the way and keep in touch once you get there?"

"Good idea," he says. "I know the girls will be happy to keep up with the news here. It won't hurt my feelings either. I'll talk with Pat. Thanks for the idea."

Kansas has ample population of White Tail deer and they provide us meat at no cost to our feed and grain reserves.

Today, Karin is back in tactical gear and accompanied by John Stubbs and Dennis Paterson. All three have pack-boards and intend to bring them home full. Karin has the only rifle but neither of the guys are hunters, today they volunteered as pack-mules.

Karin knows exactly where to go and though the terrain is flat, the guys struggle to keep up with her. They got a late start and she has little time to get into position. Finally, a solitary oak stands nearly fifty feet atop a subtle rise. Karin hardly stops between walking and climbing, swiftly she assumes a position among the branches. The guys are more than grateful to stop and now painfully aware that they are not in as good shape as they thought.

Talking softly as she glasses for her quarry; "While I'm setting up, you can gather those acorns. This is a Chinkapin Oak and they make the sweetest acorns. Deer love 'em, but make sure any you get off the ground don't have wormholes. Just keep very quiet and remain low."

With her rifle set and herself in a comfortable spot, Karin takes a moment to notice the beauty around her. The only significant color comes from a cloudless, intensely blue sky. During humid times the sky feels like it's right on your head but today it looks endless. Nothing is green this time of year. The brush near the river is gray and the dry prairie grass has turned from summer's gold to winter's dirty brown. From her perch, Karin commands a view of the only natural swale between the river and another large stand of brush. Deer use this path for cover to migrate between water and where they bed down for the night. In late afternoon, deer should be starting to move. No sooner is she set than the first doe pokes cautiously from brush near the river. It's a three hundred yard shot; not much of a challenge but she never shoots the first deer out. Bucks are smart and cautious. They send a small doe to test the path. Predators usually go after the first prey, allowing the breeding buck to escape. It appears cowardly but the practice protects the herd's most valuable member. Karin is lurking.

Once the doe is in the open a larger doe steps out. She keeps looking back and then forward. There's a buck behind her. Karin has seen this before.

A third doe joins the first two and then a fourth and fifth. This is an established herd. The grid failure and resulting die-off occurred too early for hungry victims to hunt these deer during rut when they demonstrate less caution. Light hunting has made them complacent but that's about to change.

Away from the doe, a spike buck emerges. If he gets too close to the herd, the alpha buck will run him off. With him is another immature buck. They will have to find their own herd next year. An alpha buck doesn't tolerate competition.

Finally, a snort and with it comes a beautiful mature eight-point buck. He's in his prime and lord of the herd. Standing half exposed from the protective cover of the brush, he sniffs the air, looking for traces of trouble.

Karin transitions from binoculars to her scope. Her breathing is conditioned and deliberate.

"Deep breath, let it out slowly, hold.... squeeze..."

CRACK! The .270 hardly finishes recoil and another round is chambered.

"Follow, lead, elevation... squeeze...." CRACK! A second deer is down.

"OK guys, our work has just started," she says. "It's going to be dark soon, we have to hurry."

Three hundred yards is not a tough shot for an experienced shooter like Karin but a second shot at a running deer takes it a step further. Either way, three hundred yards is still a fair walk. Arriving at the carcasses, John is first to notice, "You let the buck go?"

"When you're shooting for the table," she says, "a fat

doe tastes better than a gamey buck. Besides, he's needed to make more fat doe next year."

John and Dennis drag the second deer back to where Karin has already begun field dressing the first. With temperature dropping, there's not much chance of it spoiling but they have to get the meat onto the pack boards to port it home.

The two doe were each about a hundred and seventy pounds. Dressed out, there will be about eighty pounds of meat for each of them to carry. Some meat is lost due to the heart/lung shot, but at three hundred yards a deer's brain is just too small of a target.

Dennis comments as he sees the wound channel. "You hit both, dead center in the heart. Remind me never to make you angry."

Karin has no comment but the subtle reference to shooting another human stirs a twinge of remorse from the depths. Her monsters are back.

It's an hour and a half past dark when they get to town. Byron, Elmer, Dick, and Keith are waiting for them and set to work preparing the meat for proper cooling before it's butchered in the morning.

"Nice shooting, Karin," says Dick. "Where'd you find 'em."

"Like always," she says, "in the draw."

"How's the herd look?" he asks.

"I counted eight with two spikes," she says. "Probably another herd up river at the bend. That herd is usually larger but more work getting to them. I went easy on this trip."

"I'll say," says Elmer. "You didn't leave me a single heart. You know I like the heart."

"It was dusk and three hundred yards," she says. "I'll get you a heart from a morning hunt."

Karin knows his banter is in fun. The only other shooter in town, who could make single shot kills at three hundred yards was Josh. Now it's just her, and as the new top shot, it doesn't mean much without Josh to share it with.

Byron offers to take her rifle and her shooter's bag home. It's one less thing to carry and after hauling eighty pounds nearly two miles after a hunt, she gratefully accepts.

Sam shows up as Karin washes blood from her hands. Field dressing and pulling meat off a carcass is messy work, even when you have a lot of experience.

"Good hunt," he says. "Can I walk you home?"

"I'm a mess and probably don't smell very good but I do like your company," she says.

"You're beautiful to me," he says. "My dad once told me never choose a girl from the prom but when you find one attractive after she's been working a hay field all day, that's a keeper."

Walking hand in hand by moonlight, their conversation is limited by fatigue.

"I'm going to sleep good tonight," she says.

"I'll bet you will. You deserve it," he says. "It means a

lot to everyone and that fresh meat is a welcome reprieve from canned and dried."

"I do it because I know it's needed," she says. "I used to enjoy hunting but now, there's a lot of demons and I'm not sure how long I can keep it up."

"I can only imagine," he says. "You've earned retirement anytime you choose. Don't ever feel bad for that. You paid a terrible price for this town's peace and I know it wasn't easy."

"I did what had to be done and I don't have regrets," she says. "Still, I close my eyes and can see every face. It's like they haunt me and I can't make them go away."

At the end of the Bennett's walkway is a picket fence and small gate. The walk is a short step up from the sidewalk. Standing on that step lets Karin meet Sam, eye to eye. As she steps up, she turns and faces him and without thinking they kiss. It's not a quick 'goodnight' peck. This is a long passionate kiss, returned with equal emotion. For this moment, her demons are gone and she is lost in her love for the only man she can open her heart to. Sam too, is caught in a rift where his heart races as time stands still. He's never been kissed like this.

She goes into the house as Sam turns to slowly walk home, unnoticed is Byron who's been standing beneath the elm tree, respecting the couple's privacy. With a mix of sadness and joy, he muses the expectation of giving his daughter away at the altar.

In the house, Karin washes and heads to bed but slumber comes slowly. Sleep is postponed by a whirl of images and thoughts of what life might hold for her.

At least for now, her monsters are temporarily chained.

Sam makes it to his bed after a long walk home. Well below freezing, he isn't cold. Resting on his bed, he has a lot to consider. Big changes should be made carefully and with forethought. So why is he thinking of making them quickly?

Blizzard:

Elmer, Fred, and Harry, are on the buckboard heading north on Center St. Continuing past the Taylor's and Connors' place with a set of welding tanks and some tools, they have their work cut out for them today.

A few hours later, they return with an old yellow grain truck running roughly on a wood gasifier like the one that runs Stan's truck. It needs some tuning but it's running on its own. Passing each intersection, Harry honks the horn in a victory salute. They seem pleased with their accomplishment. Elmer follows with team and wagon. There's a peaceful connection he enjoys with slower times when life was less complicated. It's the life his dad and grand-dad knew and behind this team, he's living it. Motor trucks and advanced technology never prospered anyone. It only made their life faster. A farmer was forced into the race because failing to modernize would put you in the poor house. In the end, however, technology only let you maintain your standard of living at a faster pace. Farms became greater in size and yields increased per acre, at the cost of equipment, operational loans, and maintenance. Farmers ended up with about the same standard of living but with a lot more to worry about. Technology is perhaps overrated.

Chris makes his way to the Tousley farm and Elmer explains.

"Rick Boresma was a new farmer on the north side of town. He lit out for his kin up in Michigan as soon as the dollar crashed and we never heard from him since. At any rate, when he bought the place, it came with this 1969 Chevrolet C-50 grain truck. I figured it was just what you needed and perfect for retrofit to a gasifier. We just finished two gasifiers for Stan and figured they had to be tested so what better way than to fetch this truck. We charged a battery with the generator at the Grange and ran up there with all the parts. She runs pretty good for a first try!"

"It looks good but how far can she go on a pinecone?" Chris asks.

Chris means it as a joke but Harry brings up a good point. "Ya know, Chris... fuel could be a problem. These things burn most any wood but it has to be in small pieces and very dry. That could be difficult to find in prairie country. Settlers resorted to burning buffalo chips when they crossed the pains and buffalo quit making those chips long ago. You might talk to Stan about proper care and feeding of his truck."

"I've been pondering that," says Elmer. "We can add a port to direct wood-gas to run smaller engines like we do the generator. You could have several small engine machines that would run off that port. One might be a chipper to process wood for fuel. Chipped wood dries faster and you can store it in feed sacks. It wouldn't hurt to have a generator either."

"Good ideas," says Chris. "But where do I lay hands on either one?"

"That's your next assignment," says Elmer. "There are several farms along Route 2 and most had generators. Besides being ready for power outages, they come in handy to run tools beyond reach of extension cords. You'll have to look close because most folks don't just leave them out for show. Chippers are a bit scarcer but I'd lay odds there's a few to be had. Just make sure the place isn't occupied. You can take the buckboard to haul back what you find useful. After this long, if owners aren't back, they probably won't be back. Make use of what you can."

Chris enlists John Stubbs and Dennis Paterson for what he calls a 'scrounge detail.' It sounds interesting and they are both growing a bit stir crazy. The only work they can find is collecting firewood and they have the grain barn nearly full. It's not that they need the store credits as much as they need something to do. Chris's plan sounds like an adventure.

As they begin harnessing the team, Elmer takes a look at the sky.

"Better hold off, Chris," he says. "That sky doesn't look right and the barometer is dropping fast. I think we might be in for a storm. Would you boys lend a hand bedding down the stock? We need all the cribs filled with hay and water buckets topped off."

Chris steps out of the barn and looks at the wall of clouds heading their way. "Woah! That's building fast. Any chance of a tornado?"

"I don't think so," says Elmer. "That's more of a front line. Tornadoes generally come along with a supercell. We're going to get a lot of rain, wind, or snow. Any combination is possible but we'll know pretty quick."

Horses are pacing in their stalls, anticipating a storm. Dick, Keith, and Sam quickly load the stalls with remaining animals and feed. All water buckets get filled along with two barrels inside the barn. Wind begins to pick up as they close the outside stall doors.

"Help me brace the doors," says Elmer.

The big barn doors hang on rollers but to keep high winds from knocking them around, Elmer has old oil well pipe casing that he wedges from the ground to the doors. It stops the wind from constantly banging the doors and unsettling the livestock.

In short order, the barn and animals are all secure.

"Thanks for the help," says Elmer. "Storms rise quick on these plains; you boys better head right home. How are you set for wood, food, and water?"

"Wood is one thing we have PLENTY of," John says. "We'll be fine but man the temperature sure is dropping. We better make tracks."

Chris, John, and Dennis leave and begin jogging to keep warm. The temperature has fallen at least fifteen degrees just during the time they spent helping secure the barn.

"Ya know guys?" says Chris. "This started off a real nice day."

"Jogging all the way; they reach Chris and Becky's house in less than twenty minutes but the temperature has fallen another ten degrees, it's snowing, and all three men are very cold. Chris insists John and Dennis stay with them 'til the storm passes and he doesn't have to argue.

Becky has the rocket heater fired up but it will take time to overcome the sudden drop in temperature. Gina is comfortably playing on a blanket pad over the heater's warming bench. Seeing the guys coming, she quickly fixes three cups of hot tea to warm them up.

"You guys look frozen," she says. As she kisses Chris, "Wow! You ARE cold. Have some tea."

The guys grab cups and head to the warming bench as Gina makes her way to hold onto Becky's leg.

Sipping the tea, Dennis says, "This is good. Thanks."

"Can I offer you a blanket? You guys look cold still," she says.

"We jogged most of the way," says John. "I think we'll be fine."

"Can you believe this weather?" she says. "This morning, Gina didn't even need a coat and now it's snowing. Any idea how bad it might get?"

"Elmer says storms come quick out here," Chris says. "Without weather satellite data, it's hard telling what we're in for. We'll just have to wait and see. I asked the guys to stay with us 'till the storm passes. As fast as the temperature is dropping, I didn't want them going any further in this."

"Not a problem," she says. "I haven't started dinner yet but we have plenty to share."

There's a knock on the kitchen door. It's Steve Stokes from next door.

Becky answers the door. "Hi Becky, did Chris make it back home yet?"

Chris steps into the kitchen as Steve continues. "Chris, I'm glad you made it back. LouAnn was worried for Becky and Gina. This looks to be a bad storm. I've been watching the weather gauges and we could be in for a real blast. This is nothing to get caught away from home in."

"Thanks for the concern, Steve," he says. "How bad do these get? It sure got cold fast."

"This is a strong front moving in on what was a lot of warm, moist air," he says. "This has all the makings of a first class blizzard with no telling how much snow might drop. It's a good day to stay indoors. It could be several days. Do you have enough water drawn?"

Chris looks to Becky for an answer. "I have ten gallons drawn but it sounds like maybe we need more. John Stubbs and Dennis Paterson only made it this far on their way home so we're five until this is over."

"Heard that," says John. "Hello Steve. Chris, do you have any more buckets? Dennis and I can at least haul water. How far is the pump?"

"If you folks need anything," says Steve, "just holler.

I'm going back home."

"Tell LouAnn, thanks for thinking of us, Steve," says Becky.

"We don't have any more buckets but I just set a water barrel in the basement," Chris says. "We can dump these two five gallon buckets there and refill them; shouldn't take too long. I'll show you where the pump is."

Two years ago, Steve and LouAnn put in a new deep well to tap into a better layer of water. The old well produced fine but had a lot of minerals in the water. LouAnn's love of antiques really paid off for both families since the well is between their houses and they found a hand pump to mount on the old well head. Suction pumps are limited to twenty-seven feet of draw and this well is nearly a hundred sixty-five feet deep. The answer is to have the pump at the bottom of the well and operate it by a long rod connected to a four-foot pump handle at the top. It's the same as a windmill pump but with a manual lever replacing the tower and fan.

"Wow, that's some pump!" says Dennis. "I've never seen a hand pump that big before. It's got to be five feet tall."

"Try to stay impressed as we work it," says Chris. "The water's over a hundred feet down and won't start out of the spout for at least ten pumps. You're lifting a lot of weight by then. I plan to run a water line from here to the barrel in our basement. That will at least eliminate hauling buckets back and forth."

John hangs his bucket from the hook above the spout as

Chris begins working the four-foot-long pump handle. Water begins to flow after only a few pumps.

"Steve must have just used the pump," he says. "The check valve leaks some and generally takes longer to get it going. They never thought this was going to be their primary water source so they installed a single stage piston pump. It only delivers on the down-stroke."

With the first bucket full, John takes over and Dennis carries the bucket back to the house. Chris takes the next bucket to the house as Dennis returns and mans the pump.

They keep it up for a few more rounds but snow is falling faster and with the sun going down, it's becoming difficult to see between the house and pump. The water they have will be enough.

Even with physical effort, all three are chilled again and come inside. At least the warming bench is good at what it does and they don't stay cold for long.

Storm:

For three long days, the snow blows and the wind howls angrily. During the storm you could see very little as even daylight struggled to penetrate thick clouds and snow. Then it was over and this morning we have clear blue skies and golden sunshine. Mother Nature has her make-up on again and everything looks clean and beautiful. It's hard to see how much snow actually fell. Unprotected areas have less than two feet but drifts against the house nearly reach the gutters. Temperature appears to be holding at twenty-three for now. Anna and I talked Dr. Whitaker into staying with us during the storm. We really enjoy his stories of growing up on a farm. It's funny that Mandy and he will share similar experiences as neither had, or will have modern machinery or electricity in their youth. Things have sure come full circle.

Hearing an odd engine sound, I come outside to find Dick Reed driving an old farm tractor with a small snow plow mounted on the front. It isn't able to go fast but he is slowly clearing a lane through the snow. He, Elmer, Keith, and Sam, obviously didn't stay inactive during the storm and they fit a gasifier to run the tractor. Dick is pleased and hardly affected by the cold.

"Howdy, neighbors!" he says. "Everybody make it through OK?"

"We're fine here," I say. "I like your new ride. Where did you find this?"

"I think Elmer has nearly two of everything," he says. "This is a 1952 Allis Chalmers WD that I never knew he had packed into the back of that barn of his. It's only twenty-eight horse but she gets a lot out of each one."

"That gasifier looks right at home in front of the radiator," I say. "You'd think they planned for it to be there. Have you been around to check on others?"

"I plowed Center Street as far as your folks, then East Dower to check on the Bennett's," he says. "Everyone is fine out there. Next, I plowed a lane from Main down to Route 2 and up to the Parkers but couldn't make the rise to the Elkhart's place; slipped too much. I backtracked to Center and West Dower and I'm heading out to the Stokes place now. So far, everyone is doing OK."

"Not everyone," says Scott. "Have you tried making a snowball with this stuff?" Scott says hello to Dick and me but he's obviously disappointed at the snow.

"It's too cold for that, Scott," says Dick. "Wet snow won't hit 'til spring. This is powder snow and be grateful for it. This tractor is all we have to push it off the roads and it couldn't do squat against wet snow.

Gotta go; catch you fellas later."

"Jason," he says, "you have no idea the disappointment of trying to clobber a good friend with a snowball, only to have it blow apart as soon as you chuck it."

"Somehow," I reply, "I think I should be grateful for your disappointment. Did you and Roxanne have any trouble in the storm?"

"We did alright," he says. "But if that storm had lasted much longer, we'd have run out of wood. Rocky hung blankets over the hall entrance to keep the heat in the living-room and we slept there. I need to build a bigger storage rack if another of these comes along. I'm guessing we tripled the regular burn rate."

"I think we all did," I say. "We could have an Arctic blast hit and put us in real trouble. This storm was a wakeup call. We need a plan for severe weather and a place we can heat against sub-zero temps."

"Sounds like a town meeting is in order," says Scott.

Sam makes good use of the cleared pathway from the Tousley farm to the Bennett's. With all his trips to see Karin, his foot traffic might have saved the need for plowing.

They don't seem to mind the cold and hold hands as they walk everywhere. When they return for lunch, Emily has a gift-wrapped present for them.

"What's this?" Karin asks.

"I think you'll find it useful and enjoyable," says Emily. "Open it."

Sitting next to Sam, she opens the paper to find two

knitted mittens and one bigger mitten with two wrist sleeves attached but no place for thumbs to go.

"This is interesting," she says.

"It's a pair of courting mittens," Emily says. "Grams used to talk about them. When she was a girl and a fella came courting, they would walk with mittens like these so they could keep warm and still hold hands. Your outer hands each have a regular mitten and your other hands share the one in the middle."

Karin has a big smile. "I always did like Grams."

"I guess this means we're courting," Sam says.

There's a town meeting after church this Sunday. To prepare against a prolonged blizzard, we decide to augment the big rocket mass heater at the Grange Hall with some extra wood stoves and keep wood, food, and water barrels ready. In the event of an extreme storm, everyone will gather at the Grange and bring all the blankets and provision they can. Food, water, and fuel will be stored to feed and house everyone for eight weeks. We'll keep it ready from Thanksgiving to Easter but for this year, we gladly don't need it. No more blizzards come.

It's funny how the daytime temperature never rises above freezing but the snow dissipates just the same. At least the ground is still hard. Chris, John, and Dennis decide to venture out on their delayed scrounge mission and meet at the Tousley Farm. The horses are anxious to get out on the road. Elmer says they get cabin fever like the rest of us. The air is clear, the sky is blue, and it's a good day to be out for adventure.

Up Route 2, and past the Elkhart place, the road seems to reach the horizon. There are several farms, all abandoned. Some have been ransacked with furniture and what's left of clothes strewn over the yard. They look through what was once a nice house to see if anything useful remain.

What a strange commentary to the way we all once lived. The center of the living-room wall is apparently where a large screen TV and video equipment once were. It's been looted but how will the takers make use of it? By now, it's surely been dumped. In the kitchen; electric can openers, microwave ovens, blenders, electric mixers... everything made as useless as the electric well pump and darkened light fixtures. In the bathroom; an electric toothbrush, curling iron, hair dryer, and electric curlers, again, all useless. All have no value without an umbilical cord to centralized energy. They rest; a silent epitaph to what we thought were life essentials.

Out-buildings are stripped clean. An air compressor must have stood in a corner where hoses now dangle. There are only a few scattered hand tools being reclaimed by rust. Under the debris, a partial box of nails and three bundles of asphalt shingles. Not much left of a once functioning farm.

What isn't stolen is destroyed. The charred remains of farm equipment give evidence to the looters senseless mind, void of reason. Continuing a search here is a waste of time.

Each succeeding farm reveals the same. What a tribute to society's death. In a vain attempt to survive by pillage, they leave only destruction.

"I thought there would be at least a few farmers hanging on out here," John says. "In six farms, there's not one with survivors."

"It was the same in Bosnia," Chris says. "Isolated farms didn't have the manpower to defend themselves and they made easy targets. Invading armies in this case were small bands of looters but one family didn't stand a chance. Hazel Creek survived because they were unified and acted as one. Farms have also changed over the years. They used to be self sufficient. Today, they depend on electricity as much as anyone. Convenience succored them to dependency. I'd guess you'll still find survivors among off-grid communities but not so much among modern farms."

Another farm grows closer. This one is different. A house in need of repair and long overdue for paint, stands idle. It was likely abandoned early but looters found little to desecrate. Still, Elmer said to check everywhere and this shouldn't take long to check out.

This house is as bad inside as out. Carpets worn through, a couch that would be refused by a thrift store, and rings of dirt circling each light switch.

"Can you believe this place?" Chris says. "I've seen dumps but I wouldn't spend the night here in a storm. I'd rather sleep in the barn."

"I've seen it before," says Dennis. "A friend of mine used to run dragsters in E-modified class. He said you never worry about pretty cars with expensive paint jobs. That's were their limited money went. The ones you needed to watch are the ugly ducklings where the money goes under the hood."

Chris looks puzzled. "How does that relate to this place?"

"With farms, sometimes the barn is in better shape than the house.   Farmer's make money by crops and livestock so it's the house that suffers."

"Hey, I think we can use this." John is in the kitchen. "There's a hand crank meat grinder in here."

"Sure can," says Chris. "Let's check the barn for tools"

The kitchen door hardly opens for overgrown weeds. It cracks when forced. The path to the barn shows it was once worn but hasn't seen traffic in some time. The barn is an old structure but sound and sporting a fairly new roof. It's obviously in better shape than the house. The door is on rollers like Elmer's and opens easily.

Inside, the barn looks untouched.   Looters never bothered to look past the house. Tools and equipment are ordered and in secure boxes.   This may be a bonanza.

Tractors and implements are just as they were left. Next to the tool room is a locked door on what looks like a tack room.

"I hate to do this but I don't think the keys are here," Chris says.

Finding a T-post driver, Chris breaks the hasp and lock from the door. Inside is power equipment. There is a four-cylinder engine powered arc welder, a gas powered trash pump, and in the corner... a 7KW generator.

"You know guys?" Chris says. "I feel dirty doing this. I have no right to take this stuff from some poor guy who worked hard for it. It's just wrong."

"I've been thinking the same," says John, "but it's what Elmer said. It's been nearly a year and a half since these places were left. If anyone was coming back, they would have by now. If it were my stuff that I had to leave behind, I'd at least feel better that it went to help someone who could use it instead of some low-life who just trashed it."

Chris looks around and says, "We'll take only what we need. If this guy ever comes back, I hope he understands. Let's get the trash pump, the generator, and what tools we can use. Leave everything else."

With the meat grinder, an old Aladdin lamp, cast iron cookware, and various animal traps, they load the generator, pump and several boxes of mixed tools onto the wagon. In all, this is a very helpful find. Heading out, there is no joy in the accomplishment. Reaping from the losses of other's misfortune brings no pleasure.

Their number one item is not found so the elusive wood chipper will have to wait another day. A bow saw and feller's axe will have to do until then but the generator was number two on the list so there is measured success.

Chris drops John and Dennis at their place and continues through town to return the wagon and team to Elmer. Unhitching the team, Dick and Chris get to talk.

"You found some good stuff," says Dick. "Sad way to get it though."

"Yeah, I felt like a common thief, going through other people's stuff like that," says Chris.

Dick stops as he's about to hang up one of the draft collars. "I had the same feeling when we made a run up Center Street to Route 804. It's one reason I didn't offer to go along. The other reason is that I don't much care to go by the Matthews' place. Did you go by there?"

"I saw it," says Chris. "Their name is still on the post by the drive. We skipped it. I didn't want to see that, even after this long."

Dick continues as they brush down the horses. "Most folks had already left but the Matthews hung on. He was a volunteer fire fighter and prior military, like yourself. He thought he could handle whatever came but he was wrong. Real nice family too."

With horses in their stalls, Dick offers Chris a ride home. "We'll unload the wagon tomorrow, how about a tractor ride home? I can show you how these gasifiers work."

Dick lights the gasifier through a small hole at the base of the big can mounted in front of the radiator. "We'll have to give it time to get hot. This bellows keeps the draft going the right way and helps get the fire hot. This second box holds more wood chips. They work like a filter to keep tar out of the engine but it will also dry out your next batch of fuel."

"How long does it take to warm up?" Chris asks.

"About ten minutes does it," Dick says. "I can guess why gasoline took over. Not many people care to wait this long to run to the store."

Dick reaches over the steering wheel and sets the throttle to half. Making sure the transmission is out of gear, he pulls the starter rod and the engine begins to turn over. The engine takes five or six cranks to begin coming to life but smooths down to a steady idle.

Collecting:

"Pretty good for running on smoke; wouldn't you say?" asks Dick.

"Sounds good. Where do I ride on this thing?" asks Chris. "There's only one seat."

"We mounted a tray to stand on in the back," he says. "You can hold onto the back of the seat. It's not too bumpy back there."

Dick drops Chris off at his gate and heads right back for the barn. "Give Becky my best. I didn't bring any extra fuel so I need to get right back on what's in the hopper."

The ride home is a lot faster than walking and Becky meets Chris at the door with a hot cup of tea.

"You look beat," she says. "Was the trip worth it?"

Chris explains how their long day unfolded but after ten minutes on the warming bench, he can hardly keep his eyes open. The day started early, ended late, and was filled with light work coupled with heavy emotion. He'd decide if the trip was worth it, tomorrow.

Other scavenging trips yield more items. Scott takes Robert and Brendon Wagoner and returns with another generator, more oil lamps, tools, and various blankets and clothes but no chipper.

A very interesting find is a Ford Crew-cab pickup truck. It's in a barn, on blocks, and under tarps but appears close to being a complete restoration. Scott wants to take Harry to see it. This may be the right vehicle for their trip to Trout Lake. Being smaller than a grain truck, it would use less fuel and should negotiate road obstacles better.

Turkey in the Straw signals Stan Richter's return.

"Good to see you, Stan!" I say. "Glad you made it through the storm. We figured you were holed up someplace."

"That I was," he says. "I was clear up near Kingman and had to lay low for nearly a week. At least I didn't get caught out in it. We lost a driver out that way. His rig got rutted-in about five miles outside Kingman and we found him froze to death after the storm. We figure he was hoofin' it into town as the weather closed in."

"Really sorry to hear that," I say. "Did he have family?"

"Not that he spoke of," he says. "We're all a bunch of road gypsies but when we get together, it's like family. We'll all miss James. SAY! Is Chris around? I have some information for him and I have an order for Sam too."

"I'm sure they'll be along," I say. "Chris has been asking about you. I'm guessing you have some route information for Iowa?"

"That I do. I think he'll be pleased."

Evening finds Pat Wagoner passing radio traffic. He has become a recognized conduit for east/west messaging. Tonight, he re-originates two messages; one to Monteith and the other to Eastern California.

K5OSI with traffic for IOWA 21 or 22.

K5OSI, KG3KQR ready to relay.

Station responding; please repeat your call sign.

K5OSI, this is Kilo, Gulf, Tha-ree, Kilo, K-beck, Romeo, do you copy?

Roger KG3KQR, copy loud and clear. QTH?

My QTH is EM48 with fair contact to your destination. QRV when ready.

Message for Dan Spencer, Monteith, Iowa, grid 21 or 22

From Chris Spencer and George Hardin

Start Text: We are well and plan PCS to your location. Eight in company. Please reply your status and ability to accept. End Text. Twenty words.

The distant radio operator repeats the message back to confirm a good copy and tells Pat that he will relay it as soon as he can. Pat calls to relay a similar message to Roxanne's family in California but no station replies to accept his message. Reception appears to be one direction tonight.

George and Jackie's house becomes a staging area for

cargo headed to Iowa. Food will be added last but their pile of essentials will leave plenty of room in the cavernous grain box. It's decide to anchor two recliners to the floor of the truck box and stack two mattresses for sleeping along the way. The canvas cover over the box should keep out all but the heaviest rain shower. Since the cab can only accommodate two or three, the rear window is removed and a matching hole cut in the front of the box so they can at least pass things back and forth.

"I'm getting excited," says Jackie. "It's been a plan for a long time but seeing this stuff pile up in the living room is making it real. Is there any word from Iowa yet?"

"Nothing yet," says George. "Pat says the first message takes longest because they have to locate them. After first contact, the message path gets faster. It's probably going to be a lot like when we first found your folks in Montana."

Jackie puts her arms around George's neck and playfully asks. "What's it like in Iowa? Do they speak English out there?"

"Last I checked they still do," he says. "Maybe that's what's slowing the messages down."

"I've only lived in Short Pump, Houston, Big Bend, and here," she says. "Is Iowa much different?"

George picks Jackie up and sits on the recliner with her on his lap. "It's a lot like Kansas; flat, corn and soy beans mostly. Not a lot of wheat. Some oats and alfalfa but a whole lot of corn and soy beans."

She turns to George and grins. "Do they grow any corn or soy beans there?"

"Some," he says, "but mostly corn and soy beans. I'm not sure what they're planting now. Those were cash crops with some held back for feed. They raise a lot of hogs in Iowa."

"I wasn't going to mention your eating habits," she says, "but since you brought it up...."

Conversation turns abruptly to a tickling, wrestling, kissing match that both sides win. A knock at the door halts the fun. Nicky comes in with another armload of things for the trip.

"It's me, you guys. Keep it respectable."

George jumps up to help Nicky with her bundle.

"What do you have in here? It's heavy."

"It's a pressure canner," she says. "I have three cases of jars and some Tattler lids for the next load. If you two aren't too occupied, you could walk back and help." Nicky has a big smile as she pokes fun at her sister.

On the walk back to Nicky's house, Jackie starts the conversation.

"George was telling me about Iowa."

"I saw that," Nicky says, still teasing.

"I mean before that," she says. "George, tell us more about Iowa."

"We're headed to an agricultural area, even more than here," he says. "Everything revolves around farming or raising hogs. The land is really flat and the Raccoon

River winds all over the place. Fishing isn't great but we used to catch catfish, bluegill, bass, and an occasional walleye. Deer hunting isn't too bad but there's not much cover so they're hard to stalk. It helps to have a blind. Everybody farms, everybody knows everybody, and everybody goes to church unless it's plantin' or harvest time. But you can't get into any kind of trouble that your neighbors won't show up to help you out. It's a good place to call home."

"I just hope we hear from Chris's brother and that Iowa welcomes strangers," Nicky says.

Chris, Becky and Gina are at Nicky's house, talking with Ron and Jen. Chris has a highway map spread out on the table and is explaining Stan's markings.

"When Stan got stuck in Kingman during the storm there was another operator there from up north. They worked out a route for us to avoid obstructions."

"What kind of obstructions?" asks Ron. "Couldn't we just drive around any we find?"

Chris points to a red 'X' on the map. "Evidently the trouble here was repeated all over. This town decided to blow a bridge that crossed a creek, west of their town. It solved their immediate problem by eliminating a path for raiders but now the town is cut off. They can't replace the bridge and the closest detour by-passes the town completely. Stan saved us about a hundred and twenty-five-mile mistake if we tried to go that way."

Rob points to a small town further up the route. "What's this circle mean?"

"A circle in a circle means the town is a closed group and not friendly to strangers," he says. "A single circle means you can pass through but it's not a good place to stay the night.   Dashes around a town mean it's friendly and a secure place to spend the night."

"I guess these water drops indicate safe sources of drinking water and the ones that are crossed out are unsafe," Ron says. "They put a lot of work in this. I hope you thanked them properly."

"Stan wouldn't take anything for it," Chris says. "He said there's a lot of mistrust from some of these smaller towns and any good word we can say for them will be pay enough."

George walks in with the girls and spots Gina. "HEY! Look who's here!" He drops to one knee and holds out his arms. Gina runs to give him a hug.

He stands, holding Gina, and sees the map on the table. "How's the road look? Are the speed traps marked?"

"Where are Becky and Jen?" Nicky asks.

A voice comes from the back of the house.   "In the bedroom! We're sorting clothes."

Daddy's Girl:

Sam spends every available moment with Karin and when she's not with Chris, she is with Byron. Karin loves her dad deeply and values his advice. They sit together in the living room next to the heater.

"You two are getting pretty serious; do you love Sam?" he asks.

"That must be what this is," she says. "I can talk with him like I did with Josh but even more, I feel safe when we're together. The monsters go away when we're together."

Byron has often helped her cope with haunting memories that she calls 'monsters.'

"It sounds like you two might do good together. Have you talked about getting married?" he says.

Looking away as she answers, "We've talked around it but he's so proper, I don't think he will go further until he has the 'daddy talk' with you."

Byron reaches over and pats Karin's knee. "It may come, in time."

What isn't shared is that he and a very nervous Sam, have already met and Sam has been given full blessing to pursue Karin for marriage. Sam is working out the right time and place to 'pop the question' but Byron is already glad for Karin and sad to think of giving his daughter away.

Later that evening, at the Tousley farm:

"Right time and place?" shouts Elmer. "Stan got ya the ring already; just ask the girl. She doesn't care about when or how, as long as it happens. I asked Meredith on the steps to her house and she never complained once. The right time and place is as soon as you decide and anyplace you find her after that."

"You have to give the man credit for romance," Keith says. "He wants to make it special and it gives her bragging rights when she tells the other girls how he asked her. They are ALL going to ask the details."

"What bragging rights?" says Elmer. "Other girls are more interested in how she gets Sam to ask her, than how Sam goes about asking. Kids these days; I don't understand 'em."

Dick has been holding comment 'til last. "Women are kinda detail oriented; in my observation. Lisa could recall how many crickets chirped as I worked up the courage to ask her to marry me. I'm thinking Sam is onto something and in ten years, Karin will still be talking about what a romantic fool her husband was when he asked her to marry him, AND if Sam doesn't waste his time, it might be him she'll be talking about."

The room explodes with laughter but Sam gets the message. He's determined to ask her hand, tomorrow.

In the morning, Scott pays a visit to the Taylor's after breakfast. Harry has agreed to go look at the truck he's found.

"Elmer sure has been gracious in lending his buckboard," Harry says. "For an antique make-over, it rides pretty comfortable."

"I bet he never thought it would get this much use," says Scott.

"How far out is this barn of yours? And you say this F-250 Ford is a crew cab with a straight six cylinder?" Harry knows his trucks and is puzzled by Scott's description.

"That's what I saw," he says. "That's why I wanted you to come take a look. I think it's mostly restored but I'm not sure if it's ready to run."

They drive the team nearly an hour before turning on an overgrown ranch road. The dirt road to the house and barn is longer than most. Harry guesses about eight hundred feet or better.

The house doesn't appear to have been looted but judging by no food left on shelves, many cabinets conspicuously empty, no other vehicles on site, and everything else in order; they surmise the owners took what they could and bugged out for a better location. The truck in the barn must have been a project they never had time to finish.

Scott carefully pulls back the canvas to expose a dark green 1972 Ford F-250 crew cab pickup truck. It's on blocks but the tires look fresh. The exterior is near perfect and freshly painted but the interior, though useable, shows a lot of original ware.

"I'd say you found a 'cherry' of a truck," says Harry. "Pop the hood and let's see what we have."

Scott raises the hood to expose a complete engine but obviously a large inline six cylinder.

"Now THAT makes no sense," says Harry. "Especially the ¾ ton trucks came standard with V-8's. This looks like an I-300. It would get a lot better mileage but poor marks from the show circuit. It's like this guy was building a daily driver instead of a show truck."

"Why is that?" Scott asks.

"Show trucks are supposed to be as close to original equipment as possible. This isn't."

Pulling the canvas completely away exposes more parts.

"Look here," says Scott. "Maybe this was the original engine."

On the floor, between the truck and the barn wall is a well-used V-8 engine and transmission.

"That's what he did," Harry says. "He re-engined this truck for the big six."

"Will it run OK with that?" asks Scott.

"It won't be fast off the line but it will out pull most V-8's" he says. "And it will do that at better than twenty miles a gallon. Inline sixes were great engines but everyone wanted high revving horse power in the seventies, and these fell out of favor."

"Do you think it will run?" Scott asks.

"No reason to think it won't," he says. "Not today, however. We'll have to build a gasifier and come back with a good battery. It's still a gamble but from the looks of everything else, I'd lay my money on the truck."

Checking fluids, they find the oil full and the gas tank bone dry. The engine turns by hand and the radiator is filled with antifreeze.

Scott and Harry carefully return the cover and try to make it look undisturbed. Scott can hardly wait to get this 'show truck' on the road.

Sam has been missing all morning but it's not like him to be off without letting someone know where he was going and how long he would be. His only explanation was that he was scouting for something and that it would take most of the day. He returns and Keith asks how it went.

"Fine," is Sam's only answer, though it's obvious he has something up his sleeve.

Pat Wagoner can hardly wait to deliver some good news. Across the street and three doors down, he knocks on the Hardin's kitchen door.

Jackie opens the door. "Hello Pat. Come on in, can I get you some tea?"

"Thanks, just the same. Marge and I just finished lunch. I came to pass on some good news from Iowa," he says.

George hears Pat in the kitchen and comes in from the living room. "Hi Pat. Always glad to see you, especially when you have good news."

Pat hands the message to George and he reads it aloud.

KG3KQR to K5OSI with traffic from Dan Spencer, Monteith Iowa, grid 21 or 22 for Chris Spencer and George Hardin.

Start Text: We welcome your arrival. Have room for all. Aunt Dee is well, Uncle Ed passed last August. Mom and Dad are well. Wife, Christi and son Daniel are fine. End Text. Twenty-nine words.

"Pat, thanks!" he says. "This means a lot. You have no idea how good it is to hear that they're OK. I knew Uncle Ed had a weak heart so his passing is sad but not unexpected. I really can't wait to see them all again."

"Glad to be of service," Pat says. "Let me know when you want to send a reply."

As Pat heads home, Jackie and George go first to the Spencer's and then to Nicky's, to share the news. They are another step closer to Iowa.

One of Sam and Karin's favorite dates is hiking to spot game and wildlife near Hazel Creek. Everything needs water and for the same reason towns locate near it, game seldom is far from it.

A daypack and binoculars provide hours of mutual entertainment as they locate various birds and game. Sam carries a pistol because you never know what you might cross but on their many outings, it has never left the holster.

Cresting a small rise, the water's vegetation line comes

into view. Sam hands binoculars to Karin to look for interesting game. She's a meticulous spotter and quickly sees what others fail to notice. It explains why she is such a productive hunter.

Along the brush-line in front of the first row of trees, her scan stops where a small bush has been removed and a sign put in its place. The sign is barely readable at this distance and has but one word... 'Karin.' Following her name is an arrow pointing to the right. Successive signs along the bank form a message... 'Will' 'you' 'marry' 'me?'

Letting the binoculars hang from the neck strap, she turns to see Sam on one knee with a ring in his outstretched hand.

Two miles away on the Tousley farm, Elmer turns to Dick. "Did you hear that?"

"Hear what?" says Dick.

"Nuthin', I guess, but I thought I heard the sound of a bachelor dying," he says.

Both friends have an understanding smile and continue with their work.

Announcement:

Small town news spreads faster by gossip than any other media and before the next day is through, everyone is talking about Sam and Karin's wedding plans.

Long ago, men of the town laid claim to the store as their meeting place; not by decree but more by the process of immanent domain.   They've always met there and it's never been contested. The store is known as The Roost. Women tend to gather at the Grange Hall when it's warm enough and in each other's homes when it's not. Homier settings are preferred and there is no desire to usurp the men's claim on the corner store. In all locations today, the subject focuses on Sam and Karin.

Stephanie and Nicky have been close, even before the Christmas dinner, and meet today in Stephanie's apartment at the Taylor's.

Sharing tea and some cookies that Rachel made,

engagement news is the subject.

"How are you handling the news about Sam and Karin?" Nicky asks. "You two were an item once. Are you OK?"

"I've been thinking about it," she says. "I'm a little jealous of Karin, that she's getting married and not me, but it's not over Sam. I do love Sam but it's like a brother rather than a husband. I want to snuggle and kiss his babies, not HAVE them."

"ME TOO!" says Nicky.

"You want to snuggle Sam's babies?" Stephanie is poking fun.

Nicky laughs and clarifies. "NO! I mean, snuggling babies is fine but I meant that I felt the same way about Karin. The nerve of that teenager; getting married before either of us dazzling divas."

Both girls are now laughing. "Someday, our prince will come," she says, "but he better get a move on, or bring a walker with him."

Rachel grows curious over the bursts of raucous laughter coming from Stephanie's apartment but for now, she is glad the girls are enjoying each other's company. Hearing them laugh answers her prayers for the young lady that she and Harry have grown to love like a daughter.

The Bennett house is a busy place. Emily and Karin's relationship has migrated over the years from parental to close friends. Right now, they are trying to plot what needs to be done so she and Sam can be married after they get married.

"Have you thought about where you will live?" Emily asks. "There are a few vacant houses still in town but none of them have heaters yet. That will take two weeks. I'm sure we can find you some kitchen things, maybe even some chickens."

Karin explodes, laughing. "MOM! We sound like Fiddler On the Roof!"

Mom and daughter swap favorite classic movie lines and reminisce how life has changed, and yet so many things remain unchanged.

"Mom, what was it like when you got married to Daddy?" she asks.

"Life was hard but we never knew it," she says. "We had an old car that was black and white with one green fender and no air conditioning. On trips we cruised from convenience store to convenience store, drinking Icee's to cool down. Your dad called it 'internal air-conditioning'. It worked pretty good too. He worked hard to support the family. He took a second job at the silo in Elma for three years so we could buy a bigger tractor, then two more years for a used planter. Slowly, we started to make ends meet, then Josh came along and fifteen months later, you were born."

"We must have been quite a burden," Karin says.

"Not once," she says. "We never regretted either of you. The struggles life throws are what make a marriage stronger. If it weren't for challenges, we wouldn't have learned to work together or appreciate the sacrifices each of us made for our family. That's one reason I keep that old kerosene lantern on top of the refrigerator in the kitchen. We couldn't afford better so our dates were often nighttime walks. That poor lantern was all we had for light. It keeps me reminded where we came from and how God has been with us every step."

"Don't you ever think about all you could have had if it wasn't for the broken arms, summer camps, and sport programs?" Karin asks.

"Look at how many wealthy people are miserable," she says. "If 'things' make for happiness, there wouldn't be any unhappy rich people, now would there? Happiness isn't about what you have; it's about who you have. In the end, every 'thing' is left behind but loved ones can meet again. Whatever your dad and I have spent on you kids has been an investment in a joyful life. I'm happy and wouldn't change anything. I think we've made some good investments."

Karin gives her mom a long hug. "I love you, Mom."

The 'Iowa Group' as they are called now, meets regularly at either Nicky's, or George and Jackie's house. Tonight, at the Hardin's, they are looking over the calendar.

"We need to stay for the wedding," says Becky. "It wouldn't be right to miss it."

Jackie agrees. "This is probably one of the best things to happen since the collapse. I know it delays us a few weeks but there is time and our trip won't be that long. We can still be there for spring planting."

Chris, George, and Ron work out logistics and with the women's help they arrive at a departure date in the first week of March.

George brings up one missing component. "What about a chipper? I guess we could all spend every waking minute chopping up sticks but that's a lot of work. Does anyone have any ideas?"

"I think Stan is going to come through for us," says Chris. "Last he was here, he said to let him work on it. That usually means he knows where to get one."

"I hope he does," says Becky. "Shredded wood chips dry in about a week but it takes months otherwise. My Granma would use a layer of sticks between layers of compost. She shredded everything else. The compost would be all cooked down but those sticks would still be strong. She said shredding opens up the fibers."

A knock at the door quiets the room as they are not expecting anyone. George opens the door; it's Stephanie.

"Just the people I've been looking for," she says. "Is there room in that big truck for one more? I think I'd like to see what Iowa has to offer."

An awkward silence fills the room as they never gave thought to who is in charge of this group. Before silence turns to rejection, Ron speaks up.

"Well? It is a big truck."

"Welcome aboard!" says Jen. "What made the decision to join this motley crew?"

"Really, guys; I was beginning to think you didn't want me," she says. "I've been giving some thought to what Hazel Creek will be like with all of you gone. There won't be a lot left for me and you guys are most of my friends. It makes sense for me to go with you. Besides,

Nicky, we two dazzling divas need to give Iowa a glimpse of perfection."

Nicky gives her a hug. "I wasn't looking forward to losing you either but are you sure? Iowa is a long way from your family in Colorado."

"I've been a loner most my life," she says. "My family is important but since I left for college, I never stay longer than a short visit. I don't think I'd feel right, moving back permanently. Someday, I'll get back there and I'll keep trying Pat's radio messages. Eventually things will get better and travel will be easier. Until then, I think I want to see Iowa."

"You're certainly welcome," Chris says. "We can always use another hand."

The group makes Stephanie welcome and they catch her up on the route and what they expect. Now they are nine.

Repairs:

Stan usually stops in front of the Grange Hall but not today. Turning right onto Center Street, he passes the store and doesn't stop until he pulls into the Tousley farm.

Dick comes out to see.

"Well, this is different," he says. "What brings you off the beaten path?"

"Hello Dick," says Stan. "I wasn't sure I was going to make it. I'm sure I wouldn't have made it if I'd stopped in town. I lost one gasifier and this one is about cooked out too. I'm in need of some repairs and figured this was the best shade tree in town."

"Harry's not here right now but let's take a look at what you have." Opening the lid to the cold gasifier, Dick removes the cleanout cap on the bottom and looks inside.

"She's burned clean through," he says. "It looks like the burn chamber wasn't thick enough. We have three more done and another near complete but they all used the same thin stock this one is made from. We'll have to get our heads together on this."

In about an hour, Harry stops by to see the problem.

"It's not the chamber that's burned out; it's the grate," he says. "Looking at the ash, I'd say it is getting shaken off the grate to soon and exposes the grate to excessive heat. Look at all the unburned bits of coal in the ash. What kind of roads are you driving? How bumpy are they?"

"The truck is bumpy," says Stan, "the roads are about what you'd expect."

"I'm thinking we need to move the gasifier off the front bumper or add some shock absorbing mounts," says Harry. "I think we can get you back on the road fairly quick; at least by tomorrow."

"Suits me," he says. "I'm interested in those gasifiers too."

"These are already spoken for," Harry says. "We're setting up two vehicles; one for Sam and another for Scott."

"I knew about Sam," Stan says, "but where is Scott going? That's news to me and I try to keep up on things."

"Scott's heading up to northern Alberta and I don't mind sharing some concern," says Harry. "It's a long way without scouting and it crosses an international border."

Stan just whistles as he takes in the news. "I don't

think I'd be up to that long of a drive on wood-gas and a makeshift grain truck."

"He's at least got part of that licked," says Harry. "He's found him a restored old pickup with a crew cab. It's more efficient and should run on one gasifier. He'll have a second one for a spare. At least he's thinking ahead."

"Harry, that reminds me. I found some eight horse leaf and branch shredders in an old Sears store. I'm always amazed at what looters don't take. They'll loot tennis shoes and leave work boots every time. All the generators were gone but if you need a lawn mower, roto tiller, or leaf mulcher, they were sittin' in rows. I'll trade a mulcher for a gasifier, if you're interested."

"Stan, save your dickerin' for Sam and Scott. They're the ones who need 'em but I'd guess you'll have a deal."

You would think Karin has never fixed a meal before. She's always been at her mother's right hand in the kitchen. Today is different. Today Emily is at Karin's right hand and Karin is preparing the entire meal herself. Normally it would be no big thing except Sam is coming over.

"Mom! What if he doesn't like my cooking? Would you taste everything first? Does the table look alright?"

Emily calmly looks Karin in the eye. "Settle down, you're a great cook. Sam is going to be pleased."

"What's on the menu?" asks Byron.

"Venison roast with whipped butternut squash, green beans, and potato rolls," she says. "Daddy, did I miss anything?"

"If he isn't pleased with that, he isn't hungry," he says.

Sam knocks at the door and Byron goes to greet him.

"Mom, if anything goes wrong, I'm going to die on the spot."

Emily hugs her daughter and gives her a kiss on her forehead. "Everything is fine, relax."

Byron and Sam join Emily and Karin in the kitchen. Sam takes Karin's hand and gives her a quick kiss. "Hi sweetheart, how's your day been?"

Karin just gives him a look, then asks, "Would you like some tea? Dinner will be ready in a bit. Why don't you and Dad wait in the living room while Mom and I get things on the table?"

"Karin seems really on edge tonight," Sam says.

"Weddings will do that," says Byron. "We fellas just show up and eat some cake but these women put their whole life in it. I guess it's what makes us love 'em. She'll be OK."

Sam continues. "Have you heard the update on the Iowa group?"

"Last I heard, the truck is ready but they still need a wood shredder," says Byron.

"Stan found them one and they'll be ready to go soon after the wedding," he says. "We're sure to miss that group."

"Well, they need to make their way in the world," Byron says. "It's the way things have always been.

We'll get by; always have."

Emily comes in, "Are you ready to eat?"

At the table, Byron asks Sam to say the blessing which he does with ease.

"How's that roast, Sam?" Byron asks.

"Really good!" he says, "tender and moist. I gotta tell you Mrs. Bennett, you are a great cook. If Karin cooks this good, I'm going to have trouble with my beltline."

Emily and Karin look at each other as their smiles turn to giggles.

"Did I say something wrong?" he says.

Byron clears his throat. "What the surprise is... Karin fixed this whole meal herself, including the menu. Consider yourself in trouble with your beltline."

"I am highly impressed," he says. "This is fantastic."

Wedding activity keeps everyone so busy they scarcely notice a new truck in town. Scott and Harry get the Ford crew-cab truck running on wood-gas and drive it back to Elmer's barn. Harry will fine tune the engine and gasifier before Scott takes it home.

"I wanted to see it," says Roxanne. "When will it be ready for the trip?"

"If we leave before late May, we could still see snow," he says. "I promise you will see more snow than you ever wanted after a very short spring and summer.

"This is a big trip," she says. "Alberta is beautiful in a lot of ways and meeting your family will be great but getting there crosses a lot of unfamiliar ground. Are we going to be OK by ourselves?"

"Pat says the country has settled down," he says. "Gangs are all gone and most communities are trading with one another. A town with a bad name means isolation and that doesn't lend itself to surviving long. I think we should have a safe trip. Once we get to the Canadian border, I'm hoping my passport and this hand drawn marriage certificate will get us by check stations, if there are any. If not, there's always back roads that aren't checked."

"Really?" she asks. "You mean the Canada/US border can be crossed unchecked?"

"You always could," he says. "A lot of small towns are way off major highways but next to the border. Residents drive both ways all the time and are never checked. People watch for strangers using their crossing and will report suspicious traffic but nobody questions locals. If we cross and stop long enough to chat, I think I can convince them I'm Canadian. Besides that, I doubt their phones are working. They were hit with the same EMP as the States were."

Big Day:

Wedding day arrives sooner than Karin and Sam expect. Events like this have a way of sneaking up on you like Christmas does. You see it on the calendar, plan ahead as best you can, yet still there is a last minute rush.

Simple weddings tend to be more intimate and Karin looks the perfect bride in a conservative white satin floor length dress with a veil, while Sam, dressed in a dark blue suit, looks handsome as ever.

The day is blessed with sunshine parting the clouds; almost heralding spring. Reception in the Grange Hall combines good food and plenty of dancing. Elmer and Nicky are quite a team at waltz, fox trot, and quickstep dances. Nicky enjoys Elmer's company and Elmer is delighted to be ballroom dancing again.

After three numbers, Elmer is suddenly out of wind, "Nicky, dear, I'm afraid you're going to have to find another partner. I'm not the young man I used to be. I need to rest."

"You're still the best dance teacher ever," she says. "We'll sit this one out."

Finding a chair, Nicky sits by.   "Can I get you something to drink?"

"I'll be fine; I just need to catch my breath. Young lady, you're so pretty I forget my age and try to keep up. You remind me of Meredith when we were first married. I don't think I've had so much fun dancing in years."

"Elmer, I'll be right back. I think Doc. Whitaker needs to make sure you're OK."

Nicky finds Doc. Whitaker sitting a few tables away. "He's out of breath and looks pale. He's been teaching me dance steps and we've practiced longer than this before. Can you come take a look at him?"

Doc Whitaker wastes no time looking to his longtime friend. "Elmer, what seems to be the matter? Have you been chasing young women again?"

"I'm sure that's it, Neal. These young ladies get prettier by the week but faster by the day."   Elmer is still winded even after sitting for a spell.

Anna comes to the Doctor's side and brings him his bag. Reading his blood pressure and listening to his heart seems to confirm what he suspects. From his bag, he retrieves a bottle and removes two small pills.

"I want you to take these and let them dissolve under your tongue."

Elmer takes the pills, then asks. "What are they?"

"They're nitro glycerin pills." I think you're having a mild heart attack.

Within a minute, Elmer feels much better but Doc. Whitaker warns him. "No more dancing tonight and I want to see you in my office tomorrow morning. Here, take these aspirin," handing him two and a glass of water.

For the remainder of the evening Elmer watches from the sidelines. Nicky doesn't dance with anyone else, but truth is, there probably isn't anyone else who knows the steps. Her greatest concern is for Elmer.

Elmer's trouble is kept from other guests, and especially from Sam and Karin. No one wants this day blemished by bad news. A lot has been prepared to make this day special. All week a bungalow on the edge of town has been readied for the newlyweds. A rocket mass heater and full cupboards are supplied by folks in town. Traditional bridal showers were replaced by work parties to provide a fully prepared "move-in ready" home. Not bad for a couple starting out; no money down and no rent or mortgage required.

Sam and Karin are escorted to the house in shivaree fashion as well wishers cheer them on. They stop at the street as Sam and Karin proceed up the walk alone. Opening the door, Sam scoops his bride into his arms as the crowd, waiting in hushed anticipation, explodes in one last cheer before heading home. For the first time today, Sam and Karin are alone together.

Mom and Dad share the only topic of interest as they return home with the Livingston's, Taylor's, and Bennett's.

"Emily, you raised a beautiful bride," says Mom.

Dad adds, "I think they make a great couple. Sam has a good heart and they sure don't hide their love for each other."

"Who caught the bouquet?" asks Irene

"I think it was Kellie Palmer," says Harry

Fred replies, "Don't you know, Brent and Kathy are worried."

Conversation is interspersed with laughter as friends enjoy the glow of celebrated love. Still unaware of Elmer's heart attack; the night remains joyful... for now.

Anna and I join Doc Whitaker on the walk home. Mandy rides behind me in an old wood sided wagon. It's a typical metal wagon with bigger tires and a wood fence that make the sides higher. It's handy for going to the store and especially for carrying Mandy; she loves riding in it and is getting bigger every day.

Anna's concerned for Elmer since we have no hospital to correctly treat his heart. She asks Doc Whitaker, "Will Elmer be OK?"

"That's up to God," he says. "There's not much we can do for him. There's aspirin, and we know more about diet now. If he takes it easy and doesn't stress his heart, he could go a long time."

"Nicky has been a breath of fresh air in his sails," I say. "I don't think I've seen him enjoy life any better."

"Oh, I have," says Doc, "but that was before; when Meredith was alive. Elmer was a different man with a lot of energy and spark. He and Meredith would go anywhere in three states for a big ballroom dance. They won competitions too. Mostly it was for fun. That's why they never displayed their trophies. Elmer danced for Meredith and she for him. Losing her might be what's made his heart weak in the first place. I know he's never been the same without her."

Turning left on West Dower Drive, we walk past a darkened porch where a young woman with wavy golden hair weeps softly for a dear friend. Inwardly cursing time's destructive nature, she is not ready to let him go.

Morning finds Keith Reed fetching the doctor as Elmer lacks strength to leave his house.

Nicky tends to him daily and enjoys their short conversations. He is out of breath so easily. The Elmer she knows is wise, romantic, kind, and full of grace. Her love for him transcends physical and has knit their souls together. Marriage would be absurd yet she could spend a lifetime in his glow. More than a father, greater than a lover, she watches helplessly as his name is called beyond eternal doors. In four days, Elmer drops his earthly mantle to join his beloved.

Nicky is awed at the emptiness engulfing her. Dad and Jen are here, Jackie lives a block away; she has many who call her friend, but none so close as Elmer. Was it the mystique of clandestine midnight dance lessons? Perhaps it was the combined investment each made for Karin's surprise transformation. There was no awakening moment between them but a slow and progressive bond of intense platonic friendship. Old enough to be her grandpa, his youthful spirit was her equal and part of him will remain with her always.

Buried in his tux and tails, silk top hat, white gloves, and cane, he is the image of an elegant suitor expecting to meet his intended at a ball. Admirable words fall deaf to Nicky's ears as she watches him lowered into the family plot next to his cherished Meredith. In her heart it is herself resting at the bottom of this grave. Dirt slowly blacking out light; isolating her to silence reserved for the dead; she feels very alone.

Iowa:

Bidding farewell to an Iowa bound group of nine brings out every member in town. The big grain truck is loaded and with gasifiers now in the truck's grain box to lessen the jarring that caused Stan's burnout. It makes them easier to tend and shredded fuel can be stored right where it's needed.

Sam still feels a bit awkward around Stephanie but she and Karin are on good terms.

"Sam," she says, "You've always been a big brother to me and the whole romance thing sorta got in the way of that. I'm really glad you two found each other but I'm not ready to just walk away. Keep in touch. We have the radio and Iowa is not that far. Karin, make him do it. We've all been through way too much to drift apart."

"We will," she says. "Our house is close to Pat's and we'll make a point of getting on the radio at least once a week." Giving Stephanie a hug, Karin whispers to

Stephanie. "Thanks for giving Sam a shove. Nicky told me about it. You're an awesome person and I'll never forget you."

Words struggle to pass the lump in Sam's throat. He casually knew who Jackie and Nicky were when they worked at Oilfield Solutions but now they are closer than blood kin. He and Chris are closer than brothers since the recon trip from Terlingua. Now he's leaving.

Jackie and Anna have been like sisters to Anna and me and I've grown pretty close to George too. Saying goodbye isn't any easier for us. Escaping Houston, we overcame challenges that would break most people; our bond is forged in adversity, tempered in trust.

Hugs and tears send the team off with heartfelt prayers and best wishes.

George brings a lighter side. "Will you look at all of us? You'd think we were going to the moon. It's only five hundred miles." Humor's shallow cover betrays him as his voice begins to crack. None of us want to say goodbye but all of us understand the draw to rejoin our families.

The big Chevy C-50 lumbers out of town carrying hearts away, connected for a time by hands waving until distance slowly blends them into the countryside and they are gone.

Scott and Roxanne walk with Harry and Rachel Taylor, past the store to the Tousley Farm. Dick and Keith assume ownership at Elmer's passing. It was his desire and he expressed it many times. His grave is prominently marked in the family plot but flowers aren't available for early spring graves. Fresh turned dirt is ringed with white limestone but John Stubbs is still working on his tombstone. A marker isn't necessary to accentuate how greatly he is missed.

"It's hard to believe he's gone," says Rachel. "I expect him to walk out from the barn any moment."

"Do you think he and Meredith danced one more time, up in heaven?" Harry says.

"If watching him and Nicky was any clue," Scott says, "I bet everyone up there cleared the floor and set the music. He almost made me want to take lessons."

"You're on," says Roxanne. "First thing after we get to Trout Lake."

"Fortunately," says Scott, "there are no dance instructors at Trout Lake."

"Too bad; I think I'd pay money just to see that," says Harry. With a chuckle, they continue past the grave plots to the barn.

Pulling off the canvas reveals Scott's truck for Rachel and Roxanne to see for the first time.

"Oh, it's really nice," Rachel says. "I have a question though. What will you do if you get a flat tire? Where's the spare?"

"It's up under the bed of the truck," Harry says, "but that does bring up a good point. You can only stop and patch small holes. It would be good to carry at least two spares. Finding another might be worth the effort."

"We're getting another spare; right?" says Roxanne. Scott just nods.

Scott removes the lid that blocks airflow from the fuel stack and fills the gasifier with shredded wood.

"The shredder idea was a good one," he says. "This stuff dries in just a couple days."

Removing a two-inch threaded cap from near the bottom of the gasifier allows Scott to light the fuel from beneath. Once the stack is lit, the cap is replaced and it's ready for priming. An old fashion bellows, draws smoke from the firebox, through the cooling stack and filter to remove smoke and tar. What comes through the filter is wood-gas that will run the engine. A bypass vent feeds a burner to test the output, the gasifier is ready to feed the engine when it burns steadily. When the flame burns steadily, Scott closes the bypass valve and opens the feed valve to the carburetor. After adjusting the air and fuel valves, he turns the key.

"That sounds purrrty ta me," Scott says as the engine comes to life.

"Are we ready for a ride?" Rachel asks. "Is it safe? Harry, you said this is safe, right? I'm trusting you that this is safe. Is it safe?"

"Yes dear. It's actually safer than gasoline," he says. "There's nothing to worry about."

Harry and Rachel get into the back seat while Scott drives with Roxanne next to him.

"What are those pipes and valves for?" she asks.

Scott explains, "The carburetor's job is to mix liquid fuel with the right amount of air to run the engine. Since our fuel is already a gas, I need to adjust the air/fuel ratio with these valves and feed it to the engine. All we're using the carburetor for is a throttle. Does that make sense?"

"No, but at least I know it's for the motor." She replies. "Rachel, I don't think I've ever been this excited to ride in an old truck. Wahhh-Hoo!"

"We've come a long way," Rachel says. "I can't even remember not having a car or truck in the family. I do remember an old Dodge we had when I was just a girl. Mom drove it grocery shopping and we kids sat among the groceries in the back seat. It was long before seat belts. I don't know why I remember it so clearly but I recall lying on my back on the shelf of the rear window, eating a banana. I must have been pretty small but now it seems rather funny."

Scott honks as he approaches Dick and Keith walking from the store toward the farm. As they pass, Dick yells out. "Looking good!"

Dropping Harry and Rachel at their house, Rachel has a sad expression. "I'm going to miss my girl." Tears fill her eyes. "I guess I blocked it out but it just dawned on me that she won't be home."

Harry puts his arm over Rachel's shoulder as they walk toward the house. With his other hand he waves goodbye to Scott and Roxanne as he says, "I'm going to miss her too, but we'll hear from her now and again. Maybe we can go visit next summer."

In a grain truck headed for Iowa, Stephanie's heart is full. Her family may be in Colorado but leaving the Taylor's creates the same empty spot she felt the day she left for college. Always independent, she never looked back, not even after saying goodbye to her mom on the first day of her first summer camp. Other kids became homesick but she never understood it. Everything is an adventure for her and after the adventure, she can return home. Why spoil a great adventure? As years pass, the expectation for adventure fades with the reality of life's limitations. Saying goodbye holds the prospect of permanence and now it weighs heavy on the heart.

Grain trucks are not known for a smooth ride. They bounce even more when they're near empty. Half loaded; the idea of sleeping on a mattress and box spring is ditched with the first good bump. It's fortunate Jennifer is nimble because she catches Gina in mid flight.

Driving through Elma is greeted by friendly waves but it's understood that stopping for a visit is more involved than deciding to. The engine supplies draft to the gasifier so stopping one, stops the other as well. Ron keeps fuel fed to the gasifier and the first four hours pass without problem. Their map shows a good water stop next to a bridge crossing. A spring fed pool overflows to feed a small stream and it's a beautiful place for lunch.

Secondary roads offer more places to stop with fewer abandoned cars but they are more vulnerable. They have little choice; it would take a long time to get past the abandoned cars on highways near cities.

"We've made a hundred and seventy-three miles," Chris says. "If we can double that today, we'll be there by early afternoon tomorrow."

"I thought canoeing down the Missouri was rough," says Ron, "but that was before I rode in the back of a grain truck."

Enjoying the stretch, they poke fun at the drivers for aiming at potholes.

"This is a pretty place," says Becky. "Did you know this was here?"

"Not really," says George. "I mean, we knew this was on the map as a good water stop but we didn't know what it looked like. We thought it was a good first stop and there aren't any towns nearby so we shouldn't be bothered."

"Bothered?" says Jackie. "Do you expect trouble?"

"Not bad trouble," he says, "but when Stan drove into town after we all thought fuel was history, we wanted to know all about wood-gas and how it worked. We just don't need to be explaining ourselves at every junction. Sharing is a good thing but we'll never get to Iowa if we're tied up in show & tell every few miles. "

"This old truck is quite a prize in a post technology world," says Chris. "I know the biggest part of gangs and violence is past but we're out here alone and I'm not ready to accept that the world is a happy place. We're being cautious and taking things slow."

"I guess that explains the gun racks you guys mounted inside the box back there," says Stephanie. "How many of us can shoot?"

"If we're careful," says Chris, "none of us will have to. But all of us need to be ready for a show of force. We have two deer rifles and a shotgun plus three more sidearms. Next to the gun racks are some pieces of half inch black pipe. From a distance, those look like rifle barrels when you stick them through the holes we drilled through the side of the box. If we come across trouble, this truck can look like a war wagon and we shouldn't have to fire a shot. The sides are too high for anyone to see into from the road and the tarp gives cover from above; they might as well think we have a fully armed platoon."

Lunch is simple. Bread rolls become sandwiches when you stuff them with canned meat and goat cheese. Along with canned fruit "it's fit for who it's for," as Elmer would say. After an hour, it's back on the road. Ron gets pretty good at manning the gasifier. After this hour long stop, the engine fires up without a prime.

Safety:

Two weary travelers pedal their way to find safe haven at a ghost town they guess is empty. At the turnoff from the highway, a sign changes their assumption.

Terlingua   Trading   Post
We're open, Welcome!

Lucas watches as bicycles near the store and announces their approach.

"Mark; Sandy; customers coming!"

Mark and Sandra Fogerty have worked with Lucas and Adelaide Maxwell for three years. They left to be with family when the power failed but returned last February to check on the trading post and stayed to help run it. Mark looks the couple over with binoculars.

"Looks like two young men on bikes," he says. "Nice rigs. Pannier bags on front and back; pullin' trailers. I can't tell if any kids are ridin' inside. They don't look to be trouble."

"We'll be careful jest the same," says Lucas. "Like Travis says, ya cain't be surprised if'n yus always 'spectin' sumthin'. If'n you'll pleez occupy yer spot, I'd be much obliged."

Mark climbs the ladder to the storage area over the counter and makes sure the shotgun is loaded. Seated in a chair, it's difficult to see him among the shadows.

Bikes parked, two travelers approach the door. The top half of the door is windowed and seeing Lucas waving them in, they slowly open the door to step inside. The first man is about five foot, eleven. The second is much smaller with lighter build, shy and awkward, with a ball cap pulled down so you can barely see his face.

"Hello friends," says Lucas. "What brings ya ta here taday?"

"We haven't been to a trading post before," says the first man. "How does it work with the money no good?"

"Well, we start with innerductions," says Lucas. "I'm Lucas Maxwell an I run this establishment. What's yer names and where ya from?"

"I'm Marty Benton and this is my brother Mike. We're from Presidio and need some water."

"You boys look ta be not headin' back Presidio way," says Lucas. "Ya got a plan or place ta go?"

"Our place was this side of Presidio but it got to be too much to defend," he says. Looters come up from the river and it's getting worse. We're looking to go north to find a better place."

"Ain't ya got no folks?" Lucas asks.

"Mom died in '04," he says. "Last week we found Dad in the barn; shot dead. He probably surprised looters. We left two days later and we've been camping in the brush since."

"Where ya goin'?" Lucas asks.

"We're not sure," says Marty. "North and away from here. Route Sixty-Seven cuts through rough, dry land so we've been following the Rio. We figured Big Bend would be safer and 385 north, might have more water."

"There's plenty 'o water here an I cain't charge what the good Lord done give us," Lucas says. "Yer welcome ta fill up what ya got to carry it. How old are you boys?"

"I'm eighteen and Mike is fifteen," he says.

"He don't talk much, does he," says Lucas. Motioning to chairs by the now cold woodstove, "Sit boys; take a load off your feet. You gotta be tuckered from pedalin' them bikes. How far ya git in a day?" Lucas sits across from the boys with a small coffee table between.

The boys take a seat and seem to relax as Marty continues. "We could do a lot better but it wasn't safe to travel by day. With the moon, we can get by without a light and we made thirty miles the first day. Today; we came the rest of the way in daylight. Night is cooler but without light we have to go slow."

Sandy Fogerty comes in with a pitcher of water and three glasses on a tray. Sandy is a stocky woman with a disarming smile and gentle manner about her.

"Boys, I'd like ya ta meet one o' our team," Lucas says. "This here's Sandy, her other half be up above watchin' us wit' a scatter gun. I don't think you boys are here for any trouble and I knows you'd be mo' comftable wit out carryin' that iron. I AM going ta have ta ask ya ta park yer artillery on the table here."

Surprised at being discovered, Marty tries to explain. "Mister, we don't mean any harm. It's just that being out here…"

With hands facing down as he would gentle an excited horse, Lucas tries to assure his guests.

"Boys, I'd think ya foolish ta be out here unarmed. Our precaution be da same reason. I kin assure ya dat you's in good company an has nuthin' ta be feared of. Jest open yer coats an set 'em on da table. No harm will come."

With no alternative, Marty slowly opens his coat to reveal two cross draw holsters pointing in opposite directions. If needed, he could shoot through his jacket either way. Removing his jacket completely, he unstraps the holsters with the guns and lays both on the table.

"Now, young man, it be your turn," says Lucas.

Reaching behind his back, Mike removes a pistol carried inside the waistband.

"An yer coat," says Lucas.

Very reluctantly, Mike first removes the hat which allows soft brown hair to fall to the shoulders. Mike is a girl.

"This is my sister," says Marty. "Her name's Michelle but I call her Mike to be safe."

"We didn't want to deceive you," she says, "but talking gives me away. This jacket is too warm anyway."

Michelle removes her jacket revealing a very feminine young lady with close family resemblance to Marty.

"Come on down, Mark," says Lucas. "We have us some guests. When did you two last eat?"

Mark gathers the pistols as he assures them. "I'll keep these for you until you need 'em again. They'll be safe and you'll get them back. Do you have anything else packed away out there?" Mark motions toward their bikes.

"I have a double 12 gage in a cut off pant leg, strapped to the frame of my bike. It's loaded and facing forward," he says. "Probably shouldn't leave it out there."

"Why don't you bring it on in and I'll put it with these," says Mark. "I'll look 'em over and clean 'em for you if they need it."

Adelaide prepares extra for her crew tonight. Beef Stew and biscuits always hits the spot.

Marty is a bit apprehensive. "That smells really good, but we don't have anything to pay you for this."

"If yer willin' ta git eggs in da mornin', feed da goats, an clean a stall," says Lucas, "that be pay enough."

"Deal!" says Michelle. "I love animals."

At dinner, Marty and Michelle open up about avoiding

bandits on roads near the border and atrocities in and near Presidio. It's no wonder they left without planning where to go.

Adelaide puts them up in the Cinnabar suite so they can each have a room but still be in the same cottage. I guess she didn't consider the stress these two are under because in the morning, only one double bed is used.

True to their word, Michelle gathers eggs and feeds the goats while Marty cleans the horse stall.

Adelaide calls for breakfast and Lucas offers a prayer.

"Lord, we thanks ya fer sendin' these two our way. Hep us to hep 'em as best we kin. Bless this good food an da hans what fixed it. Amen."

"Did the chickens give you any trouble, Michelle?" asked Adelaide.

"The dominecker was guarding her eggs pretty good but it was no trouble, she might be getting broody," she says.

"You seem to know your way around a farmyard. What animals did you have?" asks Adelaide.

"Well... chickens. We ran some Barbados sheep, a couple cows, and some horses. Not a lot of animals but those can be a lot of work," she says.

"Marty, ya did a fine job wit da stall," says Lucas. "Hard work don't run ya off like most kids taday."

"Thank you, sir. Dad had us working stock since we were little," he says. "I guess it's in our blood."

"Ya could do worse than stayin' on here wit us, if'n ya

has a mind to," says Lucas.   "We kin use da extry hands."

"You're good folks and I appreciate the offer but Dad wanted us to get away from the border and I owe it to Michelle to take her someplace safe up north," he says.

"Do you have family up north or any idea where to go?" Mark asks.

"Not really," he says.   "We have an aunt, uncle, and some cousins out in North Carolina but that's too far to go. I guess we'll go north and see what we find."

"We know of a place you might try," says Adelaide. "It's a long way but there's good folks at the end. Lucas can show you on the map after breakfast.

Spring:

In Hazel Creek, the stalks of last year's garden are pulled up and stacked on the compost pile, soil is worked with a hoe to prepare it for spring planting. Seeds have been sprouted in cold frames and in about a week, plants will be ready for the garden. Composted solids from last year's manure tea enrich the soil and promise a good crop.

Stephanie has trained the garden workers in every step of each process. They are competent and capable but still miss her oversight.

Dick, Keith, and Sam have been working some ingenuity of their own. Dick accumulated a large amount of pulverized limestone and saturated it with manure tea. As it dries he saturates it again to concentrate nitrogen along with the mineral content of the limestone. He intends to broadcast it on their wheat field, hoping to replace commercial fertilizer.

"I'm tellin' ya Keith," says Dick, "you should have won

that lady's heart while you had the chance. You let her get away."

Sam and Dick both enjoy ribbing Keith about his love interests. Truth be told, Keith doesn't mind it either.

"Sure would make things easier with Stephanie here," Sam says. "Maybe Keith could catch up on that bike Chris left him. I'm just sayin' Keith, I think she left with a broken heart."

"Not from me," says Keith. "I only danced with her once."

"That's what broke her heart, Keith," Sam says. "She was waitin' and waitin' for you to ask her again, but you never came callin'."

"All right," says Keith, "enough of this. Let's get to work."

Home grown fertilizer feeds well in the broadcast spreader and should put them ahead for the May planting. Running the tractor on wood gas re-mechanizes the farm, allowing more planted acres and more production to sell through a growing network of merchants. Their future is looking hopeful.

"I'm going to talk with Stan about moving our extra wheat this year," Dick says. "He can't carry more than a ton and that's after off-loading a lot of other stock. We could back ourselves into a corner where we grow more than we can get to market."

"Too bad you can't run a train on wood gas," says Keith.

"Maybe not wood gas but this would be a great time

for an antique steam engine to go back in service," says Dick. "Remember those old Christmas steam train rides? I wonder where those engines are today. A man could turn a good profit running freight up and down the line."

"There's a whole lot of gaps that could turn a profit if filled," says Sam. "I guess it's only a matter of time before someone puts the pieces together and gets rich for it. Once again, America is the land of opportunity."

Keith isn't encouraged. "Is there an America anymore? Where do we go from here?

"We start over," says Dick. "Just like we did the first time. Communities develop and some fail; states, or something like it, form and begin to construct some kind of order. We establish trade with other communities and states; develop a standardized currency; organize some means of defense and elect corrupt leaders to destroy it all over again."

It's gallows humor but the three men can't help but chuckle at the sad truth of human behavior.

Scott and Roxanne spend more time planning and staging belongings for their migration to Trout Lake.

"May is going to be here before we know it," he says. "At least we don't have to pack more than what we need to get there."

"That depends," she says. "A bachelor's cabin might need a few things. What kind of curtains are there? Bedspreads? Nice towels?"

"Unless I miss my guess, Mom, my aunts, and cousins will probably have 'girlyfied' my cabin to where Uncle

Ed may need to show me where it is," he says.

"Let's hope so," she says. "But I'm still packing a few things if there's room."

"I think we'll have plenty of room," he says. "The back seat will stay dry and we can put a tarp over what's in the bed. Once we get to Canada; even in summer you can count on rain."

Roxanne answers a knock at their door; it's Karin.

"Well, hello Mrs. Karin Elliott," she says. "How are you adjusting to the new name?"

"I'm kinda liking it," Karin says. "How are you two, today?"

"We're fine; trying to sort out things to take to Canada," she says.

"Good morning Karin," says Scott. "Sam's not with you?"

"No, he's working with Keith and Mr. Reed; getting ready for spring planting," she says. "Farming sure is a lot of work. There's a lot more to it than putting seeds in the ground."

"I'll say," says Scott. "There's a lot of work in anything, I guess. But I'm better suited to trapping, hunting, and fishing."

"That's really why I dropped by today," she says. "Canada sounds so interesting. When you have some time, I'd like to know more about it."

"Can you stay for lunch?" asks Roxanne. "We're about to fix something to eat and we can talk as we go."

"If it's not a bother," she says. "I'll help you in the kitchen."

"And I'll supervise as I tell you all about the place I call home," Scott says.

"Is Sam like this?" says Roxanne.

"Just like it," Karin says. "But that's not such a bad thing. Sometimes I think Sam could burn water."

Scott has to take a back seat to the lady's laughing. Roxanne sets between them a bowl of hard boiled eggs that have been cooling since this morning. They peel them for an egg-salad while Scott shares.

"If you ladies are finished trashing the dignified legion of manhood... I'll attempt to amaze you with descriptions of the far north," he says.

"Please do, in your humblest fashion," Roxanne says.

Scott continues. "Without apology, Trout Lake, Alberta, is one of the most beautiful places on earth. Rolling hills, tall trees, snowy winters, ice skating, ice fishing, great hunting, wild berries to pick... it's hard to beat. Canada 688 is the highway through but more people come by air than road. There's a big airstrip with one end at the lake edge and the other at the highway. Float planes can land on water and taxi up the ramp to the strip. Fishing draws most visitors and there aren't more than 350 people living there year-round. Town's that small don't need police and can't afford a fire department. If anyone gets injured or real sick, an air ambulance can take them to Wabasca Desmarais Hospital. Winters are long and snow isn't fully melted until late May in most years. That's why we're planning to leave about mid to late May. We'll get there in plenty of time before snow falls again."

"It sounds wonderful to me," says Karin. "Kansas is all I've known and it's so flat here."

With the eggs peeled and chopped, Roxanne adds chopped pickles, some pickle juice, chopped garlic, spices and yogurt instead of mayonnaise. It tastes great on sourdough bread.

"That was a great dinner," Karin says, "thanks for asking me; and Scott, thanks for telling me about Canada. I'd love to go there someday."

As Karin heads for home and the door closes, Scott comments. "I guess I should have told her that 'dinner' in Canada is served at the end of the day."

With a chuckle, Roxanne and Scott resume sorting and packing for the trip.

The Maxwell's enjoy having Marty and his sister Michelle, help out around the store at Terlingua but Adelaide is concerned that spring is growing warmer.

"I'd hate to think of those sweet kids on bicycles under that hot sun," she says. "How many days can they go between water stops?"

"I asked Marty an he 'tol me theys kin make three days betwixt water," Lucas says. "That's pert' near two-hunert-fifty mile."

"That seems like such a long way," she says. "Have you looked over their map? Is the way safe? What did they say about Hazel Creek?"

"It be about good as ya kin reckon," he says. "Marty's a

cautious sort so I figure they be alright. He looked kindly on Hazel Creek. Might work out fer 'em."

"How long would it take them to go that far?" she asks.

"That be what give me the notion they was kindly toward it," he says. "He had it figured right off at fourteen day."

"By the way the days are warming up, they best get started but I hate to see them go," she says. "I will worry over them until they get safely there. I'm so glad God sent them to us. Michelle is sleeping in her own bed now and Marty takes such good care of his sister."

"Well, you done right good by 'em, y'self," he says. "You'd a guessed they'd died and gone ta gramas."

"They're easy to love," she says. "Easy to love."

Sandra helps load essentials to Marty and Michelle's pannier packs and trailers, being careful not to make them too heavy. One extravagance is a bag of Adelaide's cookies but Marty says they won't last too long.

Mark returns their guns and as Marty 'guns up' Mark explains, "These are cleaned and chambered with safeties on. I found a couple old leather belts to strap your double twelve to the top bar of your bike. They'll hold better than the bale twine you first used. We're going to miss you two around here. Try to remember us from time to time."

"You folks have been good to us and for us," says Marty. "I don't know how we could ever forget you."

Hugs sometimes say more when words fail. Adelaide's

tears certainly can't be expressed in words but they may have been missed as nearly everyone struggles to control their own.

It's 7 a.m., late by traveling time but Adelaide filled their stomachs with a big breakfast and their hearts with loving goodbyes. Their trip north begins again.

Family & Friends:

Looking through her kitchen window, across the pond and toward F-51, Christi Spencer spots a single grain truck coming their way.

"Dan! It's them! They're here, THEY'RE HERE!" she says.

Dan comes from the barn, wiping his hands on an old towel. Spotting the truck, he starts waving both arms, using the towel as a flag. In a few moments, the truck horn accompanies blinking headlights. Chris and George are back home.

"Hey, big brother! About time you came home."

Dan bear-hugs his brother, nearly lifting Chris off his feet.

Obviously glad at seeing each other after so many years, both men are laughing. "It's good to be home and if you'll let me go, I'll introduce you to the family."

"GEORGE! How ya doin' buddy!" Dan releases Chris

to wrap George in another bear-hug. The sight of his only brother and his best friend, after years of separation is almost too much for Dan. His 230 pounds look lean on his six foot four frame; lending credence to his nickname "Fireplug." He still looks like a linebacker.

As George regains his footing, "Hey big guy; when are you going to grow a neck?"

"I got one. It's in there."

Christi joins them from the kitchen. "If I didn't know better, I'd think you three were still in High School. Hello Chris." She gives him a hug and then George. "Good to see you George. What's this I hear about you getting married?"

George gets an embarrassing twinge for neglecting Jackie. "Dan, Christi, I'd like you to meet Mrs. Jackie Hardin, her sister Nicky Chambers, their parents, Ron and Jennifer Chambers, and our good friend Stephanie Sweeny."

"Welcome!" says Christi; taking Jackie's hand, "We might as well get used to this; boys will always be boys." Seeing Gina holding onto Becky, Christi gets on her knees to be at eye level. "Hello, you must be Gina. I've not met you before. The last time you were here, you were still in Mommy's tummy. I'm your Aunt Christi. Would you like to come to my kitchen with your mommy and have a cookie?" Gina smiles and looks up for Becky's approval.

Let's all go inside. Are you hungry?" Christi leads everyone inside.

"Like I told you in the radio-grams," Dan says, "there's room for you here. You remember the Baxter place?"

"That old place?" says Chris. "I remember scaring the younger kids into thinking it was haunted and making noises from their bushes to frighten kids on Halloween."

Dan's grins, remembering the pranks. "That's the one, but now it's the NEW Baxter place. Old man Baxter short platted his west hundred acres to the Simpson's and built a new house. All brick too. Then he died of a heart attack two years ago. Mrs. Baxter tried to stay but said there were too many memories here and moved to her family in Connecticut. She listed the house but it didn't sell before everything fell apart. There it sits, just waiting for you and Becky to move in."

"I guess things have changed," Chris says. "What did they do with the old house?"

"There wasn't much to save," says Dan, "so they donated it as a controlled burn for the fire department to train with. They even dozed the block foundation. There's a garden plot there now."

"Did many families leave Monteith?" asks George. "Maybe I should ask if there's anyone left from when I was here."

"Not many," Dan says. "Aunt Dee is still here; looking to see you too. Mom and Dad should be here shortly; I'm sure they saw you pull in. The Simpsons farm is vacant and they have a second house for a farm boss. I thought you and your in-laws can stay there. "

"Where'd they go?" Chris asks. "Any chance they

might be back?"

"Not likely," Dan says. "You know how she hen pecked him. If he wasn't a piece of work on his own, I'd felt sorry for him. His son Mike was just like him. He knew how to farm but would stop traffic to chisel a dime off the interstate. Her family was in Atlanta where she thought 'everything is better' so they packed it off at the first sign of trouble. I tried to hold a going away party on the Monday after they left but Christi stopped me."

"That's enough bad talk," Christi says. "If I don't stop this, Dan can go on for hours."

Jackie says, "I get the idea the Simpsons weren't the best of neighbors."

"They had their ways," Christi says, "but they did take good care of the house and property. You'll find little that isn't real nice. Even as they were, I'd sooner have them back than assume the worst. Atlanta saw terrible trouble and it's not likely they will ever be back. Good or bad, I'll miss them."

Dan can't resist one more dig. "I missed Mike once, but my aim was off."

"Dan!" Christi glares as the rest try to suppress giggles and laughs.

"There's not much chance anyone is coming back if they were caught in big cities," Chris says. "Same for most of the east coast."

"What do you mean?" Dan's grin quickly fades. "What's wrong with cities and the east coast?"

"How did you get your news out here?" he asks. "What was your last update?"

Christi answers. "Satellite TV is the only source out here. Even our radio comes off the dish. We heard there were a lot of riots but everything stopped when the power quit. We assume that's all over now and things are settled down. What have you heard?"

"It has settled down but it's not like you think," Chris says. "The riots began when the money failed; you got that news. When the EMP took out the satellites, you lost all TV and radio but that's what shut down the electric grid and that shut down everything else. There wasn't enough police or National Guard to stop the riots and it boiled over. Fires couldn't be stopped, police couldn't communicate, hospitals were overloaded, and factions of every city were at open war with each other. Social control has collapsed. The estimated death toll starts at 70% and rises. Violence claimed a lot but most have starved or died from bad food and water or sickness. No city is safe to even visit, much less live in."

"We never knew," says Dan. "What about outside the cities? You mentioned the whole east coast."

"Most nuclear power plants in the US are east of the Mississippi," Dan says. "They had high population densities and few locations for hydro-electric dams. The problem wasn't the reactors but when fuel rods are replaced, the spent rods are stored in containment ponds until they cool down enough to move to long term storage. Twenty-four feet of water is enough to protect us from contamination but without power to run pumps that keep those tanks full, they eventually heat up and boil dry. Radiation goes airborne and spread for up to 200 miles downwind. That doesn't leave a lot of room between east coast nuke plants."

Dan grows somber. "So that means neighbors who went east, and especially to big cities, aren't stranded. They're most likely dead." All this time, Dan considered his neighbors alive but isolated. Realizing how awful their death might have been; perhaps must have been; changes his demeanor and for once he pities the ones he enjoyed mocking a few moments ago.

"It doesn't look good," says Chris.

"Look who's here!" Oren and Francis Spencer come in the kitchen door.

As Chris, Becky, and George go for hugs and kisses, introductions start all over and conversation leads to stories and laughs of growing up on Iowa's farmland.

Stephanie and Nicky stick close to Ron and Jen. Feeling a bit outside the loop, there is a vicarious sense of belonging that draws them toward this family. Watching them reminisce, laughing with funny stories, getting a glimpse of what built the character of these 'boys become men,' she wonders what Iowa may offer two single women with interesting lives of their own.

Adjusting:

Anna and Mom establish a tradition of their "breakfast" meeting. Most times it surrounds a cup of tea since we make it a point to share breakfast with Dr. Whitaker and Mom usually eats with Dad, but they still call their tea time a breakfast.

"I'm having a hard time adjusting to everyone leaving," Anna says. "Jackie and I were close and George is a good friend. Nicky and Stephanie were fixtures at camp and it feels so strange with them gone."

"Chris and Becky quickly became part of the family too," says Mom. "Gina is a delight and I'll miss her too."

"I've learned to accept friends coming and going but never so many, so fast," she says. "We've also lost Josh, Kristine, and Elmer. I think it's easier to be the one leaving than to stay behind."

"It isn't easy but it's the way things are," Mom says. "I

went to a girl's 'day camp' they called it. For a week during summer, we met to do crafts and learn outdoor skills. They taught us a song and it helps me even now. Make new friends, but keep the old, one is silver but the other's gold. We sang that almost everywhere we walked. It's kept me reminded that life will be filled with making new friends and parting with old ones. We never lose friends unless we choose to forget them."

"I'm all for that but we're running out of prospects in Hazel Creek," says Anna. "We need to fill these empty houses."

"Somehow, they always get filled," says Mom. "Sam and Karin joined the ranks of the married. Others will come."

The store is now called by several names. Some still call it a store while most have grown accustomed to 'trading post,' but when the men are gathered, everyone knows it by "The Roost." Elmer Tousley was a central figure of the group and with his passing; none wanted to disband the morning meeting. Dick, Keith, and Sam, are joined by Dwight and now Harry. Others come and go but these five are regulars.

"We have a deal with Stan to market some of our wheat," says Dick. "He'll take up to twenty sacks on each southbound trip and give us ten credits per sack as long as the market holds. He's working another deal for corn and should have numbers when he comes back through."

"That's a start," Dwight says. "It seems fair enough and there's no other way to get it to market. It works for me."

"That Stephanie was a smart young lady," Dick says. "We adapted manure tea to make fertilizer the broadcast spreader can handle and now the tractor runs on wood-gas. We'll triple our tillable land this year. We should have plenty to trade."

"Any word on what Stan can bring back this way?" asks Harry.

"Stan hoped to be bringing back sorghum grain and dried beef," Dick replies, "but we'll have to wait and see."

While Sam attends the morning meeting at The Roost, Karin visits her folks.

"Hi Mom!" she says.

"I'm in the kitchen," Emily says. "Would you like some tea?"

"Love some. It's still chilly in the morning but I'm glad for this warmer weather," she says. "Spring is coming."

"And I'll be glad to let the stove get cold," says Emily. "They've been nice but I have a mountain of ashes and not enough fat to make soap. Come fall, we'll have mountains of fat but the stoves won't have run long enough to make lye from the ash. I guess this is what helped farmers always think ahead."

As Karin sips her tea, "I guess that's why farmers have barns. You store what you have plenty of now, so you can use it when you have plenty of something else.

"How are you and Sam doing?" Emily asks. "How's

your food holding out?"

"We're fine, Mom. Sam has plenty of credits at the store. But guess what; I found out I have credits at the store too."

"What from?" Emily asks.

"Mrs. Eckerd gave me credit for those two deer I shot last fall," she says. "I just did it because folks needed something different from pork and chicken. She didn't have to do that."

"Vicki is a good woman and a smart store manager," Emily says. "You earned the credits and it was good of her to give them to you."

Emily hands Karin her tea and picks up a subtle change in Karin's demeanor as she shifts topics.

"Mom, have you ever grown tired of this Kansas prairie?" she asks.

"If you mean the constant wind, hot summers, and dusty harvests, I guess there have been plenty of times," Emily says, "but never enough to pack up and go. Your Dad's a farmer and we've grown into the land. I've seen pictures of oceans and mountains and tall forests; they're all beautiful but not something I could call home. It would be fun to poke my toes in an ocean but I call Kansas home."

Karin doesn't talk more of this but in her deepest longings she does want to kick sand on an ocean beach, explore alpine meadows, and walk among trees so tall you can't see their tops. All she has known is the prairie but she hungers for more. Love for parents and home is strong but the call to places yet seen is growing and Emily senses it.

"Hello? Is my beautiful bride in here?" Sam is back.

He's barely in the door as Emily greets him from the top of the three steps to the kitchen. "In the kitchen, Sam; would you care for some tea?"

"Thanks anyway," he says, "I had plenty at the store. How've you been?"

"Real good," she says. "Byron's in the field already; getting ready for planting. Dick said he'd run the planter for him with Elmer's old tractor."

Karin has her jacket on and gives Emily a quick kiss and hug. "Thanks Mom. See you soon."

Putting her arms around Sam's neck, she kisses him deeply and pops her heel up on one leg. Looking back at her mom, "It's still there."

Emily grins wide, "That's a good thing. Your Dad and I are going on thirty-nine years and still going strong."

Decision:

Sam and Karin, walking home hand in hand, have been silent for almost a block when he comments. "You're being quiet."

"I've been thinking a lot about Nicky and Jackie and George and the group that went to Iowa," she says.

"You want to go to Iowa?" he asks.

"No," she says, "but what if I said I was interested in us going with Scott and Roxanne to Alberta?"

"Wow," he says. "That's a long way. What brings this on?"

"All I've ever known is the flat plains of Kansas," she says. "It's my home but it doesn't take long to know all there is to know about it. I mean, over the next rise is a repeat of where you came from and over the next rise is more of the same. I've been talking with Scott and Roxanne. Alberta sounds so interesting and it's so different from here. I can't stop thinking about it."

"Are you sure your desire isn't a reflection of their motivation?" he says. "Both Chris and George were going back to their homes and the rest followed to stay with family. For us to go to Alberta would be really cutting a new path."

"Like Stephanie did?" she says. "She doesn't have family there. Change is what moved her to go."

"I'll grant you that," he says. "Alberta would be a big change. How long have you felt like this?"

"Josh and I talked about it several times," she says. "He told me about a visitor when he stayed at the fish shack, who said there are two kinds of travelers. One is at peace wherever he is so he travels; the other can't find peace so he travels hoping to find it. Josh and I were both the second kind but I never had a chance like this before. Here are friends going on a long journey to a place I'd like to see, and they could really use another couple to make the trip safer."

"They aren't going on a vacation," he says. "This is a one-way trip. What if you get there and decide you want to come back?"

Karin stops, looks Sam in the eye and says, "Then my strong and marvelous husband will figure something out." Before Sam can answer, Karin throws her arms around his neck and covers his mouth with a kiss. Both laughing, Sam begins tickling her as she breaks away running to their house.

"Anna, are you happy?" I ask.

"What brings this on?" she says.

"I was talking to Sam and we got into the difference

between being content verses complacent. We know people who've found a comfortable rut and never left but were never really happy either. They became complacent with a life that met their needs but left them wanting more. I got to thinking about us. Are we happy where we are, or have we grown complacent?"

Anna has stopped what she was doing and gives me her complete attention. "You are so sexy when you get philosophical."

I guess I need the humor to lighten the mood. "...and I love you when you love me, but the question is still out there. Maybe it's for both of us. Are we happy here, or have we grown complacent?"

Anna, now next to me with my arm around her shoulder, "I'm not sure if it's being here that makes me happy or that any other place wouldn't make a great difference. I was happy on Intrepid but I was also happy at camp. Terlingua was the same except we couldn't stay through summer. Maybe that would have become an unhappy place but it wasn't because I was unhappy; it simply would have become unpleasant. If you're happy inside, the outside may not matter. In the same way, I guess if you're not happy inside, where you are won't change that. I am happy. My husband loves me, I'm with people I care about, we have an adorable daughter, and my work makes a difference to people. Are YOU happy?"

"I think I am," I say. "I don't have any suppressed desires to wander but talking with Sam got me re-evaluating where we are and if it's where we want to be or is it where we have accepted as the home we can't change."

"If you could make changes by the snap of a finger," she asks, "would you, and what would change?" Anna's question has meat behind it. She has learned from Mom to ask questions that unlock answers.

"I could change a lot of things but they would be superficial," I say. "The things that matter are all here. You are here and we love each other, Mandy is my delight, Mom and Dad are here and we all get along. Even better, we aren't battling a repressive economy. We're like the children of Israel entering the Promised Land. God told them they would not have to build homes or plant orchards or vineyards. I guess you can't improve on that."

"Remember Golde from Fiddler on the Roof?" she says. "Tevye asked her if she loved him and it went into that song, Do You Love Me. I always liked that part. I guess it's easy to get trapped in the patterns of life and forget why you're there. I do love you, and I love our life here..... SO, Jason?" Anna breaks into song.... "Do you love me?"

"Well, it hasn't been twenty-five years, but..." now I'm breaking into song. "And I suppose I love you too."

Taking Anna in my arms, I add one more line from Fiddler. "It's nice to know."

Traveling from Terlingua on bicycle is an arduous task. Marty and Michelle pace themselves to conserve water and stop to refill at every opportunity. Adelaide and Sandy packed several types of food. Most can be eaten without any preparation but included among their stuff was provision for a delightful break from sustenance alone.

"Where are we?" Michelle asks.

"Almost half way if we keep on to that place in Kansas. That town we past about twenty-five miles back was called Post." Marty says. "That was White River Reservoir back there."

Michelle rolls her eyes. "I can't believe we're still in Texas. We've live here all our lives but it still amazes me how big this state is."

"We'll be crossing Oklahoma in a couple more days," he says. "It's looking more green up here. How's our food holding out?"

"There's enough, I think. But how do you feel about bacon tonight?" she says. "We haven't had a hot meal in days and we're running low on cold food."

Marty prefers a low profile and a fire with the smell of bacon violates that on two bold counts, but his gut overrides his caution this time. "That sounds real good. If we stop now a fire won't be noticed too much, and let's hope the wind doesn't carry the smell too far. Let's fry up all the bacon so we can eat it cold if we have to."

Finding at least some cover provided by a drainage ditch next to the road, Marty and Michelle make camp in the bottom of it and cover their bikes with brush as best they can. A Dakota hole keeps the heat under the pan and soon, bacon begins sizzling.

"Where did Adelaide get bacon?" he asks.

Michelle continues to turn the cooking bacon while

slicing more as she talks. "Remember Travis and his sons that came to visit? They caught several feral hog piglets and raised them in a pen. Adelaide said they grew to about two hundred pounds and this is their bacon. Willie smoked it. He sure did a good job."

"Hello the camp!!" Marty dives for cover and draws both pistols from his coat. Michelle sets the pan aside and snuffs the fire with a sweep of her hand, pushing sand into the Dakota hole.

A man on horseback waits about fifty yards up the road; next to the brush.

Marty can see him through the scrub bush he took as cover.

"Can I approach your camp? I mean no harm!" The man says.

Marty looks him over and sees no weapon drawn. There is a rifle in a saddle scabbard but it's laced down. He motions to Michelle to get cover as he calls back to the horseman.

"Who are you?" he asks.

"My name's Glen Thatford. I live on the land adjoining this road," he says.

Marty calls back while slipping his second pistol into his coat pocket. "Tie your horse and come on foot."

Michelle is hardly visible. She's hunched down with her coat covering her legs in the tall grass and behind a small oak tree. Pistol drawn, she's ready if trouble starts.

Glen is not as tall as Marty by about two inches and

approaches with both hands open and half way raised. "I was ridin' fence line and smelled your bacon. I haven't smelled that in a while. You're welcome to be here but we don't get many travelers and you'd me more comfortable at the house. If you've lived this long after all the trouble, I don't figure you're a problem. I'm unarmed except for the saddle gun; you can put the gun away."

Marty holsters his pistol as Glen reaches out his leather gloved hand. Marty relaxes and extends a handshake. As hand meets glove, Glen yanks Marty toward him and in a fluid motion, has a knife at his throat and his right arm locked behind his back. He has Marty as cover between him and Michelle as he barks orders to her.

"Put the gun down and come out from behind there," he says. There is a commanding nature to Glen's voice that allows no alternative. Slowly, Michelle stands and tosses her pistol to the ground in front of her.

"Now step over there." Glen motions to where the Dakota hole was. "Ankles crossed, on your knees, hands behind your head." Once Michelle is seated, he removes Marty's holstered pistol, then the one in his coat pocket. Marty is surprised that he knew where it was but there's not much he can do about it.

"Now sit next to the girl," he says. "Same way."

With both in defenseless positions and unarmed, Glen begins to ask questions.

"Who are you?"

"I'm Marty Benton. This is my sister Michelle."

"Where are you from?"

Marty is not happy with being suckered and he's only answering what he has to. "Our ranch was outside Presidio."

"Where are you going?"

"North" is all he answers.

"Where's your folks?"

"Dead, it's just my sister and me." Marty's voice begins to crack.

Glen's voice seems to soften as he gives a nod to Michelle. "How long have you been on the road?"

Michelle has more complete answers. "This is day six since we left Terlingua. We stayed there almost a week."

"That's a long way over some rough land. You have any kin to go to?" Glen asks.

"There's a place in Kansas that we were told of," she says. "We were going to check it out and maybe live there."

Glen walks over and picks up Michelle's pistol, dropping the magazine and racking the slide to empty the chamber, he comments, "Clean. You take good care of your hardware."

"OK, you can get up slowly. You may want to untangle your feet and sit a minute. That position can cause your legs to go to sleep. Sorry to put you through all this but when I saw you with a gun on me, I didn't take to the idea of an ambush. I suspect you were being cautious. My name really is Glen Thatford and me, my wife and son live just up the road. Get your bikes packed up and I'll take you to the house. I figure you could use a place to clean up after nearly a week on the road."

Deadeye:

Scott packs three trash cans with dried wood chips into the back of the truck. They will help feed the gasifier on the way to Trout Lake. Roxanne visits the store to pick up items for a weeklong trip. As she settles up with Vicki, she sees Karin.

"Hi, Karin. You ready for spring? Sometimes I think it will never get here," she says. "Then before you know it, summer's all around you. I'm heading home; I'll walk you back if you're going that way."

Karin confesses. "Actually, I saw you headed this way and followed you here. I want to talk with you about your trip. Would you possibly have room for Sam and me to come along? We've talked it over and neither of us feels anchored to Hazel Creek and both of us feel wrestles. Hearing about Alberta was like opening a book and reading all my dreams."

Roxanne stops and the girls talk eye to eye. "Have you talked with your parents about this? I know you're married and on your own but it would be a big impact to them."

"Mom and Dad know I'm not happy here. They told me I have to make my own way in the world. I'll miss them but I feel trapped here," she says.

"It sounds like you've been thinking this through for a while. I know Scott isn't real comfortable with us traveling alone. Why don't you and Sam come for dinner tonight and we can talk more?"

Thrilled at the possibility; Karin accepts and heads home to prepare something to bring. Excitement grows as dreams become possibilities but is she fully prepared to see the possible become real? Growing next to her excitement is the fear of embracing an unknown that might fail her expectations.

Scott is my brother in law and best friend, closer really; more like a real brother than a friend. With all we've been through, it's going to be lonesome without him.

"Hey Scott, I have something for your trip." Scott's eyes widen as he knows what lives in the padded canvas case on his kitchen table.

"The .308 from Intrepid? Thanks!" he says.

"It was your dad's so you've always been the rightful heir," I say. "Think of all the memories this thing holds. Pirates, security…"

"Nearly going to prison," Scott says. "But in all that, we've never had to pull the trigger. Do we know if it even works?"

"Only one way to find out," I reply. "When can you

go?"

Scott leaves a note for Roxanne and we start the gasifier on the truck. We no sooner start the engine when Roxanne turns up the driveway.

"All right you two," she says. "Caught you, and where might you be off to? Doesn't look like work related to me."

"Oh, but it is, dearest princess." Scott hams it up again. "Why don't you come with us? I promise it will be fun." Lifting the gun case is all the explanation she needs.

She sets her bag in the house and jumps in the truck. "Let's swing by and pick up Karin. She's headin' back from the store. I've never seen her shoot but I'm told she's good."

Karin joins us with Roxanne's coaxing and we head out of town to one of the few hillsides near town. Obviously a regular place to zero in rifles, we set up old cans and bucket lids for targets. About a hundred yards back, Scott loads the .308 and barks off three rounds that print about three inches high on the target.

Karin spots with binoculars and 'matter of factly' says, "It's zeroed at two fifty. Good enough for short shots."

"Short shots?" says Scott. "What do you consider medium to long?"

"That .308 is stable to 800 yards and with the right cartridge you can press it to a thousand," she says. "Range and wind gets critical after 600 yards and it turns into a mortar after 800. For practical purposes it takes skill to 600, luck to 800, and a miracle at 1000."

Karin's command of ballistics and cartridge performance is obvious. This isn't boasting, she really knows this stuff.

"I'd like to see a 600 yard shot; can you do it?" Scott asks.

"Not here," she says. "There's not enough room but we're pretty close to where we can if you'll drive."

Karin collects a plastic lid from a five-gallon paint bucket and tosses it in the back of the pickup. We drive another fifteen minutes to the crest of a rise, overlooking a bend in the stream that passes Hazel Creek. The hill is turning green as spring wakes winter's slumbering grass. Even the short grass paints a beautiful pattern as the wind does its magic. At brush line next to the stream, three plump doe emerge.

"Oh, look," says Roxanne. "Aren't they pretty?"

"They're scared," says Karin. "Deer don't break cover in midday unless something pushes them."

Using the rifle scope, Karin glasses the brush as the deer nervously move and duck among the protection of the trees. Exploding from cover, five coyote send the deer flying. Karin racks the .308 and cracks off three rounds in about as many seconds. Three coyote lay dead and the remaining two break for the stream.

"How far was that shot?" Scott asks.

"Four hundred yards," Karin says. "This is a favorite watering hole for whitetail. I've measured most of it. Six hundred yards is where the stream bends south." She points to the spot but Scott can barely make it out.

"I couldn't even see a deer that far, but after watching you drop three coyotes on the run at 400 yards, I'm a believer."

"Are we going to skin those out?" I ask.

"A month ago we would, but they're starting to shed out and the pelts aren't worth anything," she says. "We'll feed the buzzards this time."

Driving back, my curiosity over Karin's shooting wants some answers. There was a day I thought myself a good shot but not compared to her. I would have had a tough time making those shots with a range finder and twenty minutes to set up each point of aim. She did all that on the fly and hit three moving targets.

"Karin, how do you adjust your point of aim between your 270 and the .308? Doesn't that take a lot of getting used to?"

With a subtle grin, she says, "Now you're asking trade secrets." But she continues with explanation.

"If you plot the trajectory curve of all popular deer rifles from 270 out to 300 Mag. they pretty much track the same out to 500 yards. After that you have to pay more attention but under 500 yards, all you need is to know any one cartridge really well. THAT's my secret and you're welcome to it."

"I think a ton of practice comes in there someplace," I say. "How much bench time did it take to master that one cartridge?"

"My Grampa taught me to shoot," she says. "He reloaded cartridges so it saved a lot of cost. Learning didn't take as long as you might think but we didn't shoot like most people. Grampa had me shooting different distances and slopes and then at moving targets. By the time I'd start to get a position and shooting angle down, he changed it. After a while you start to learn the cartridge and not your surroundings. Grampa said conditions change but the bullet's the same. On humid days, you can actually see the bullet path. Now, when I shoot, I know the bullet path and can see it overlaying my target. Once you can visualize that, it's simply breath control and trigger squeeze."

"And all these years I've been paying a gun range to teach me wrong," Scott says. "I'm going to need a much bigger range."

Karin asks to be dropped off at her house and I walk home from Scott and Roxanne's. I learned a lot about shooting today.

New paths:

An old woman walks to her house with eight fresh eggs in her apron pocket. She once let her hens free-range but the years aren't agreeing with morning searches for each new nest the birds make. The pen is wired on all sides and the top. Cattle panels laid flat around the edges, stop foxes and raccoons from digging in. Her chickens don't know how good they have it.

Aunt Dee has been managing her own farmyard since before last August when her husband died. Ed's heart was slowly failing and with it, his strength. She keeps a kitchen garden and feeds three pigs along with her ten chickens. Her name is Dee; sister to George's mother. Since she and Ed took George to live with them after his parents died, the title 'Aunt Dee' stuck and everyone calls her that. Farming has slowed since the collapse. Subsistence farming with a little to share or trade with others, takes less land than before. She questions the purpose of it all. When the country was going strong, it took all their land and two hired hands to make enough to barely keep the place going. Now she hardly needs more than the kitchen garden, a few chickens, and three pigs to meet her needs. There's still tasks that she's grateful to have help with. Dan comes each year to fill her woodshed, butcher a hog, and do repairs she can't do any longer. "He's a good boy," she says, even when no one can hear her.

"Hi Mom!" it's George. She knows his voice instantly.

"Oh my, Oh my, my, my. Look at you! Let me hug your neck." Tears fill Dee's eyes as she reaches to hug her sweet Georgie.

George hugs this precious woman longer than politeness demands. She invested her life in his at a time when he needed it most. She is loved perhaps more than a mother, at least an equal.

"I have someone I want you to meet. Mom, this is Jackie. Jackie, this is my Aunt Dee."

"George has told me about you," she says. "I'm glad to finally meet you. Let me hug your neck too. George, you sure got a pretty one. Won't you come inside?"

Dee's kitchen is typical for an older Iowa farm house. A sink to the right beneath the window, a small wood fired cook stove has replaced the electric one that occupied the wall across from the door, a small refrigerator sits next to the stove but without power it keeps pans and dry goods now. A sturdy kitchen table serves as workspace and where informal meals are eaten. It's the place where friends sit and talk. George's Uncle Ed had a saying, "Company comes to the front door but friends to the kitchen."

Dee takes Jackie's hand, "So tell me about yourself. Where do you call home?"

Jackie finds Dee's open heart and soft eyes, welcoming. "I was born in Richmond VA but grew up in a tiny place called Short Pump. My sister, Nicky..."

"Didn't I hear that she and your folks came with you?" Dee asks.

Jackie smiles. "Yes they did. They want to meet you too but I think George wanted this time just for us. Anyway, Nicky went to college and then down to Texas for work, I followed a year later. When the crash happened we ran to the company owner's property in Big Bend, Texas, where we stayed during most of the bad time. That's where I met George and we got married in Terlingua before we went to Kansas. Now we're here and I couldn't wait to see where George grew up."

Dee shares memories of George's early years on the farm while he sits patiently, hardly finding space to join their conversation. Finally, Dee turns to him.

"George, you found a wonderful treasure in Jackie. I only wish your mom and dad could have been here to see you both."

Walking to Scott and Roxanne's house seems longer than two blocks when carrying a hot pan of bread pudding.

"How did you come up with bread pudding without sugar?" Sam asks.

"Stan's Trading Post to the rescue," Karin says. "A while back he had sorghum syrup AND alfalfa honey so I bought some. I mixed the honey with the goat milk and used gooseberries in place of raisins. I even found a source of vanilla and cinnamon."

"Where did you find vanilla and cinnamon?" he asks. "And how much did THAT cost us?"

"It wasn't bad," she says. "I learned a little secret about the preacher's wife."

"You mean Christi Duncan?" he asks.

"Yup, Christi's a bit of a moonshiner," she says. "They brought a still with them from Texas and she's been making alcohol for Dr. Whitaker. She also brought a bunch of vanilla beans they got from Mexico somehow, and she's been making vanilla extract to earn credits with Stan. She gave me a big bottle as a wedding gift. The cinnamon is from all we collected from vacant houses before all you came. It seems so long ago."

"It's hard to believe our two groups are starting into our second year together," he says. This has been a very busy year with a lot of change."

Arriving, they turn up the drive to the kitchen step where Roxanne answers the door.

"Come in, welcome! That smells good. Sam, let me take that for you, come on in."

Scott comes in from the dining room. "Hey Sam, glad you two could come. Karin, how's he treating you?"

"Like a princess," she says.

"Your timing is perfect," says Roxanne, "I made a pork and venison meatloaf that came out of the oven only ten minutes ago. Let's eat."

Dinner's small-talk gives way to Scott and Roxanne's upcoming trip. Sam asks, "How close are you to leaving for Alberta?"

"We could leave almost any time now," says Scott. "We're all packed but the last of the snow can take 'till the end of May to clear."

"Karin and I've been talking and we're interested in going with you if it could work out," Sam says. "Could you use the extra help on the trip?"

"Your help would take a lot of pressure off this drive. Extra eyes and hands are more than appreciated and you're more than welcome to join us," Scott says. "It'll take three to four days if we can drive straight through. The problem might be at the border. I have no idea what to expect. Neither of you are Canadian citizens so if the border is closed, it might even be enforced by our military. Even the secret back-doors may be shut. Like I said, you're welcome to come but there's a possibility you could get stranded at the border. I'd hate to see that happen."

Karin takes a deep breath and asks, "Where do you plan to cross?"

"US-15 meets AB-4 at Sweet Grass Montana and Coutts Alberta," Scott replies. "There's a border road with multiple uncontrolled crossings but if you look suspicious, you're sure to be followed and watched by authorities. There is little room for trial and error. Another problem is the firearms we'll be bringing. That .308 of my Dad's is clearly not allowed but I can't see leaving it behind. The same goes for hollow-point pistol ammunition. But I can assure you, ours won't be the only non-compliant firearms in Canada."

"You know," says Roxanne, "Canada has had some of the same difficulty as we have had down here. Fuel shortages, economic downturn without US support, and they don't have electricity either. I'm thinking that after two years past the US collapse, they don't have much traffic across that border. They may not have resource enough to man a full time border patrol. Our truck must be one of perhaps only a few hundred operating on wood gas between both countries. I think we stand a good chance of crossing without any trouble."

Either way, Karin isn't deterred. "I'm ready for Alberta but I'll take the Rockies as a second. If we can't go all the way, at least we can get that far. I want to live someplace that's not flatland."

Sam isn't as confident. His role of provider and protector is intensified with Karin's boldness. Adversity will always become his problem to resolve and he isn't too sure what to expect from Montana's wilderness. "Let's just get across that border... Will we need to build a cabin once we get to Trout Lake?"

"When we get there," Scott says. "We'll be good to go. Trout Lake made the largest share of their income from fish tourism. Almost every resident has a cabin or two for rent income during fishing season. Everyone competes for that income so the cabins are made as attractive as possible. Uncle Ed has three rentals that I'm sure aren't seeing much business. You and Karin can stay in one of those at least for now."

"See," says Karin, "it's all working out."

Sam feels yet another weight is added to the enormity of his burden.

Hospitality:

Extracting their bicycles from cover, Marty and Michelle quietly load their belongings into their trailers and pannier bags. Michelle takes care to wrap and pack their half cooked bacon. It's been way too long since they've had any, and bacon is way too precious to waste. Observing from a distance, Glen no longer believes his arrested guests intend harm but safety demands caution. Watching every move, he notices the pant-leg covered bundle tied to the crossbar of Marty's bike.

"If that's what it looks like; you both best step away from your bikes." Glen motions back toward where their fire was, locates and removes the shotgun, and removes both shells. "You won't need that at my place and we don't want any shot flying by mistake. I'll give you back your rounds when you leave." Glen steps back again and motions Marty and Michelle back to their bikes.

Two bikes roll on paved road with a rider following.

"Next gate on your right, watch the cattle guard," he says.

A modest home sits over the first rise. The two story white sided house has a green trimmed veranda on front and one side. A grassless void separates it from an all metal barn with a three sided tractor and implement shed completing the shape of a 'U'. Drawing closer, a windmill comes to view pumping well-water to an elevated cistern at the top of the tower. Alerted by the singular bark of a well trained dog; a woman peers from an open window.

"Sherri!" he says. "We have some guests. You two can park your bikes. I want you to meet my family."

There's a look of substance that grows on country people. It may be the confidence from growing your own food and embracing hard work as life's expectation; regardless, it's evident in this woman.

"Sherri, I'd like you to meet Marty and Michelle. Marty, Michelle, this is my wife Sherri." Nodding their acknowledgment, Sherri is a bit confused. Glen chuckles as he explains.

"You two can relax. You're here as guests and can leave whenever you choose but I'd stay for dinner and a shower if I was you. Sherri's a real good cook."

"They were camped across from the reservoir and we needed to overcome a bit of apprehension before getting neighborly." Glen is trying to stifle his amusement. "I'm afraid some of that apprehension may still be hanging around."

Sherri looks from her husband to Marty and with an

understanding smile, says, "Don't tell me you shook hands with Glen.   He was a Texas Ranger and developed some habits that I don't share."

Extending her hand, she says, "I'm pleased to meet you both."

Marty's tension eases as he takes her hand.   A slight smile begins to show.   Michelle joins to exchange courtesies and begins to speak.

"When he grabbed Marty, I about died.   I had no clue what to do but I'm glad you folks are friendly."

Conversation grows more comfortable as Sherri and Glen show interest in their ambitious trek.   With dinner not quite ready, Sherri helps Michelle gather a change of clothes from her bike and then shows her where she can shower.   There's no hot water but with the sun working on the cistern, their cold water isn't chilly. Glen invites Marty to join him as he tends some chores.

"You're set up pretty good out here," Marty says.

"We didn't used to be," says Glen.   "Sherri and I once lived outside of Dallas.   We were invited to a meeting about self-reliant living and started seeing indications that trouble may be coming.   We moved out here and began shifting toward off-grid living as much as we could.   That's when we put up the windmill."

Glen's horse is hitched to a pole outside the tack room. Fetching a grooming box, Glen turns to find Marty already has the saddle and pad off to air out on a fence rail.

"You know your way around a horse," he says. Handing him the grooming box, he takes the pick and begins checking each hoof. Marty explains as he combs and brushes the horse, "Our ranch was small but we kept some horses to tend the cows. We didn't have very many cows but they had to cover a lot of ground to find pasture."

Brushed and stalled, Glen tosses some hay in the feeder before he and Marty head back to the house. Sherri has the table set as Michelle emerges clean and feeling it.

"It feels good to have clean hair again. Thank you so much."

"You're entirely welcome," Sherri replies. "I imagine traveling by bike and camping on the road makes it tough to stay clean."

"We do alright to some extent," she says. "When we come by a stream or pond in a safe place, we get all cleaned up for the next few days. In between, we take sponge baths. The worst part is not getting to wash my hair. What kind of shampoo is that? It smells really good."

"Why thank you," Sherri says. "I make it myself... or at least I used to. It's castile soap; made from olive oil and a few other ingredients. The scent is lavender oil. We never realized how bad things were going to get but I started a cottage industry making soaps and lotions. It just got started when everything fell apart."

Sherri's wood cook stove sits on rails with a removable wall section that lets her roll it into the kitchen during cold seasons and out to the veranda when it's hot.

Noticing Michelle's curious look, "Isn't this great? It

was Glen's idea. We bought and restored this Monarch stove years ago but the first time we fired it up, we about cooked ourselves out of the house. It's great when it's cold but murder when it's hot. I love my little stove train and there's another chimney connection out there."

Glen and Marty wash up at a sink on the veranda before coming in for dinner. Michelle helps fill glasses with tea as Sherri sets a one pot casserole on the table by a basket of rolls and says, "Let's pray."

Reaching for Sherri's hand, Glen extends his free hand toward Marty and Michelle, "We hold hands for prayer, would you join us?"

As Glen is about to pray, a young boy comes into the kitchen, rubbing his eyes.

"Look who's up," says Sherri, scooping her son into her arms. "Did you have a good sleep? I have two friends for you to meet. Alexander, this is Michelle and Marty. They're going to have dinner with us. Are you hungry too?"

Alex looks over to Michelle and smiles as he nods his head that he's hungry. Joining the circle, Alex bows his head for prayer.

After dinner it's Marty's turn for a shower while Michelle helps wash the dishes.

"That was a really good dinner," she says. "We've been eating on the road for so long, you almost forget what real food tastes like."

"I'm glad you enjoyed it," Sherri says. "Would you like to stay an extra day and I can help you do laundry? I

KNOW that's a challenge when you travel."

Michelle's eyes light up with the offer, making it too late for a polite decline. Clean clothes AND clean hair; this is turning out to be a very good stop; even if it wasn't their choice at first.

Two days pass and they are finally ready to resume travel. Marty spends an extra full day helping Glen with chores and Michelle does the same for Sherri. Dinner that evening is quieter than normal, anticipating farewells in the morning.

"You know," says Glen. "We could use your help right here. You could stay on if you'd like. "

"It's tempting," Marty says, "but we have a place up in Kansas that we need to check out first. If the offer remains open, we could head back if it doesn't work out there."

"You have a deal," says Sherri. "I want the best for you but I hope you don't mind me praying a bit selfish."

Glen returns their guns and helps Marty attach the shotgun to his crossbar so he can fire it in place or quickly draw it to his shoulder. Dawn begins to reclaim the sky as Marty and Michelle make their way back to the highway and on toward Kansas.

Departure:

No consolation will quell Anna's tears. She's become comfortable with her big brother being near and has developed a bond with Roxanne as well. Now she's losing both and the pain is deep. It was different when she married and left home. Then she was fully occupied with the newness of marriage; now she must watch Scott and Roxanne leave her behind and an awareness glimmers for what her mom and dad must have felt.

Anna's tears have company with Emily and Byron's. Raising Karin, they always knew she would one day leave their nest but parents are seldom prepared for the day when it arrives. When words and hugs are exhausted, Byron passes a gun case to Karin.

"Dad would want you to have this."

Opening the case, it's her grandfather's 'Big Gun' as she called it. A bit more gun that necessary in Kansas, but perfect for Alaskan moose and Colorado elk.

"The 270 is yours already and I'm sure it will come in handy but you'll find game more suited to Grampa's 300 mag. in Canada. I know it's in good hands with you. I love you sweetheart."

Tears finally fill Karin's eyes as she wraps her arms around her daddy's neck. "I love you too, Daddy. I'm going to miss you and Mom so much. We'll contact you on radio when we can."

Whether the giving of Grampa's 'big gun' signaled her dad's surrender to letting go, or that this gift clarified the reality that she was really leaving her parents and home, Karin's tears are flowing.

Turning to give her mom a hug, Emily says. "Mail will have to restart somehow. This can't last too long, you'll see." But in the depths of our hearts, none of us can say what will resume or how long anything might take.

For this Alberta bound crew, two farewells are required. Most of the town is waiting at the Grange Hall to give family some privacy for difficult goodbyes and blessings. These times are never easy and they give pause to appreciate the cultures where newlyweds merely add on to their parent's house and live next door.

Scott's truck is re-arranged to empty the back seat for Sam and Karin. All the cargo fits into the pickup box and for now, a tarp will keep weather out. There should be an RV or truck center somewhere along the way and they can look for a cap then.

With the gasifier lit, there are a few more minutes for extra hugs, handshakes, and blessings. I doubt the crew of Apollo Eleven had this many goodbyes.

Packed with loved ones and their belongings, Scott drives slowly to the center of town while family takes the shortcut between the Whitaker's and Jason and Anna's house, arriving before the truck can navigate the streets.

Another round of goodbye's tug at each heart but departure must come and so the journey begins. Alberta bound; not knowing what may come; an adventure unfolds before them.

Anna finds few words walking back home. Mom and Dad go with us as I suspect Mom understands Anna's feelings and her needs right now. I'm holding her left hand, Mom has the other. There are few effectual words but none are needed, knowing she has the support of those who love her. Anna's Viking cannot find her and its strength fails against these tears. Is it time for Anna to return home? We have lived most of our married life within a few miles of my folks. She loves them and they her, but perhaps it's time for me to take her back to her roots. I know she would never ask, but it's my job to understand her needs and find a way to meet them. Time will tell.

"Welcome to Oklahoma! I thought we'd never get here!" Michelle says. "How much further to Hazel Creek?"

"If we don't shake hands with anybody, we should be there in another three days." Marty says.

"I wouldn't mind shaking hands with folks like the Thatford's again. Glen and Sherri turned out to be pretty nice," she says, "and I could use another shower and home cooked meal."

"Yeah, I'll hand it to you," he says, "it turned out to be a good stop."

"What kind of Ranger was Glen?" she asks. "I'm guessing he wasn't a baseball player so that leaves the Army or Texas Rangers."

"Texas Ranger," he says. "Glen was like a super-cop. He told me he's been with them for twelve years but didn't say much about the things he did. They must have some kind of rule about keeping work private."

Marty and Michelle stick to side roads and see few people along the way. It's safer to avoid contact but there are times that children will wave to them as they pass a small farm. Twice they abandoned caution, turned in to ask for water, and ended up camping there for the night. Whatever destroyed trust among people seems to be passing. Marty hasn't felt the need for his weaponry since they left Terlingua but he isn't about to surrender it yet. People they meet are friendly, sharing, and hungry for news from anywhere they've been. Could it be the terrible loss of human life has somehow cleansed the humanity that survived? Perhaps with so few remaining, life has become something more precious. Whatever the reason, Marty and Michelle have enjoyed traveling a long but un-perilous ride.

"Three hundred and thirty miles our first day," says Scott. "Not bad for running on smoke"

Roxanne has been sleeping to pass as much travel time as she can but now she is even tired of that. "Where are we?"

Sam has been navigating by the trucker's atlas they brought from Terlingua. "We are flat dab in the middle of nowhere but that nowhere is in central eastern Colorado."

"How much fuel have we burned?" asks Karin. She seems to be keeping tabs of supplies. No official jobs have been assigned but each has taken interest in particular areas.

"I think we burned through nearly one full can of wood fuel," Scott says. "There's a small town and an old military site up ahead. I thought we'd look for dry wood there. We can shred branches if we have to but pre-dried is better."

Past the town, signs on a chain link fence indicate they've found what they were looking for. The gates are open and hanging. Something big must have crashed through. Everything looks abandoned, no sign of activity.

"Not much to see here," says Karin. "What kind of military site is this?"

"Back in the sixties, this was a Titan missile site," says Sam. "They tried converting some to Minuteman sites but this one appears to be abandoned long ago. We should be good to spend the night here and the fence should limit any animal traffic."

Some mounds have concrete pads on top. These must have been the silos for the missiles. Other buildings probably held support equipment. Rounding one of the mounds exposes a tour bus parked with its nose against metal double doors of the middle silo. The nose of the bus is damaged, maybe explaining how the gates were opened.

"That's not from the sixties," says Scott. "Why would that be here?"

"No telling," Sam says, "but it's been here quite a while. I'd guess from soon after the blackout. We have some cover and protection between these mounds, let's make camp and get something to eat."

Sam and Scott begin scrounging the handful of outbuildings for anything wood. Door trim and floor planking will heat their dinner and fascia trim fills nearly another can of fuel for tomorrow. Roxanne and Karin prepare a simple dinner before spending their first night beneath the stars. The air is cool but dry so instead of tents, a tarp under their sleeping pad and then over their blankets, will suffice against the morning dew. Sleep is so good.

"Scott," says Sam, "are you awake?"

"I am now," he says. "What do you need?"

"I think you need to open your eyes," says Sam, "we have company."

Scott rolls over to see a man sitting on their packed truck bed, with a shotgun pointed their direction.

"Good morning," he says. "I trust you slept well."

Roxanne and Karin are now sitting up and looking at the stranger, eyes wide open.

"Let's start with you telling me who you are, where you're from, and where you're going," he says.

Scott clears his throat. "We're just passing through. This place looked abandoned and the fence gave us some protection. We didn't mean to trespass."

"Since following directions doesn't seem to be your strong suit, let me repeat myself," he says. "Who are you?"

Sam answers. "He's Scott Iverson and that's his wife, Roxanne. I'm Sam Elliott and this is my wife Karin. We're from Hazel Creek Kansas and headed for Alberta Canada."

"Now that's better," he says. "You must have gone to better schools than your friend."

Something about this stranger indicates he doesn't mean harm. It could be the slight smile he shows while poking at Scott.

"What did you do for a living before we lost the country?" His voice appears more serious about this question.

Attempting to redeem himself, Scott answers again. "I'm chief engineer and owner of Can-Geo, we locate tar-sand and oil shale. Sam is a project manager for Oilfield Solutions Incorporated, a company we're associated with in Houston."

"Son, you just climbed a few notches with me," he says. "I was afraid you were with the feds." Setting the shotgun aside, he continues. "My name's Rick Yeager, former site engineer for this complex. I'm sorry for the scare but I need to be careful who pokes around here."

Black Swan:

"You mean this site is active?" says Sam.

"Not active like you'd think," says Rick. "This is a clandestine 'Continuity of Government' site. Its code name is Black Swan but you won't see that on any signs. In fact, it's supposed to look just like you found it. An old abandoned missile site. I don't mean you folks any harm."

Hopping down, Rick reaches a hand to help Scott to his feet and shakes hands with him. Sam is on his feet with a little less anxiety. Roxanne slowly stands next to Scott as Karin peals back her blankets and tarp, exposing Sam's pistol in her hand. She is in no way amused at her rude wake-up today. Rick's eyes widen as he notices.

"Good thing we just got to be friendly. You can put that thing down, young lady. I'm unarmed and sorry for our rude introduction. I think you'll understand after I give you folks a tour and tell you about this place."

Karin lowers the pistol but still isn't smiling. She has the look of a cat caught in the rain.

"Let me start with a peace offering," he says. "How long has it been since your last taste of genuine roast coffee?"

Roxanne is still a bit edgy and not sure what to make of Rick but he's touched a soft spot with her. "Where do you find coffee after this long, in Colorado?"

"Do you have a pot to make some in?" he says. "I can explain while it's getting hot."

Roxanne isn't the only one exhibiting caution. No one is jumping to get breakfast going and Rick isn't winning their confidence yet.

"OK," he says. "I guess I need to explain first. Black Swan is the code name for this complex. It only looks like a missile site but has been converted to a high grade bunker to protect essential government personnel in the event of nuclear attack. If you'll recall, many older missile silos were converted to house the newer and larger missile systems. Trouble is, it was faster and less costly to build new sites than bust up and re-design the old ones. They knew this from the start but calling it a conversion gave them a good cover to do something entirely different... like expanding a few of these to become super bunkers. This site has capacity for eight hundred personnel and it's completely provisioned for five years. Water, sewer, medical, dental, cafeteria, even a chapel, library, and a working crematorium; everything was planned for."

"You're telling me there are people down there; right now?" Scott says.

"Not that many, but some," says Rick. "This was a prototype site. When completed, they realized they would have to build a lot more of this size or fewer much larger ones. The Cheyenne Site is deeper, stronger, and holds three thousand personnel. These smaller facilities were kept as backup for lesser personnel and this one as a model to show people who had a need to know but weren't on the guest list."

Sam sets a fire in the Dakota hole while Roxanne fills a pot with water. Everyone is listening intently.

"So, if this site wasn't actually meant to be occupied," asks Sam, "who's down there now?"

Rick scoots a discarded box closer to the fire and sits. "We best get comfortable; this will take a bit."

Reaching into his insulated vest, Rick removes a plastic bag and hands it to Roxanne. She hasn't seen fresh coffee in a long time but hasn't forgotten what it's for. Opening the bag, the smell of fresh coffee brings back memories from better times.

"When we lost communications and after that, grid power; key federal personnel went missing. They were apparently on the Continuity of Government guest list and were whisked away. Those left behind panicked and came here. They weren't authorized to enter but I had no security detail and a few of them knew how to operate the doors from previous site tours. They decided to make their own rules about who was 'in' and who was 'out.' They crashed the gate with that bus over there and two other busses followed. State and city big-shots from Denver, with their families, entered the site with their security detail and their families. There was nothing I could do to stop them."

"So why are they still down there?" Scott asks. "Don't the doors work?"

"They're prisoners of their own fears," says Rick. "They were convinced this was a nuclear attack and thought they were more important than anyone else, they killed anyone in their way. The bus drivers were told they could return to fetch their families but one had none to go back for, so he stayed behind and let the driver who crashed the gate take his bus. After the other drivers left, he was told none of them had access and when he protested they shot him dead where he stood. Right then, I knew I didn't care to survive if it meant being with 'leaders' like that. It didn't matter; they made it clear my service as security guard was no longer necessary. 'Security guard,' that was a mistake."

"Why is that?" asks Sam.

"Because I'm not just the security guard; I'm the site engineer. I helped build this complex and know every system and sensor in it. They asked me to lead other bunker projects but my wife, Sarah, was in final stages of leukemia and I couldn't leave her. I took early retirement and accepted this site maintenance position to keep medical coverage for her. I live about a mile from here. Sarah passed right after things collapsed and I buried her on our place."

"I'm sorry to hear that, Rick," Roxanne says. "Do you have any other family?"

"None that's close," he says. "Thanks for asking. I

have things to do and I'm helping several elderly couples that aren't up to gardening or hunting. We do OK." Then, he says with a chuckle, "I have to watch over my underground zoo down there too."

"I still don't understand why they don't come up," Scott asks.

"Like I said, their afraid to," he says. "Remember, I built this place and those blood thirsty, merciless souls thought a nuclear nightmare was upon them. There's room for nearly three times the people they have but they shut the doors and sealed others out. In taking Sarah to the Denver cancer treatment center, I had a lot of waiting time as she underwent procedures. In the waiting room I read up on every kind of treatment for every type of cancer. Denver is one of the first centers for radioactive brachytherapy and I found it interesting. It works on isolated cancers like tumors that are too close to sensitive organs for regular radiation. They take a very small gamma implant and insert it in contact with the tumor to shrink it. Micro radiation at just the right place; slick idea really. Six weeks after we lost power, the riots petered out in Denver and I rode back on my dirt-bike. The cancer center was all beat to pieces but my previous interest in brachytherapy got me a tour and I knew where they kept the gamma implants. I brought back a whole lined case and seeded each radiation sensor to the control room down below." In a condescending tone, he says, "Site engineers know where each one is hidden."

Rick continues, "There's no radiation to hurt you up here but down there they think Denver was a direct hit.

All their sensors are reading high radiation levels. Remember this site was only a demonstrator site so communications were never made active. They're isolated and unless they open the doors from their side, no one can get to them."

Karin is getting over her affront at being awakened to a shotgun and asks, "Are those the only sensors they can go by?"

"The sensor plan was limited because this was supposed to be a demo site," he says, "but they also had four cameras, anemometers, thermometers, and barometers to make a good show. It wouldn't do to have them see people walking around while sensing deadly radiation so one moonless night I disabled all but the rad sensors and drove that bus into the outer doors. I figure they might have heard the boom and with the loss of most of their sensors, they would assume a near nuclear strike."

"But why?" Karin asks. "Why keep them down there?"

"Those are the same tax and spend government leaders who bankrupted this country and then demonstrated a ruthless disregard for the lives of those they were supposed to serve. Besides that, they have plenty of minions with weapons. If they come up here, they'll continue taking what they want from people who can't afford to give. I figure I'm protecting a whole town from them, and them from a town that sees little use for their kind. It's ironic really. The prison guards are the terrors of their own thinking. I can't open the doors to get to them and they won't open the doors to come out. I guess when they run out of food they'll have to come up but that should give us nearly fifteen years to establish a stronger government."

"Coffee's ready," Roxanne says.

She pours a strong cowboy coffee into several mugs and the taste is fantastic.

"Not to change the subject but where did you get fresh coffee, here in Colorado?" she asks.

"I took a lot of interest in stocking the bunker with realistic supplies to impress visitors and the question of coffee kept coming up.   Ground roast coffee in a vacuum can, only lasts a year at best and instant coffee was unacceptable.   These are liberal, citified Latte drinkers, mind you. I did a little research and found that green coffee beans last for decades and you can roast them in a cast iron pan. I requisitioned a few hundred pounds and displayed some in the cafeteria stores.   The problem was shelf space.   Everything was designed for what's down there already with little room for two huge bags of beans.   I only got it for display to stop whiney questions over coffee so we kept the rest up here. "

Rick looked over to the sealed blast doors and sarcastically toasts his subterranean prisoners, "Here's to you. So sorry you don't have any."

Regardless of how any feel about deceiving officials into self-imprisonment, Rick's toast is funny and they all get the humor.

There's nothing they can do for, or to, the self-incarcerated. We offer to share breakfast with Rick and ask about the road heading north. After sharing what he knows from travelers coming south, he makes us another offer to help with our breakfast.

"Part of my duties made me the supply officer and it was important to rotate food stock so the bean counters wouldn't complain over dates on cans. I never threw anything out. Could you use a few pounds of canned bacon? How about some of my favorite; corned beef hash?"

Roxanne and Karin make a fast breakfast fit for company. After breakfast, Rick asks to see how we're running a truck on wood-gas. Being an engineering type, he doesn't take long to get enough understanding to replicate the process.

Tummies full, an extra few pounds of food, AND a couple pounds of green coffee beans, our truck is running again and we're headed north.

Roxanne and Karin take the back seat for a mid-morning snooze while Sam and Scott take turns driving.

"What do you think's going to happen when those people finally come out?" asks Sam.

"I'm not sure but Alberta may be just enough distance for that Ground-Hog Day," says Scott. "You think Rick will have a prison fence built by then with gate guards?"

"He just might," says Sam, "and maybe it's called for.... it just may be."

Canada:

The trip north goes without incident. Society's ills may be from too many people trying to live close. I'm reminded of a verse I once read in the Bible;

"Woe unto them that join house to house, that lay field to field, till there be no place, that they may be placed alone in the midst of the earth!"

Maybe the rise of violence was from living that woe, or from men reacting to an oppressive government that sees its people as a tax resource instead of constituents to be served. Whatever the cause, life is more precious these days and we all have plenty of space to be 'alone in the midst of the earth.' Simply seeing a traveler now invites welcome and the sharing of news. Kindness is a new normal; not that travelers can go defenseless, but knowing that nearly everyone you meet is armed and capable, for having lived this long, it engenders a mutual respect and polite demeanor.

Scott is navigating secondary roads, especially near previous population centers but now he diverts to farm roads.

"Scott, are you lost?" Roxanne is aware that Scott knows the Canadian border better than most.

"Sweet Grass, at least WAS a controlled border crossing," he says. "I'm headed for an agricultural crossing that's uncontrolled."

"You've been here before?" Sam asks.

"See all these fields?" says Scott. "This is wheat country and these farmers cross the border on farm roads all the time. If you follow the border road, it will lead you to those crossings. Normally, farmers living here will report anyone crossing who they don't know but I'm guessing things are much less strict these days."

"Let's hope so," says Sam.

"There it is," Scott says. "Oh, Canada! We're home."

Motorized vehicles draw attention almost everywhere there are people to notice and this farm town is no exception. Hardly a town and smaller than Hazel Creek; it has fewer buildings but claims a small store. Scott pays a social call for anyone who may be curious.

"You from the States?" a man asks. "I'm Curtis Andresen." He offers a handshake and both Scott and Sam reciprocate.

"From the States but heading home," Scott says. "I'm Scott Iverson, this is Sam Elliott, and our wives Roxanne and Karin, over there," pointing to where the girls are perusing shelves.

"My family's up at Trout Lake; that's my home but I got caught in Houston when everything fell apart," he says. "I've been away longer than I planned."

"I was up there a few years ago," Curtis says. "Nice place. Stayed at a fish camp run by Ed Iverson; any relation to you?"

"He's my uncle," says Scott. "How was the fishing?"

"Well worth the trip," he says. "Is that your truck?"

"It's not registered to me but I didn't actually steal it either," Scott says. "It was abandoned so we converted it to run on wood gas and used it to get us here."

"I was noticing the plates," he says. "I'd change them out or you won't get far without being stopped. Wood gas, eh? My dad told me about running their tractor that-a way back during the war. Yours is the first I've seen up close. Must work pretty good to get you here all the way from Houston."

"Not from Houston," Scott says. "We migrated from Texas to Kansas last year and found this truck there. We've been on the road most of this week and hope to get home in a day or two."

Curtis' welcoming smile quickly changes to a more serious countenance. "OK son, welcome home. Now listen carefully. You need to pack up and head north about two 'k,' then turn onto my farm road, marked 'Andresen.' Drive around back and get your truck into the barn. Stay inside and out of sight. I'll come get you when it's safe. You folks not being local are sure to have been radioed in. Border patrol should be along within the hour and I'll send them looking another way. Be quick now; there isn't much time."

Sometimes trust has to be from the gut as time doesn't allow much else. Scott, Sam, and the girls load up and head north following Curtis' directions. As he said, they come to a dirt road marked with a small wood sign 'Andresen.' The barn has two roller doors on each end. The side facing the road is closed with the rear door open. Scott pulls in, shuts the engine down, and waits.

Roxanne is first to start the questions. "Can we trust this guy? We don't know anything about him. He's either looking out for us or setting us up."

"I thought about that too," says Sam. "What do we do?"

"He was checking us out pretty good," says Scott, "but I think he heard the right answers. I felt a little better when he knew about Trout Lake and Uncle Ed. I think we can trust him."

"He reads OK," says Karin. "At first I thought he was hiding something with that overly friendly salesman face but that dropped at the end and I think he came clean."

Sam grabs the binoculars, "Still, I want to keep a lookout," he heads to the loft where a small window offers a commanding view of the road.

Twenty minutes seem like hours when a diesel truck motors southbound on the road out front with 'C.B.S.A.' emblazed over a maple leaf on its doors.

"Scott," says Sam. "What's CBSA stand for?"

"Canadian Border Services Agency," he says. "Looks like Curtis knew what he was talking about."

"Unless he was the one who called them," says Roxanne.

"If this was a setup, why would Border Services pass us by?" says Scott. "So far, I think we can trust Curtis."

"Hello, Mr. Andresen. We got a call regarding another unchecked crossing. Have you heard anything?" Agents from the Coutts check point frequent Curtis' store. Primarily for this being a busy crossing for illegal entry into Canada but also because he seems to access trade goods that are otherwise difficult to get in Canada. Picking up a can of spaghetti sauce, canned in Omaha, he asks, "How is it that you have so many products from down south? Doesn't ConAgra deliver out here?"

"It could be the stock from down there was returned and distributed up here. How should I know? Am I not supposed to sell what comes in?" he says.

"About that crossing; did they come here?" the agent asks.

"Two men came," he says. "They were nervous and tried to say they were Canadian but they were fooling no one. They bought some medicines with Canadian currency and left."

"Did you see which way they went?" the agent asks.

"They went north but I watched them turn east on 500," he says.

"AB500 is quite far from here; how did you see them

turn east?" The agent's suspicion is growing but Curtis remains cool. Reaching behind his counter, he retrieves binoculars, chuckling as he says, "Some think I watch birds. I couldn't see their truck but the wind always puts up dirt on that turn and I saw the dust."

The agent smiles as he pays for the contraband spaghetti sauce. "Perhaps you should work for us with your keen sense of observation. We could use men like you."

"Who would run my store then?" he says. "And where would you find sauce for your spaghetti?"

The agent smiles, accepting his change, and returns to his truck. Curtis watches it head north but there is no dust. The agent is heading back to Coutts.

Getting on:

Jackie has been Anna's closest friend and her brother Scott was certainly mine. With them gone, we're spending more time at Mom and Dad's. We have always enjoyed our time together but now we have more opportunity. Tonight, we're playing Mexican Train Dominoes and the Taylor's have joined us.

"Any word from Chris and them in Iowa?" Mom asks.

"Pat said they all arrived OK and they're settling in," Harry says, "but they need to raise their antenna higher. As it is, they can only rely on text. They did say we are all missed and that planting will start soon."

"Speaking of planting," Dad says, "we need to start plants in the cold frames about now. Who's heading up the garden with Stephanie gone?"

Harry sets a double domino, followed by a second. "John Stubbs rose to the task. He helped Stephanie from the start and has a green thumb but I saw a lot of plants in the cold frames already. It looks like they're way ahead of you.

Anna sets a marker on her line and draws a tile. "I hear Dick is looking for more hands for planting this spring. Without Elmer and Sam, they have their hands full."

Dad plays a tile on Anna's line. "I think Eric Stokes might fill in. He will be a big help."

No mention is made of Scott and Roxanne, Sam and Karin. It's too early to expect word but it doesn't stop a flood of thoughts on their regard. There's no quenching memories of moose, bear, and picking berries from Anna's heart either. Nearly all her idle thoughts migrate north to cabins and lakes and snow; lots of snow.

"I can't believe we're in Kansas already," Michelle says. "It's taken us two weeks to get out of Texas and only a few days to cross Oklahoma. They sure make states smaller outside of Texas."

"I hear Alaska is bigger but I'm glad we aren't headed there to see," says Marty. "Hazel Creek should be another day's ride from here. How are you holding up?"

"I'm doing fine but my thighs are getting huge. Keep this up and I'll look like a bullfrog. You hungry?"

"Yeah, let's stop for lunch," he says.

There's been no trouble along the way but keeping to back roads is still their plan. Besides being difficult to navigate, main highways always lead to cities where you can't trust the water.

Here on the side of a country road, in the middle of

nowhere, they can eat their lunch in peace.

"What if Hazel Creek doesn't turn out like we hope?" Michelle asks.

"The way Lucas talked, it sounded pretty nice, but things can change," Marty says. "I figure we'll ride through and stop for a visit like we're on our way west. If we like what we see, we can decide to stay. If not, we keep going."

"How about going back to Glen and Sherri's?" she says.

"I'd like that. They turned out to be nice people," he says.

Michelle gets a big grin, "You going to shake his hand again?"

A smile is all Marty answers but more is not needed. Michelle loves her brother. Marty is her rock and she feels safe with him near. She loved her dad but when their mom died of sudden onset pneumonia in 2004, he was so caught up with grief, caring for two children, and the farm; he hadn't much left. Marty grew tall in those anguished days. His chores grew; taking on some of Dad's so he could tend to Mom's affairs. Tending a small ranch is work enough without added burdens and theirs were piled high already. Still, Marty didn't assign tasks and set her loose. He kept his sister beside him as they tackled chores together. Small talk through the day sometimes gave respite to tears but her greatest comfort was knowledge that her brother cared more for her than if the chores were completed. Somehow, each day managed to end with nothing amiss but there was little daylight left to spend mourning. Perhaps that too was a help.

A broken heart may have contributed to their dad's death. He may have noticed earlier that something was wrong in the barn if his mind wasn't distracted by lingering grief. More than a decade after death claimed her; the untended spark she nurtured in his life had grown cold. Thoughts of death brought peace but he could not embrace it with precious souls depending on him. If he were to die, it would have to be God's call, and that day in the barn; it came from a looter's gun.

Marty grew tall again as he buried their dad and set plans in place to care for his sister. Presidio wasn't safe anymore and his idea to use mountain bikes with child carriers as cargo trailers was well thought. Their propane fueled tractor could only drive until the extra bottles ran out but without a means to refill them, they would make about 300 miles and be stranded. Motorized transportation would also attract bandits but bikes make little sound. Traveling by moonlight allows early recognition of roadblocks and often, a silent passing on paths too narrow for other means. Dawn offers enough light to find shelter among thick brush to wait the day out until the safety of darkness returns.

Distance from the border brought a measure of safety; enough to travel again by day. Marty still thought it best to keep Michelle's long hair under a hat. She didn't understand why girls attract trouble but that didn't dull the truth of it.

Pedaling endless hours on a bike gets you in shape but beyond that, it opens your mind to fill the void with thoughts seldom afforded time otherwise. You come to know more of who you are and what values matter most. Lately, Michelle is thinking of what kind of man she hopes to spend her life with and she hopes he will be a lot like her brother Marty.

It may have been anticipation of the journey's end or an unperceived favorable slope but after today's ride, Marty's map puts them barely two hours out of Hazel Creek. Sleep comes quickly to the exhausted but not this night. The stars are bright and the evening cool but their minds are caught between expectation, hope, and the unknown until dawn finally ends a slumber that took way too long to start.

Normally, they are on the road quickly; twenty minutes or less. Breakfast is on the road, usually after at least half an hour of pedaling. Today, Michelle boils water for tea and finishes cooking the last of their bacon.

"This isn't going to keep much longer," she says. But it's more excuse than reason. Inside, they are both apprehensive. What will Hazel Creek be like? After all this time avoiding people, are they ready to ride right into a town now?

Michelle prepares fry bread and bacon with hot tea. It chases off the chill but so would thirty minutes of hard pedaling. They are finally packed and back on the road but making poorer time than yesterday.

The Andresen barn is spacious enough but is growing cramped after nearly an hour with no sign of Curtis.

"Maybe we should go now and make tracks away from here," Roxanne says. "If they haven't come for us yet, maybe it's safe." She is asking more than telling.

Drawing on past experience, Scott makes the call. "Not

yet. Curtis will come when it's safe. If he wasn't to be trusted, Border Services would have been here already. His delay tells me it's not safe to expose ourselves yet. We can stay put for a while longer."

Curtis closes his store at four p.m. every day, and does this day like every other. Ten minutes later, he turns up the drive.

Sam sees it first. "Scott! There's a car coming up the drive."

"How many in the car?" he asks.

Sam takes another hard look. "Appears to be only one and the car is alone."

Karin reaches for Sam's pistol they previously buried among their cargo but Scott intervenes. "That won't work. We stand a better chance without a show of force. I think this will be OK."

Uncomfortable with going unarmed, she defers to Scott's better knowledge of Canada's border region. Right now she longs for a perch in a tree on the Kansas prairie.

The car parks at the back of the barn and looking through the crack between the barn doors Roxanne sees a man coming.

"It's Curtis," she says. "Whew! I thought he would never get here."

A voice at the barn door confirms it. "This is Curtis, are you here?"

Opening the door, he enters and explains. "They are looking for you but I sent them away. I doubt they believed me but we have an understanding about such things and I don't have trouble with Border Services. I would have come sooner but we have an informer in the village and it would be curious for me to close my store early."

Curtis hands Scott a package wrapped in brown paper that resembles a package of bacon. "Here, I brought you these. They are Canadian plates for your truck. Those Kansas plates will get you caught for sure. There are few cars and trucks on the road these days. Most are government vehicles or merchantmen such as myself, so you will be noticed. The further north you go, the better."

Sam asks, "When do you think it will be safe for us to continue?"

"If you don't mind, be my guests for a day or two," he says. "By then, they will assume you crossed back and things will go back to normal. Until then, they will be watching all the major roads."

"It will be dark soon. The kitchen door is open, come in and I'll have some food for you. Welcome home." Curtis extends a hug to both Scott and Sam and kisses the hands of both Roxanne and Karin before stepping out to his house.

Karin holds her hand out like she's displaying evidence. "Ooooh, I'm glad I didn't shoot him. He's nice."

Roxanne giggles, "I rather like his style, myself. I already like Canada."

Sam takes Karin's hand. "I'd place a kiss on this fair

hand but I see the space is already taken."

Dinner is a hearty pork soup with plenty of potatoes, carrots, and peas. It fills the stomach and calms the soul. The evening passes with childhood stories and more details of the adventure that brought them here. Then a knock comes at the kitchen door.

Outed:

None heard the truck creep up the drive with its lights off.   None heard the barn door open or the soft footsteps scale the stoop to the kitchen door but the soft knocking at the door penetrated hearts like thunder.

Curtis goes to the door as four travelers remain riveted to their chairs.   It's the agent who visited him this afternoon.

Curtis put on his best plastic smile as he opened the door. "Can I help you?"

"We need to talk. I'm alone. Let me come in."

Curtis steps aside as the agent walks in.   Scott, Roxanne, Sam, and Karin slowly stand as he enters.

"Please keep seated. I have some questions and need honest answers from you. Before you answer let me inform you that I have all I need to have you and Mr. Andresen arrested and imprisoned so your answers can do you no further harm."

Taking a seat in a camelback chair, he continues. "We've known about Mr. Andresen's activities for some time. He has helped us at times and other times, has sent us on goose chases. He is well known for acquisition of merchandise not generally available in Canadian markets but it brings no real harm. Your being here may change that."

"Start by telling me your real names and where you are from."

"I can speak for the group," Scott says. "I am Scott Iverson, of Trout Lake. I'm owner and president of Can-Geo, a Canadian owned and operated oil exploration corporation."

"Then you are Canadian?" he asks.

"Yes," Scott says. "My sister and her husband were sailing back from Hawaii when things fell apart and I joined them at Sitka to warn them off and travel with them to Mexico and then into Texas where I met and married my wife Roxanne."

Roxanne acknowledges by lifting her hand half way. She says nothing.

"That's where I met Sam Elliott also." Sam softly acknowledges, "That's me."

Scott continues. "With short cold winters and long hot summers, we couldn't remain where we were and traveled north to Kansas where we merged with a small farming community. That's where Sam met Karin and they were married in April."

Karin nods her head once as the agent looks her way.

"Roxanne and I planned to return to live at my home at Trout Lake. Traveling alone can be hazardous so we welcomed Sam and Karin's request to join us and live in Canada."

The agent is listening carefully; he looks at the carpet for a silent moment, takes a long breath and makes a summary.

"So, you are the only one with documentation of Canadian citizenship. I assume you have some record of your marriage but it can't be official since it occurred after this confusion." Looking to Sam and Karin, "And you two are clearly not Canadian but have no way to properly immigrate without a functioning home government."

"Yes sir," says Scott, "that's about it, and we are at your mercy."

"It takes a reasonable man to know the difference between letter of law and intent," he says. "I am such a man but this puts me in a difficult position. Letting you go would mean not only my career but would also make me complicit with your criminal act, according to the law. Our concerns at Border Services are to stop black market trade especially for arms and munitions from US military stockpiles. There are many looking to buy them and our border is a likely corridor. You do not look like arms dealers nor smugglers to me. This meeting never happened; you have never seen me nor do you know my name. When you depart here, go directly north by way of side roads only. All main highways are watched. After Edmonton, you will be safe. In time, the world may find normal again;

whatever that is. When it does, you need to contact the Provincial Magistrate, tell them your story, and apply for citizenship."

The agent stands and goes to the kitchen door with Curtis following. On the stoop, he turns to have a few words in private.

"I never came here tonight and we have never met outside of your shop. Stay within bounds or you will be prosecuted." Turning to leave he stops and speaks with his back to Curtis. "And for God's sake, tell them to hide the guns better. It took me less than two minutes to find them."

"Matt?" Cynthia asks. "Do you think the kids will end up back at Trout Lake one day?"

"You mean permanently?" he says, "like moving there?"

Cynthia sips her tea, sets her cup down and looks across the table to her husband. Her eyes are somewhat fearful and her heart feeling pain of expectant loss. "I think Anna is getting homesick. I saw it when Scott left. She's seen him go back many times when visiting or passing through Houston but this is different. I sense she's missing her mom, her extended family, and the home where she grew up. Now she has Mandy and I think she would like for her to share the childhood she knew as a girl. Where could Mandy see a moose down here?"

Matt has always been a good listener; better than that, he knows his wife's heart. "It must be a heavy load for you. Knowing how important it must be for Anna and for Mandy because of how important it's been for you to have them here with us. The spirit we cherish in Anna is partly from how she grew up. Depriving Mandy of that would be unkind but letting them go is undesirable."

"So, you think they will go back to Alberta?" she says.

Leaning forward, Matt holds both her hands. "I don't know what they will decide.   Anna is a very responsible young lady and she is very important to Doc. Whitaker and this town. I'm sure she's weighing this too. If God gives her peace to go to Alberta, our same God will give us peace to let them go. Until then, let's leave this in God's hands and enjoy our children as long as they are here with us?"

Arrival:

Stan has helped promote our manufacture of wood-gas generators and business is growing. Anna and I leave Mandy with Mom as we head to the store to meet Dad, Fred, and Harry, and so Anna can pick up some things. Stan's Trading Post is like a catalogue store. He is resourceful at finding things otherwise unavailable. The price may be high but asking is always free.

Even from a distance, it's evident something new awaits us. Two bicycles with trailers are parked in front of the store. Their riders are inside, talking with Vicki Eckerd and the men.

Seeing us at the door, Vicki greets us with a brighter than usual smile. "Hello Anna and Jason; no Mandy today?"

"We left her with Mom," Anna says, "who are our visitors?"

With Vicki's interest level, you would think these were her own children. "Marty and Michelle Benton, I'd like you to meet Jason and Anna Connors. Anna is our RN in town; not many communities have both a doctor AND a qualified nurse."

Anna steps forward and offers Michelle her hand and I do the same with Marty who seems a little reluctant at first. As he finally takes my hand, he explains.

"I'm sorry, I had a handshake go wrong on me once and I've been a bit gun-shy since. I'm glad to meet you."

"Marty," Dad says, "Jason is my son I was telling you about." "Jason, Marty and Michelle have biked here from Presidio TX by way of Terlingua. They met Lucas and Adelaide who sent them here."

"You've come to a good place," I say. "Hazel Creek is at the crossroads of plenty. We grow enough food to trade and we have a small industry starting up. Best of all, we're in the middle of a motorized trade route with connections to other markets in all directions. Are you two looking for a place to settle down?"

Marty feels at ease after the welcome and begins to explain how it is that they left their place in Presidio to find a home farther north.

"Well, you and your pretty wife could make a lot bigger mistakes than setting roots here in Hazel Creek," says Harry.

Both Marty and Michelle's face turn red and Michelle can't help but giggle.

"A lot of folks think that," Marty says, "but Michelle's my sister."

Now it's Harry's turn to get red faced. "Oh, I'm sorry. You two look so natural together, I just assumed wrong. Michelle, please forgive me."

Still giggling, Michelle replies, "If I find an available man like my brother, I couldn't ask for a better husband. I don't take that as any insult."

Now everyone is laughing but Anna breaks the awkwardness. "You've been on the road a good long time, why don't you come to our house and get freshened up? We can have lunch and share what we know of this part of Kansas."

Marty and Michelle accept and as they thank everyone for making them feel welcome, Michelle takes Marty's arm and says, "Come on Hubby, let's go." Laughing inside the store follows us into the street where the bikes are parked. It's a good thing Harry is good natured. He's going to wear this for a while.

Sam changes plates on the truck as they share teary goodbyes with Curtis Andresen. Staying an extra day may not have been necessary but he nearly insisted; he hosted them for two. His wife passed several years back and he so enjoys their company. Curtis turns out to be quite a chef. Quiche Lorraine for breakfast the first day and ebleskivers the next; lunch is rye bread with goat cheese and pickles; dinner is lamb and rice the first night and his own creation called 'lamb wellington' last night. Both Roxanne and Karin offered to help cook but Curtis explains that he has not had the pleasure to cook for anyone but himself for way too long and truly enjoys the opportunity. At least we all help wash the dishes and clean up.

Last night at dinner, Scott says, "Curtis, you could make a fortune as a chef and another fortune with a weight loss clinic." Curtis enjoys the compliment and our gratitude.

Finally, on the road, we stick to farm and side roads as we make our way north.

Endless hours seem to pass between sleep, talk, and silence for no apparent reason. Roxanne breaks a silence by announcing, "I'm hungry. Let's turn around and head back to Curtis."

Karin replies, "If we do, I may have to start my first diet."

"He was a gracious host," says Sam.

"And a God-send," continues Scott. "I know we would have been caught on the road if he hadn't helped. That agent probably wouldn't have helped us if it wasn't for Curtis, either."

"How much further? Are we there yet?" asks Roxanne.

"There's a sign coming up, we'll know in a minute," Scott says.

The sign reads 'Edmonton 25k'

"We'll cut to the main road in another hour and be half way there in another three hours," says Sam.

Karin hugs Sam's arm with both of her arms, "I hope we have plenty of blankets, it's getting colder up here; and you are my hot water bottle tonight."

Sam grins, making reply, "Are you going to put your icy toes in the back of my knees like other nights? I just love that."

Roxanne and Scott can't help cracking up. "Sam, I think that's a common female trick." Scott says. "Rocky, until now, I thought you invented that move."

Still laughing, Roxanne playfully gives Scott a shove.

"We could be there sooner if you'd stop driving like a grandma," she says.

Scott replies, "This is about all the gasifier can do. If I go much over fifty, the engine starts to starve out. If it helps any, we're going eighty kilometers per hour. Does that sound faster?"

Sam and Karin can't hold back laughing in the back seat and Roxanne gives Scott another shove.... but she's laughing too.

Kansas is fading to history. Green grass and leafing trees taking claim from a stagnant winter hasn't visited northern Alberta yet. When it does, the visit will be short. There is evidence that spring is imminent though; an occasional patch of spouting grass, a few wild flowers, but patches of lingering snow endure under the shade of trees, and this is Edmonton. Farther north, around Trout Lake, snow will barely be melted from the roads, and fields will retain their blanket of white for several more weeks. Scott is energized. It's surprising, even to him, how much he's missed the rugged majesty of deep forested hills and the thrill of hunting and fishing to provide food for a family. More than once, he's had to outwit a bear or cougar that thought to reverse roles and make him the prey. He is a hunter, and a good one. Karin may be an excellent marksman and may know Kansas deer, but up here in

Alberta, there is bigger game to hunt and greater predators to elude.

To the east, a curl of smoke catches his eye. Scott's woodsman skills are awakening form too long in hibernation. Only a wisp of smoke but he knows it means a cabin rests beyond the trees. Easily missed, a narrow dirt road between trees gives a singular clue to finding the occupied shelter and perhaps warmth for the night.

"Where are we going?" Sam asks.

"It's going to get cold tonight and this is no country to be sleeping out in the open," Scott replies. "This road's been traveled recently. I'm going to check it out and I'm hoping for a place to stay for the night."

In the cover of trees, a road; if you can call it that; it's more like a wide trail but it follows a tree line around another dense grove to expose a small cabin and large shed. From the looks of several cord of seasoned firewood in the shed and the trampled space where much has been fetched during this winter, the residents here have come through in fine shape. It testifies to good planning and knowledge of how harsh north Canadian winters can be.

Scott pulls the truck to a safe distance from the cabin and steps outside awaiting acknowledgment. Light sprays on the ground from a door opened on the side of the cabin. A bearded man steps out and Scott walks toward him. They meet and from the truck their words can't be discerned but the nature of their conversation appears congenial.

Returning to the truck, he has good news. "We can

stay the night but it's important that we remove all food and take it inside. They've been having bears making a lot of trouble lately."

Once inside, introductions begin. "I'm Jacob Martin, my wife Gloria, and my two sons, Hudson and Trevor."

There's no mistaking Jacob's sons. Jacob is a tall man with the look of an outdoorsman. His red wavy hair blends beautifully with his full red beard. Hudson and Trevor share his same red hair. Jacob looks to be in his late thirty's and his sons are fourteen and twelve. Gloria is Irish with a telling accent, perhaps in her early thirty's, though it's not polite to guess a woman's age. She has coal black naturally curly hair.

Scott pulls the truck up to the cabin with Sam and Jacob helping remove their food to the safety of the house.

"You run on smoke?" asks Jacob.

"Trout Lake is my home but we started in Kansas," Scott explains. "There's no gas down there so some folks found a way to run on wood-gas. I might keep it this way."

"I've heard about it from Morfar," says Jacob. "He said they ran lots of things on smoke during the war when gas was rationed."

Seeing Sam's puzzled look, Scott explains. "Danish names for Father and Mother are Far and Mor. Grands on your father's side are Farfar and Farmor; your mother's side is Morfar and Mormor."

The light comes on for Sam. "I like that. You don't get them mixed up that way."

Hudson and Trevor sleep in the loft over the kitchen and Jacob and Gloria have the only bedroom; we bed down in the living room. As we settle after a good dinner, Roxanne whispers to Scott, "How did you know we could just drive up and be invited like this?"

"We are getting away from populated centers out here. There are no motels or restaurants so it's the way we've come to live. We welcome travelers because in time, it will be us who needs a safe place to stay. This time it IS us who needs the welcome but you know what I mean. It's how you do up here and we'll get plenty of chances to repay the kindness."

Home:

Marty and I talk as we walk the bikes from the store to our house while Anna gets to know Michelle.

At the house, Anna begins to open jars and puts together a good lunch. After firing up the rocket stove to heat our lunch, she spends more time visiting and making our guests welcome.

A knock at the door is Mom with Mandy. "Hello! Special delivery. Look Mandy, you have company."

"Michelle, Marty, this is my mother-in-law, Cynthia Connors. Mom, this is Marty and Michelle Benton form Presidio, TX. They came here on bikes after meeting Lucas and they're shopping for a home."

"I'm pleased to meet you." Mom says. "You've come to the right place. We have homes available and God's blessed this place with a bounty of His provision. I do hope you can at least stay a few days to check us out. I believe you'll find Hazel Creek a friendly place."

"We'll at least do that," Marty says, "but we've already

discovered the friendly part."

"Tomorrow is Sunday and I'd like to invite you to join us at Church," I say. "Most of the town will be there and we'd love to introduce you."

"Jason, I don't think we brought any church clothes," Marty says. "There's not a lot of room on our bikes."

"That's no problem at all," assures Anna. "We have a very informal church and you can come as you are."

Emily and Byron welcome Marty and Michelle to stay in their guest room where Jeanie often stays and Michelle can stay in Karin's room; one wall away. They could have their pick of several houses but it will take at least a day to make them ready with food and supplies. The Bennet's enjoy their company and it helps to fill the void with both Josh and Karin gone.

At church, they are welcomed and the town falls in love with these two brave young people.

There appears to be a virtual tug-of-war in the hearts of both the Bennet's and Taylor's. Karin's empty room and Stephanie's empty apartment are available and both families are taken with Michelle and would love to have her stay with them.

For now, she sticks close to Marty but comfort is growing.

Marty and Keith act like long lost friends who've just met and Marty's interested in Sam's room at the Tousley farm. Time will tell.

Iowa is growing on its newcomers. Arriving just as field work calls for plenty of hands, they are welcome to the community. The church is active as several smaller denominations have combined into a larger one and everyone seems to get along fine. Ron and Jenn Chambers settle in the Simpson's large house. They resisted of taking such a nice house at first but everyone thought it best. There were too many unpleasant memories for some to live among their past. Nicky and Stephanie decide to share the ranch hand's house. There are plenty of available places but they have grown to be the closest of friends and being close to Nicky's parents is a bonus. Chris, Becky, and Gina, settle in the Baxter's newly built house. Chris notices Becky's tears as he helps unpack their things.

"What's wrong? Are you unhappy here?" he asks.

Becky stops and turns her tear streaked face to Chris. "It's not that at all. I'm just overwhelmed at how God has cared for us? Back in Lubbock, we struggled to pay for a house that was quickly becoming too small. Now look at us? We're moving into a beautiful new home, we're near your family, the people here are kind, and our future looks good. It's humbling; I don't feel like I deserve all this."

Chris has nothing to explain their needs being so well met. Taking Becky in his arms he simply holds her. As they stand embraced in the living-room, Gina comes and hugs their legs. God has certainly blessed this family.

Jackie quickly grows attached to Aunt Dee. She and George find a vacant house close by and plan to help her with the farm. There are nicer homes available but none so nice as being close to someone you love.

The pilgrims, as they have come to call themselves, meet and share how they are adjusting to their new community. Without exception, they all miss their friends at Hazel Creek but the move to Iowa was a good thing. There are no regrets except that distance keeps them from frequent visits.

Jacob and Gloria Martin enjoy visiting with Scott & Roxanne, Sam & Karin. Hudson and Trevor were shy at first but now seem saddened to say goodbye. Jacob helps Scott and Sam as they light the gasifier and load their food back into the truck.

"Good thing you got your food out of there," Jacob points to Scott's feet. "We had a visitor."

Looking down, Scott sees a huge paw print nearly as large as his own foot.

"Big brown, I think," says Jacob.

"That could have done a lot of damage. I'm glad I wasn't in a tent last night," says Sam. "Let's not tell the girls until later."

"How cold do you think it got last night, Jacob?" Scott asks.

"When I checked this morning, it was ten below," he says.

"Ten below! Man, it didn't feel THAT cold." Sam says.

"That's Celsius, Sam. About 14 degrees Fahrenheit. Still pretty cold." Scott says.

"How cold will it be at Trout Lake?" he asks.

"This time of year... it will get above freezing at

midday and drop again at night." Scott replies.

"A lot different than Texas," says Sam. "I can get used to it."

The girls join them, still talking with Gloria and sad that they can't keep in touch by phone or email. At least Canada's mail is working and they can write.

Back on the road after a good breakfast, Jacob and Gloria have a permanent place in hearts and prayers.

It's smooth traveling for all but the last roads into Trout Lake. It's a long day but anticipation of their journey's end buoys their spirits and carries them through.

Scott lays on the horn as he makes the last turn on the road into town. Fun as it may have been for him, it isn't necessary as a small crowd is gathered at the Trout Lake convenience store. Edna and Uncle Ed are front and center with Scott's Uncle Frank and Wilma Lofstedt, from Edna's side, next to them. Cousins Gretchen, Louisa, and Rory, wait impatiently next to them. Even the neighbors are here. The Bailey's and Archambeau's look as pleased to see the 'travelers come home' as the rest of the family.

Coming to a stop in front of the store, Scott bursts from the door for hugs and handshakes. Sam puts the snuffing lid on the gasifier as it appears to be well away from Scott's radar.

With the sun already set, cold drives the need to unload quickly. Scott's cabin awaits and another for Sam and Karin. It's a grand welcome home for everyone. Even with Sam and Karin's first visit, they are welcomed instantly as neighbors; not guests. Scott takes

Roxanne's hand, leading her to the door of his cabin. Smoke from the stovepipe tells of a family that cares to have it warm for them. Lifting Roxanne into his arms, he opens the door, stepping into the lamplight.

"What have they done to my cabin!" he cries.

"Nice curtains!" Roxanne replies. "Love the doilies."